Roman Retre

# Roman Re

**Book four in the Sword of Cartimandua series**

**By Griff Hosker**

# Roman Retreat

*Published by Sword Books Ltd. 2014*
*Copyright © Griff Hosker 2014*
*The author has asserted their moral right under the Copyright, Designs and Patents Act, 1988, to be identified as the author of this work.*
*All Rights reserved. No part of this publication may be reproduced, copied, stored in a retrieval system, or transmitted, in any form or by any means, without the prior written consent of the copyright holder, nor be otherwise circulated in any form of binding or cover other than that in which it is published and without a similar condition being imposed on the subsequent purchaser.*
*A CIP catalogue record for this title is available from the British Library.*

# Contents

Roman Retreat .................................................................. 1
Chapter 1 ........................................................................ 4
Chapter 2 ...................................................................... 12
Chapter 3 ...................................................................... 26
Chapter 4 ...................................................................... 37
Chapter 5 ...................................................................... 44
Chapter 6 ...................................................................... 54
Chapter 7 ...................................................................... 67
Chapter 8 ...................................................................... 82
Chapter 9 ...................................................................... 96
Chapter 10 .................................................................. 108
Chapter 11 .................................................................. 120
Chapter 12 .................................................................. 132
Chapter 13 .................................................................. 143
Chapter 14 .................................................................. 154
Chapter 15 .................................................................. 166
Chapter 16 .................................................................. 180
Chapter 17 .................................................................. 190
Chapter 18 .................................................................. 199
Chapter 19 .................................................................. 210
Chapter 20 .................................................................. 222
Epilogue ..................................................................... 235
Maps .......................................................................... 239
Chapter 1 .................................................................... 241
Author's note .............................................................. 257
Glossary ..................................................................... 258
Other books by Griff Hosker ...................................... 259

# Chapter 1

Centurion Marius Vestrus stroked his chin as he peered over the walls of the cohort fort; almost the last in a thin line of forts the wooden ramparts and stakes were still almost new. His chin felt rough. He would have to punish Sallustus, his slave, for the shaving blade had not been as sharp as he was expecting. Marius demanded the highest standards of his men and he displayed even higher standards himself. He was a veteran of almost twenty-five years and he knew that the only thing which kept the Roman Empire intact was soldiers like himself having the highest standards and never accepting less. As the first rays of dawn peered over the wooded hilltops he ruminated, once again, about the news the messenger had brought the day before. The legions were being withdrawn. The northernmost outpost of the Empire, Inchtuthil, was being abandoned and the legion sent south to bolster the depleted forces there. Domitian had decided that there was nothing in this remote part of the Empire which necessitated a legion and he was taking legions from Britannia and Gaul to replace those lost in Dacia. Marius found himself in agreement with the Emperor for he had seen nothing worth dying for in this desolate corner of the Empire. The winters were cold and the summers filled with biting insects and irate warriors intent on emasculating every Roman they could lay their blue-painted claws on.

"Sir!"

The Batavian Centurion did not even glance round as the sentry attracted his attention. "Report then."

"Over to the north, Centurion, there is some movement." Turning to the sentry beside him he said," Go round to the officer's quarters. I want every man armed and on the walls but silently. Understand?"

"Yes, Centurion." The soldier did not question Marius' orders. The veteran of twenty years in Britannia had earned him the respect of everyone in the elite first cohort.

"Now then where are they?"

# Roman Retreat

"Over there. You can just see them emerging from the tree line." Even as the sentry spoke Marius could see the twenty men break from the woods and head for the fort.

"They're ours, sir. Should I open the gate?"

Turning his head the sentry knew he had said the wrong thing. "And how do you know they are ours laddie?"

"They're wearing Roman uniforms, sir."

"Oh well that is alright then isn't it? I mean it isn't as though the heathen barbarians couldn't have found it eh? Or" he added tapping the soldier on the side of his head, "stolen it from dead Romans?"

As his comrades grinned at the sentry's discomfort he shook his head. "No sir."

"Then we will wait until they get closer." By now the walls were silently filling with the rest of the cohort. Marius nodded. Five hundred Batavians armed and rested would see off whatever danger was approaching.

"Romans! Romans!" The voices drifted across the killing ground before the walls.

"Prepare pila!" Although his men wondered at the command they were trained well enough to obey instantly.

The twenty men were now less than a hundred paces from the walls and the garrison could see their wounds. Marius did not order the gates to be opened. "Halt and identify yourselves."

The twenty men halted and while most looked nervously over their shoulders one voice spoke out. "Gaius Salvius Agrippa, Optio First cohort, Second Gallorum auxiliary."

"Who is the First Spear?"

"Decimus Saenius Galba..." There was a pause. "He's dead sir."

Satisfied Marius shouted down. "Open the gate. Surgeon, see to these men."

By the time Marius had descended from the palisade the Gauls were assembled on the Via Praetoria and the First Spear could see that many were wounded. The Optio stood to attention despite the bleeding head wound. "Right Optio while your wounds are being dressed fill me on what happened."

"Sir, we were woken by men dressed in Roman uniforms. They said they were Gauls from the northern outpost. The sentry let them in and suddenly there were thousands of Caledonii in the fort. We were the only survivors. First Spear led us out of the Porta Decumana. By the time we had cut our way through we were the only ones left."

Marius nodded. He would have done the same as the Gaulish Centurion. "You did well Optio, Centurions and Optios to the Praetorium."

The grim-faced officers were under no illusions. The two forts north of them had been overrun. The legion to the south had been removed. They were now the only Roman force north of the Tava. Marius scanned their faces. He had known all of them since they were recruits and he had promoted all of them. They were reliable but they have never been in such danger before. "Well, lads it looks like we are in deep shit. If the blue arsed barbarians have destroyed the two forts north of us then they are a large force. We should retreat and head for the forts south of Inchtuthil but I don't want to risk being caught in the open. Here is my plan. We will send riders south to warn the other forts and, hopefully, to summon a relief force. Meanwhile, I want every drop of water and food inside the fort. I want the ditch deepened, the bridge over it removed and the tree line cut further back. I want hot food prepared and the men fed in relays. This could be a long day. Well go on, get on with it. Decius, you stay with me." His Optio nodded. "Find as much spare oil as you can. Bury two amphora of it halfway along the main walls about thirty paces the other side of the ditch and then lay a trail between the two."

Decius nodded, "You want to fry the bastards."

Nodding he added, "When they have filled the ditch with their dead, they will be able to attack the walls and they will bring up their reserves. If we can fire that area it will buy us time."

"Will do."

Marius went to the stables where the mounted troopers were saddling their mounts. "Right. You ten are all that stand between us and disaster. Split into pairs and head for the forts south, south-east and south-west of us." He pointed to each pair as he listed their directions. "Tell the senior officer there what has happened." He looked at each man intently. "If a relief force doesn't get here in the next three days then we will all be dead. Understand?"

A chorus of "Yes sir" told the first spear all he needed to know. These men would bring help or die trying. "Right don't waste time here. Go." As the gate slammed shut behind the ten troopers Marius wondered if he would see any of them again. Sliding his gladius out of its scabbard he was determined that his Batavians would fight to the last man and the blue-painted savages would know they had been in a battle.

In the woods to the north of the fort, Ninian, one of the sons of Calgathus looked at the forces arrayed before him. The two forts had cost him men but, thanks to their subterfuge less than might have been expected from an assault on a Roman fort. He gestured for his elite warriors, his oath kin and the finest troops he had, to come forward. They were all garbed in auxiliary armour, bearing scuta and pila, looking, to all intents and purposes, like Romans. "Brothers once again we will attack the fort and you will lead the way. You must make the garrison believe that you are fleeing from an ambush. As soon as they open the gates you must secure them and we will destroy them."

The warriors banged their scuta with their pila. They had all been chosen not only for their skill in war but the fact that they spoke Latin. Each individual was keen to win honour. Looking at each other they could see that they were the last twenty of Ninian's oath kin for their comrades were now with the Allfather having sacrificed their lives to free their land of the yoke of Rome.

"Go my brothers. Go."

Marius chewed on the dried horsemeat and gazed across the freshly cleared killing ground before the main gate. The trees had been cleared back another ten paces and the ditch was now as deep as a tall man. He nodded with satisfaction as he heard the stakes being driven into the bottom. When sharpened they would thin out the numbers of barbarians and make it more difficult to assault the walls. The amphorae had been buried and his Optio already stood with the rest of the first century on the walls. "Decius, make sure the men on the walls have bows as well as pila. I want these bastards thinning out before they get to the wall." The aquifer stood expectantly waiting for his commander's order. He was Marius oldest friend and knew him better than any other living man. They both came from the same village in western Gaul and had joined on the same day. Gnaeus Rullus never moved more than five paces from the Centurion, especially during a battle. He was the protector of the most important warrior in the cohort. "Right Gnaeus, signal the work party to return. We have ridden our luck as much as we dare."

Expecting the order it was initiated as soon as it was spoken and the auxiliaries returned swiftly to the fort. As they passed beneath the Centurion, he shouted down. "Feed the work parties. This will be a long day lads."

He took the time to scan the walls. The perimeter was totally manned. The reserve century lounged near the headquarters building, ready to plug any gap or to react to any incursion. Pila were stacked in neat piles along the walkway and arrows were being distributed. Marius had done all that he could and now he had to wait. The longer he waited the more he liked it for it meant that his messengers would have more time to bring help.

It was fortunate that Marius did not have second sight for he would have seen six bodies lying stripped and mutilated where they had been ambushed by waiting scouts sent by Ninian to prevent just such an attempt. Two other messengers were also fleeing for their lives as the whole of the Caledonii and Pictii took advantage of the departure of the legions.

"Sir! Movement." The sharp-eyed sentry in the tower pointed towards the woods where the twenty disguised tribesmen ran towards the walls.

"So the sneaky bastards want to repeat their trick eh?" The men nearest to him looked up in anticipation. "No one fire until I give the command." He pointed to the reserve century. "As soon as we let them in I want you to kill them and then bar the gate. You men on the door; they will go for you as soon as the gate is opened so move away from the gate."

The warriors ran towards the walls somewhat confused by the fact that there was no bridge across the ditch. Undeterred they descended into the ditch and climbed apprehensively out of it. In the woods, Ninian had moved his troops as close to the edge as he could, trying to hide behind the bushes and thin trees. His young men would have to hold the gate for longer than he wished but they were the best he had. His men would have to cover over three hundred paces before they reached the ditch. It would be a long hard run and the Romans would do their best to destroy them before they could close with the gate which Ninian was counting on being open.

"Help us, we Romans. We ambushed."

The poor Latin would have warned Marius even without the survivor's account. He shouted down, "Open the gate."

The young Caledonii were exultant. Their ploy had worked again. Even as the gates swung open they were drawing their daggers, swords and axes ready to kill all behind the gate. Their joy was short-lived, for, as the gates opened they were faced by eighty soldiers armed with pila. The odds of four to one meant that they all died where they stood and the Batavians did not suffer a single casualty. Ninian saw none of this for his men were racing across the ground towards the gates. By the time they were halfway to the ditch, the gate was closed and the leading warriors sensed that this time they would not have it as easy as the first two assaults. The ones at the front heard a command from the fort and the next thing they knew was that a torrent of arrows rained down upon them so thick it was as though a cloud had come from nowhere. But they were the Caledonii and they were not to be put off by a few dead men. They ploughed on, those in the rear leaping over the bodies of their dead comrades to close with the hated enemy. The arrows continued to thin out the attackers but still, they advanced. The ditch filled with bodies and still, they came on. Those at the front were close enough to hurl their spears and war hammers at the armoured men on the wall.

Ninian could see that his subterfuge had failed but he knew there were less than five hundred men inside those wooden walls. He signalled to the war bands to his left and right and thousands of warriors hurled themselves towards the other three walls. The Romans would be hard-pressed to fight off all attacks from three sides. He looked over his shoulder. His own war band was eagerly pressed close together. When the walls had been weakened they would attack and then the fort would fall.

Marius was unconcerned when the runners arrived from the other walls. He had expected them to surround him. He had anticipated that the barbarians would have had a force ready to ambush him had he tried to escape by the Porta Decumana. If death were to come he would face it behind his walls with his men. The scorpions on the towers were taking a heavy toll on the warriors as they emerged from the woods and the arrows were effectively decimating the enemy but Marius knew that the bolts and arrows were limited and soon they would be using swords and shields. The result of that action would determine the outcome of this battle. He could see that one group of warriors had armed themselves with Roman shields and were using their war hammers to smash the palisade down.

He shouted to the nearest scorpion. "Realign your weapon and take out those warriors." While the shields were effective against arrows and stones they were no match for the steel-tipped bolts and soon the warriors lay in a heap of dead and dying. Their work had not been in vain for Ninian could now see the beginnings of a weak spot and he ordered his men to concentrate on the weak section of the wall. Marius waited until they were near to the oil and then gave the order. Ten fire tipped arrows plunged into the oil creating an inferno that engulfed the attackers. The Centurion's trick also had an unexpected benefit as some of the warriors had been carrying pitch with which to burn the walls and the whole of the assault force was forced back leaving many writhing blackened bodies, unrecognisable as men.

Marius looked up at the sun which was past its zenith. He had used his last trick. The next time the enemy came forward they would be able to attack the weak section of the wall. He hoped at least one of his messengers had got through. He shouted down to the reserve century. "Bolster the north-west wall where it is weak." As the men began to hammer wood against the inner walls Marius turned to the messenger. "Go around and tell the men to piss against the walls when they need to go." The man looked at his commander as though he had gone mad. "Tell them it is to make the walls harder to burn." If the messengers got through, then some of the walls might still be standing.

Two more messengers were lying in bloodied heaps, their heads adorning the spears thrust into the ground and the last two were being pursued by mounted Caledonii who sensed that they were close to victory as the Roman auxiliaries tired.

# Chapter 2

Decurion Julius Demetrius was downhearted. His men were surprised for the normally cheerful officer was never less than happy. Julius was unhappy because he knew that the Rome he loved had given up on the province. The dismantling of the fort at Inchtuthil had been as momentous an event as Caesar crossing the Rubicon. Julius was intelligent and well-read. He knew that had Julius Agricola been allowed to continue in Britannia then the whole province would have been conquered. But he was also intelligent enough to realise that Dacia was but a few days march from Rome itself and posed a greater threat especially to a paranoid Emperor who was desperate to stay in power. The conquest of Britannia had been tantalisingly close but now was as far off as the mystical land of India.

He halted his men for their noon rest. This patrol was the most northerly patrol of Marcus' Horse. Their first fort had been abandoned along with Inchtuthil and now they had another one south of Alavna. He remembered with sadness how he had felt as they had destroyed the walls, buried the nails, and filled in the ditches so that nothing could be used that they could not carry. It also meant that there was no sign that Rome had ever been there. The grass would soon grow over the land which masked the blood shed by Julius' comrades. They had held the land won by Agricola for a mere three years. Soon the northernmost forts, the Batavians and Gauls would be joining the retreat south to the Tava. Perhaps the Prefect was right, perhaps a new line of forts closer together would be the answer. He wondered how his father would view this. He would probably regard it as a defeat. During his time as prefect of Marcus' Horse, he had always held the barbarians in the lowest esteem. Prefect Marcus Aurelius Maximunius had never made that misjudgement. It was why the whole ala was constantly on patrol for he knew how cunning and determined the enemy could be.

# Roman Retreat

His thirty men had automatically set pickets and shared out the roles related to noon breaks. Julius felt justly proud of their professionalism and their loyalty. He gazed northwards beyond the skyline to the last three outposts of Roman influence. Just fifteen hundred auxiliaries stood between Julius and the hundreds of thousands of barbarians. Despite the defeats inflicted upon them they still came back with a seemingly inexhaustible supply of men. Despite their lack of armour they fought ferociously aided by a landscape that seemed to be an ally of the warriors. Certainly, Julius had chosen his noon stop with great care. They were in a clearing, on the top of a hill, giving them ample sight of approaching enemies. He was about to order the men to saddle up when he heard "Sir! Riders."

His men quickly mounted and the added height enabled Julius to see two Roman auxiliary messengers being hotly pursued by eight barbarians. The turma was so well trained that not a word was spoken. Julius led them down the hill and as he signalled with his left hand half the turma headed towards the rear of the attackers. Four men in each column held his bow in his left hand whilst the rest held a javelin in their right.

The two Roman messengers were becoming desperate. Having ridden hard for seven hours their mounts were frothing heavily and labouring. They, and their terrified riders, were almost exhausted to the point of death. The two troopers glanced frantically over their shoulders and they could see their own ultimate fate as the blue-painted warriors closed upon them. They would all die. They were doomed to perish in this ice-cold land forsaken by the gods themselves. Looking at each other they drew their swords. If they turned to face the enemy one of them might survive. The exchanged nod was all they needed. They began to slow up their horses and they turned together. The leading blue-faced warrior bared his teeth in joy and began to let out a scream, a war cry of victory. His joy was short-lived as the arrow plunged into his throat and out of the back of the neck. Two more died as quickly and the remaining five looked around to see the source of the danger. They just had time to register the red cloaks and mounts of the Roman auxiliary before they were all despatched with arrow and javelin.

"Are we glad to see you, sir."

"Where are you from?"

"Cardean. The First Spear sent us. The two forts to the north of us have been sacked and our unit was surrounded. He didn't have time to march away."

The other trooper had caught his breath enough to speak. "Ten of us set out. We found the bodies of two of the others. We may be the only ones left."

Thirty-two pairs of eyes looked at the Decurion. This was when he earned his pay. The decision he would make could affect the next year's warfare. "Gaius, Decimus. Ride back with these men to Prefect Strabo. He's at Bertha. Give him the information."

"And you sir?"

"I am going to find the rest of the ala and see if we can help the Batavians." The two Batavians smiled with relief. "Remember their horses are tired. Feed them and rest for an hour and don't push it. Prefect Strabo can't leave before first light anyway."

Leading the turma west, Julius pondered what to do. He knew that he was the furthest north. There were three turmae to the east but the other eight were to the west. His chosen man, Livius Helva drew his horse next to him. "Sir?"

"The horns of a dilemma Livius. The horns of a dilemma. If we split up to find more of the ala we may suffer the same fate as the rest of the messengers but if we stay together we may not find them in time."

"What about the fort sir? Will they hold?"

"I would have said 'yes', Livius but for the fact that this enemy has destroyed two already which means he will be better armed with Roman swords, shields, spears and helmets." He scanned the horizon. "Take two men and station yourself a thousand paces east of us. Take Albius with you." Albius had a buccina and both men knew that its sound carried a long way.

The woods were thick with pine and scrubby undergrowth. Not only did it make movement difficult but

## Roman Retreat

every rider no matter how skilled had to watch not only for enemies but dangerous undergrowth. Every trooper had a weapon in one hand and his shield looped over his shoulder rather than being hung from his left leg. None had ever heard of two forts being taken and the occupants slaughtered; it was a sobering thought.

Julius was relieved when it was a shout he heard from Livius and not the Buccina of Albius. It meant that they had met with friends. When Decurion Princeps Decius Flavius rode into view Julius knew that the gods smiled on him for the Decurion Princeps was one of the two officers Julius held in the highest regard. The grizzled old soldier should have retired three years earlier along with the prefect but Governor Lucullus had persuaded them both to stay on until the north was subjugated.

"Problems Decurion?"

Julius smiled. Decius never changed. He cut to the chase every time with the minimum time spent on words. "Looks like Calgathus has destroyed two cohorts and is besieging the third one at Cardean."

"Shit! I assume you have sent word back to camp?"

"I sent three men back to Prefect Strabo."

"He cannot get there before tomorrow evening. What were you planning then?"

"I was looking for more of the ala. I thought if we had enough men we might be able to help the Batavians out." He tailed off lamely. "Now that I explain it, it doesn't seem such a good idea."

Decius spat between his horse's ears. "Don't be so hard on yourself. It's the only idea. If we sit here on our arses they will be slaughtered. If we go to help they may still be slaughtered but they might last a little longer. We'll carry on with your plan. Besides, I hate the blue-painted arseholes." His men all laughed and Julius smiled. "Stop laughing Annius. Take two men and head west. Keep going until you have collected the rest of the ala and meet us at Cardean. Minius take two of Decurion Demetrius' men and head east. You should catch us sooner rather than later. Right, let's ride. Sixty of us against, how many barbarians are there around here twenty thousand? Now that should guarantee a fight."

They pushed hard through the forest until they came to the north-south trail which led to the fort. The hawking and screeching of the crows and magpies alerted them to the first of their dead comrades. They found the mutilated bodies next to the skulls planted on a spear. Every man's resolve hardened. There was no point in surrender; this enemy never took prisoners and the death would be a slow and lingering one.

"We'll bury them and have a short rest."

They had just buried them when they heard the thundering of hooves coming up the trail. The two turmae went into a defensive position and then relaxed as Decurion Macro rode up with the other two Eastern patrols. While Julius mounted the two turmae Decius told Macro and the other decurions what the plan was. Despite the odds, none of the officers of Marcus' Horse disagreed with the assessment. They were confident enough in their own ability to believe that no matter what the odds they would emerge triumphant.

By the time night had fallen the whole of the ala was gathered together. The last turma, led by Decurion Gaius Metellus Aurelius arrived as the camp was being finished. From his side hung the fabled Sword of Cartimandua and the mere sight of it raised the spirits of every trooper. To them it was more than just a symbol it was a good luck charm, Carried first by Ulpius Felix and then the Prefect, they had never lost whilst it was carried by their leader. While the men ate the decurions discussed strategy.

"We have almost one thousand men."

"There are five hundred in the fort."

"There were five hundred in the fort and there could be twenty or thirty thousand barbarians surrounding it and just waiting for us to arrive."

"Good point Gaius. We need to know what the situation is. Macro take half your turma and scout the fort. Do not be seen and do not stay for a fight." Scowling Macro left. Despite his admonition, Decius knew that Macro was the stealthiest of warriors and would return without being discovered. "Julius, you are quiet which means you are thinking. Come on give us ignorant shit shovellers and plebeians the benefit of your fine patrician education."

Blushing Julius cleared his throat. "Well, there aren't enough of us for a frontal attack. But we have three things in our favour. We have horses and speed; we can escape. We have arrows and can fire from distance and thirdly we have surprise."

They all looked up at the last point."How does that help us?"

"When their scouts do not return they will assume that messengers got through and that a relief force will be coming."

"Makes sense."

They will be vigilant and waiting for an attack from the south."

"And how does that help us?"

"We attack from the north. They came from the north; they will feel safe and they will be preparing across the valley not beyond."

"I like it, Decius."

"Yes Gaius but how do we get around them?"

"That depends on Macro. If the fighting has died down and they are resting then we may be able to slip past them."

"Which they should be if they have fought since dawn."

"Right Cilo then we have a short rest and use the hours of darkness to get beyond them. It works in our favour if they send a force to ambush Prefect Strabo."

"Right. " Decius stood up. "Annius get your sorry arse here."

Grinning Annius stood vaguely at attention." Yes, Decurion Princeps?"

"Take a trooper and go down the trail until you meet Prefect Strabo. Tell him we are going to attack the Caledonii from the north which means he should be prepared to be ambushed as he moves to relieve the fort. Got it?"

"Yes sir."

"Well go on then and don't get caught. I am the only one allowed to kick your arse not the blue-painted sheep shaggers."

"First Spear!"

Marius looked up wearily as another wounded Centurion reported to him. "The third century is down to forty who can still fight."

Marius looked at the Centurion, one of his older friends. He could see in his eyes that the forty who remained included many wounded soldiers. In the dying embers of the day fighting still raged sporadically around the ramparts. They had repulsed so many attacks that Marius had lost count. All of the officers had suffered wounds. He had had his leg slashed open by an axe. Gnaeus Rullus had lost three fingers of his left hand as he had fended off three warriors trying to gain the honour of killing Marius.

"Thank you, Centurion. You have done well. All your men have done well. I believe the fighting will die down. Feed half of your men and repair what you can. On the morrow, they will attack again." The unspoken words were that it would be the last attack and they would all die.

"So, First Spear, will our friends arrive?"

Marius shook his head. "I fear not. Even if the riders reached the fort Prefect Strabo could not be here before the day after tomorrow. If he forced a march he might arrive by nightfall tomorrow but you know, old friend, that we will not survive past noon."

The aquifer nodded. "We will make these barbarians pay for these old bones." He looked around as the fighting died down and nightfall fell like a smoky blanket about the wrecked and burning fort. "What a place to leave our bodies eh Marius? This place, forsaken by the gods filled with blue-painted monsters who do not know when they are beaten."

Marius laughed. "Had General Agricola still been with us I know that they would have known defeat but this boil will fester and grow until the whole of Britannia feels its poison."

"Aye but take comfort for we shall not be here to see it."

"No, we will be supping at the Allfather's table."

"I wonder what good food and fine wine taste like?"

Laughing, First Spear said, "Well by tomorrow eve we shall know."

Marius was awake long before his slave came with the jug of water and hard bread. Nodding to him he said, "Today if you get the chance save yourself. They may not notice an old man dressed in rags slipping away."

The old slave nodded. "Thank you, First Spear. It does you great honour that you think of an old man on this day of days but I shall remain here and die with the rest of you for I would perish alone in the woods and I would prefer to end my days here with comrades."

Marius nodded for the slave was a Batavian and understood the concept of honour and comradeship. "Then arm yourself and sell your life dearly."

The fort looked far worse in the cold early morning light. The repairs had been done, hastily completed before the soldiers fell asleep through exhaustion, and Marius could clearly see that they could be brushed aside if the Caledonii made a strong attack. He nodded and the buccina sounded. The red-eyed and weary warriors dragged their reluctant bodies to the ramparts and the Centurion did a quick head count. There were barely two hundred men left standing. Their wounded companions numbered less than a hundred and many of those would not see noon. Marius smiled wryly to himself; none of them would see noon."Stand to."Silence echoed like a bell and every eye was drawn to the bloodied figure. "Today we make our last stand against the barbarians. Today will see the end of this cohort and its noble history. We will all be together in the afterlife at the Allfather's table where we will talk of this day, this battle and this honour. We may die today but we will not be defeated for we will have remained at our posts and died like men. I salute you." The men responded by hitting their swords against their shields and cheering rhythmically.

Ninian was gathering his forces when his men suddenly looked up as they heard the cheering. "Have the Romans been relieved?"

"No, they are preparing for their death. No one is coming to aid them. There are warbands to the south of the fort watching for the relief column and we will end their resistance in our first attack." He looked around the war bands and saw, with some sadness that many of his oath kin had died in the terrible fighting of the previous day. The Romans had fought well and not yielded a single piece of their fort. Some of his younger warriors looked less confident and that was no bad thing for it would make them better warriors in the future. "Today, when we attack, there will be no arrows, no missiles. There will be no fire and the spiked ditch is no more. We will push down their flimsy wooden wall and fight them man to man and this time, my brothers, we will win. When we have destroyed this fort and the Romans who come to their aid we will join with my father, King Calgathus, and fall upon the rest of the Romans like wolves upon sheep. We will retake our land and then take the land the Romans stole from the Brigante, the Novontae and the Carvetii. We will not stop until they are driven all the way back to Rome." This time it was the Batavians who heard the cheers and then they saw the hordes of Caledonii marching in step from the woods. Those who had shields were banging their swords against them; the noise seemed to increase the size and numbers of those coming towards them.

Inside the fort, soldiers clasped hands with comrades and prepared to sell their lives dearly. Marius' voice boomed out as he gave his last order. "Centurions I want one man in two in the centre of the camp. Those on the walls, when the buccina sounds, retreat to the centre. We will make a shield wall and make them pay a high price for this little piece of worthless land." He turned to Gnaeus the aquifer. "Watch for my signal. I only want them close enough to the walls so that they are committed to the attack."

"You think that a shield wall will hold them?"

Marius shrugged. "I would prefer legionary shields but it does give us the best chance we have. Fate has loaded these die against us Gnaeus but we must play with what we have."

Marcus' Horse had made it through the forests to appear behind the Caledonii. Macro and his scouts returned. "They have a camp a mile into the forest."

"Are there warriors?"

"A few and old men and some women and children. They have carts and draught animals."

Decius nodded. "So they plan on advancing further south. Decurion Cilo. Take your turma and destroy the camp burn everything." He paused and looked significantly at the Decurion. "Kill everybody." The soldier opened his mouth as though to speak but Decius continued. "I know it goes against the grain but our arses are hanging out here. We may not survive the day. Do you want this army unleashed on the rest of the province?" Cilo shook his head. Decius glared around at the rest and they all shook their heads. "Right, and when we go in I want no mercy. We haven't got that luxury. Our only chance is to surprise them, get the cohort out and meet up with Prefect Strabo. That is the only way we will survive. We go in two lines. The second line will be made up of archers. Tell the lads to wait until the arrows have hit before they give their war cry and then hit them." It was a mark of the training of the ala that Decius did not need to say when their arrows would be loosed. Each man knew that.

"Usual formation?" Macro looked questioningly at Decius. Since Gaius had inherited the sword of Cartimandua his turma had led the line from the centre. The ala regarded it superstitiously as a sign of good fortune whilst the men of the Second Turma regarded it as a mark of honour.

Decius grinned at Gaius. "Usual formation. Keeps me safer a bit longer. Decurion Cilo when you have fired the camp follow up and mop up any survivors. If we come through this we will meet at the Batavian camp and see who is left alive."

Ninian was confident that his four thousand men would be victorious. He could see from the walls that barely a hundred men remained twenty-five per wall. His decision to send the other six thousand to meet the relief column was a wise one. The four hundred men on the far side of the fort, hidden in the forests would ensure that any survivors would be dealt with. "Forward." The line of blue-painted warriors moved slowly across the battlefield still littered with the detritus of the previous day's conflict. There was no need to rush for they did not have to run the gauntlet of missile fire and they would arrive fresher. They had also learned that the auxiliaries preferred their enemies to come at them piecemeal. Today would be won by the weight of numbers.

The pall of smoke from the burning camp was behind the advancing barbarians but the ones at the rear could smell the smoke. They feared some trick by the Romans and paid it no mind. The first they knew of their danger was when they felt the thud of arrows into backs and the shouts as men fell. The attack by Marcus' Horse coincided with the roar as Ninian's men leapt forward and the buccina sounded. The Caledonii were perplexed; had the Romans retreated and were they attacking the defenders placed on the far side of the fort?

Decius heard the buccina and shouted over to Macro. "Looks like some are still alive. Sweep your turma around the left flank. See if you can turn them." Macro nodded and his turma swept majestically and magnificently in a line to the left. The first of the ala's javelins were now raining home. The Caledonii were climbing over the crumbling wooden walls. Decius shouted to his aquifer, "Sound the buccina. Let 'em know we are coming." The strident notes of the buccina echoed across the field and those warriors still to cross the wall looked around in panic. The spathas of the ala cut and hacked the unarmoured bodies of those to their front for the armoured warriors were already climbing the walls.

Inside the fort, Marius looked at Gnaeus. "Was that a Roman horn?"

"Aye, but it is coming from the wrong direction. "

"Do you think they have captured one and are playing tricks with our minds?"

Gnaeus shook his head. "You have to be trained to play one of these. A Roman blew that. We might just survive yet old friend." With renewed heart and optimism they fought even harder.

Marius shouted his order as the first wave of warriors surged over the wall destroying whole chunks in the process.

"Lock shields. Go for the legs first." The men who were heading towards him were dressed in captured Roman mail and Lorica segmenta. Some also had helmets which meant they were almost as well protected as the auxiliaries. Romans knew how to defeat such warriors. Go for the legs and when they fell, the unprotected neck. Although tired with arms heavy with fatigue, the auxiliaries performed like a well-oiled machine and the first Caledonii fell to the waiting gladii. Some of the warriors at the back began hurling their war hammers and this began to take its toll as the heavy weapons of war struck shields and helmets, incapacitating all that they struck. The second ranks stepped up to take the place of fallen comrades but the weight of warriors was taking its toll and the depleted Roman ranks became even thinner.

Macro had taken his turma to the very edge of the barbarian attack. When they wheeled to charge those on the left of the Caledonii line found themselves assaulted and attacked by men from the flank and the rear. It was too much for unarmoured men and they began to flee towards their comrades in the middle. It was a confused mass of men who were trying to escape the vengeful Roman blades. They became compacted and the arrows began to fell more men as every arrow found a target. Some of the warriors evaded the Roman line and ran back to the safety of the tree line. Their escape was short-lived for Decurion Cilo and his grim-faced turma cut them down before they were halfway there.

In the centre Gaius wielded his mighty sword, its gleaming blade glinting majestically in the early morning sun. Such was the power of the sword that none could stand in its path and Gaius found himself the tip of the arrow as his turma forged forward through the warriors who fell like wheat before the relentless blades of the ala. The gate had been destroyed by the Caledonii and Gaius headed for it. The warriors inside the fort heard the thunder of the hooves and two lines of armoured barbarians turned to face their enemies. These warriors would not flee for they were blood brothers of Ninian and Lulach. They would die fighting. Gaius could see the war axes and hammers awaiting him.

Dropping the reins of his horse he slid out his last javelin and hurled it at a red-bearded giant. Thrown from a few paces it ripped through his throat and struck the man behind in his arm; as the two fell a gap opened and Gaius headed for it the sword of Cartimandua slicing down on the unprotected neck of the warrior to his right. The small opening became larger as trooper after trooper crashed through the weakening line.

Marius saw the weakening of the line and gave his own order. "Forward." No longer on the defensive, the whole line punched their shields and slashed with their gladii. For the first time in two days, the Caledonii were unsure of victory. They were being assaulted on two sides and although they could not see the numbers of cavalry it was a large enough force to put their attack in jeopardy.

Ninian saw the big Centurion rallying and leading his men. He was the leader. If he could kill him then the rest would succumb. He hacked down one auxiliary and thrust his spear at the unprotected side of the Centurion. Suddenly the blade was knocked down by the standard of the cohort. "No, you don't you sneaky bastard." Gnaeus stabbed with his gladius at the groin of the huge warrior but the sword in Ninian's hand beat it down. Slashing with his spear Ninian caught Gnaeus across the thigh and he dropped to one knee.

Ninian sensed his victory and drew his blade back to despatch the brave standard-bearer still grasping the cohort's standard for all to see. As the blade crashed down it met a jarring jolt as Marius blocked the blow with his shield. Before the spear could do any more damage, the Centurion chopped it halfway down its length leaving the Caledonii leader with just his sword. Marius had fought too many times to waste a moment and, as he punched Ninian in the face, he sliced back hand diagonally to cut through the warrior's throat. The blood sprayed all around. The infuriated Caledonii fought even more ferociously but all order had gone and the inexorable tide of Roman blades ended the blood kin of Ninian.

Those warriors who could flee got out of the fort any way that they could and Decius watched with dismay as some hundreds streamed towards the woods. Had his horses not been exhausted Decius would have ordered them to cut them down but he knew that his task was only half complete. They still had many more enemies to defeat before they would be safe.

# Chapter 3

Prefect Marcus Aurelius Maximunius and Prefect Strabo had pushed the weary relief column as hard as they could. As they rested the two prefects discussed the parlous state they were in.

"Centurion Vestrus is the best man to defend a fort. He has forgotten more than I know but even so, the force he faces has already defeated two forts and killed their men."

"The message from Decius was that the ala was going to their aid."

"I know Marcus and for that I am grateful. I was just pleased that you were still training these fifty recruits. Otherwise, we would have had no eyes and ears."

"I would not like to throw them into combat yet but at least they prevent us heading into an ambush. The trouble is, Furius, that this country does not suit my men. There are far too many trees and too many rocks. My cavalry likes open fields and space to wheel and turn."

"Aye but now that the Emperor has summoned the rest of the cavalry to Dacia you are the only ala left in the north."

"The Emperor asked for us to be sent to Dacia."

"But why? Surely there are Eastern alae who are closer. I thought the Eastern cavalry was supposed to be the best in the world? The Parthians and the Scythians."

"It seems that General Agricola extolled our virtues and Emperor Domitian wanted us and, I think, the Queen's sword."

"Why are you still here then?"

"The Governor said we were under strength."

"If Domitian finds out that that is a lie then both the Governor and you will be in danger."

"For myself, I am going to retire as soon as I can but the Governor," he shrugged, "they all play a dangerous game." Dismissing the idea as though no politician was worth a second thought he continued, "Now if you were the barbarians what would you do?"

"I would assume that a relief force would be sent south to ambush them in this valley and they would seek to ambush them. they know this area well."

"Luckily we know this area quite well; we are not far from where our first camp was. I will lead the scouts myself when we advance for I think I know where they will be."

"Be careful Marcus. If anything happened to you Decius would have my balls for his breakfast."

"Do not worry old friend I have fought in these lands too long to die in an ambush."

Decius and Marius met amidst the carnage which was the fort. They clasped arms. "Thank you Decurion Princeps. Your arrival was timely. But for you and my friend here I would be with the Allfather now."

"We may yet all join him. There are still warbands out there. We must leave and leave quickly. Gather your men together. We will need litters for the wounded." Decius shouted. "Macro! Time to volunteer again."

"Macro galloped up looking as fresh as a man who has had a full night's sleep instead of the snatched cat nap he actually had. "Yes, Decurion Princeps?"

"Choose the ten men who have the best mounts and you think are the best for the task. Find the barbarians who are south of us." Macro vaulted easily onto the back of his mount. "Oh and Macro, just watch them and report back. I know there are only a few thousand but don't try to beat them all on your own."

"As if," Laughing Macro rode to the rest of the ala to choose his men.

Marius looked up, a half-smile on his lips. "Were we ever as keen?"

"No one was ever that keen. If you sort out your men I will make sure we aren't disturbed. Decurions."

Marius looked down at Gnaeus who was being bandaged by a smiling Sallustus. "Well, my old friends we still survive although I fear, Gnaeus, your days in the cohorts are numbered."

"What this little scratch? I can still march faster than you."

"I think not old friend. That was bone I could see."

Decius addressed his officers. "Well done lads but we are not out of the woods yet, literally." They all smiled at the grim humour. "Casualties?"

Gaius had already been around the ala, "Six hundred ready to ride and fight. Fifty who can ride and we have twenty empty mounts."

"Decurion Cilo? The camp?"

"They were all killed. We lost three men and we brought along five horses."

"Good that means twenty-five of their wounded can have litters."

A grim-faced Centurion marched towards them. "We only have two hundred soldiers fit for duty. I have over a hundred wounded and there are thirty who will not make the journey."

Decius looked at the Centurion. "Would you like us to…"

The unspoken words were greeted with a thin-lipped smile. "Thank you Decurion I will drink with you later to thank you for the gesture but these are my men and I will do them the honour of sending them to the Allfather myself."

Gaius watched as the Centurion walked over to each badly wounded warrior, spoke a few words and then despatched them with his pugeo. He wondered would he ever be able to do that with his troopers; those who had fought and bled alongside him. By the time the Centurion had finished the column was ready to move.

"Centurion, if you would take the lead my ala will form a cordon around you. Gaius, you take the lead. Julius. You take the rear. The rest of you spread yourselves on either side." As they moved as swiftly as the exhausted Batavians could manage the fort was fired, its black smoke joining that of the burning barbarian camp. "The whole country will see that. I just hope they think it was Caledonii celebrating victory. Gellius come here."

A young trooper rode next to Decius. "Yes Decurion Princeps?"

"Your horse looks to be fresher than the rest. Ride to the hills to the east, skirt the barbarians and see if you can find Prefect Strabo. Let him know what happened and alert him to our predicament."

"Yes sir."

"And son…"

"Yes sir?"

"Be careful."

The Caledonii warbands had chosen their ambush site carefully. They had chosen the place lower down the valley from the deserted fort at Inchtuthil and the surrounding auxiliary camps. The valley was narrow but the cleared land near the camps gave them room to manoeuvre. They assumed they would be facing infantry and the war chief, Teutorigos wanted to draw the Romans forward to the wide part of the valley so that he could envelop the meagre force with his overwhelming numbers. He knew the numbers of Romans who could be spared and he expected no more than three cohorts. Fifteen hundred men were no match for his thousands. He had not envied Ninian attacking a defensive site with all the Roman artillery but here, on the open fields, numbers would count. He glanced to the hills to the east and west and waved his arm. When he received the correct response he knew that his trap was in place. As soon as the scouts returned to warn of the arrival of the relief force his men would stand and prepare to slaughter even more Romans.

Marcus led the twenty young recruits through the tree line. He held up his hand to halt them and then slid from his horse. He pointed to one of the taller recruits and then pointed up the tree. Grinning the recruit stood on his horse's back and then shimmied up the tree. He soon disappeared from sight and Marcus and the rest waited patiently. Marcus' plan was simple. Eliminate any scouts and then find the enemy before he found them. The recruit slid down the bole of the tree and came next to Marcus. He had enough sense to speak in a whisper. "Ten warriors sir waiting in a line twenty paces apart. The first one is about two hundred paces down the valley."

# Roman Retreat

"Well done." For the first time, Marcus wished he had brought more, for each pair would have to take out one warrior and Marcus was under no illusions the Caledonii scouts were better than his barely trained recruits. He gathered them around. "We are going to form a line four hundred paces north of these scouts. You four, he pointed to the most experienced recruits, "will wait with the horses." He noted their disappointment. "Your job is to kill any who escape. I will be with you." He smiled to himself as he saw the grins creep back on their faces. "You four," he pointed to another four, "will each take a scout from the middle. The rest will be in pairs and you will kill the scouts. This is your first real task and make no mistake it is difficult and would be difficult for someone who has fought in these lands for years, not days. You have to kill them and kill them quickly, one sound and they will flee like frightened deer and if they do then the main army will know where we are. Understood?" Their eager, determined faces told him they understood.

As Marcus waited with the four reserves he realised, not for the first time that he preferred to do than to wait. He wished he had been on patrol with Decius and that, even now, his fate would be in his own hands but he also knew that his days in the ala were numbered. He was getting too old and, as he shifted uncomfortably on the back of his mount, he knew this would be his last patrol. There was a sudden movement ahead and Marcus levelled his javelin. The recruits did the same. The Caledonii scout had no chance as two javelins struck him in the chest. The second scout was alerted and he dropped to the ground making the missiles hiss harmlessly above his head. As he rose to race off through the woods one of the recruits leapt from his horse onto his back and, in one fluid movement, slit the scout's throat.

"Well done trooper. What is your name?"

"Titus Albus sir." The young man was beaming with pleasure. Fifteen recruits joined them. With a heavy heart, Marcus realised that one was dead. They found the boy, for he was barely seventeen, with his throat cut, it seemed to grin at them in an obscene sort of way. Glancing at the rest of the troopers Marcus knew that it was a lesson learned. They had seen death and knew its smile.

Decurion Julius Demetrius was in the best possible position to witness the distress of the wounded and after two hours of helping the survivors, he rode to the middle of the column. "Decurion Princeps I have to report that some of these wounded won't survive the next mile, let alone the twenty we have to travel."

Decius looked at the eager young officer and his sad, worn face registered the pain that was spreading across the boy's face. "I know son and that is the problem. What we should do is leave them here rather than slowing down the column. They are going to die anyway but," he gestured to the back of the limping Centurion, walking next to the litter containing his best friend, "as long as they walk we'll stay with them but we won't and we can't stop. I put you at the back because you are their best chance to get out of this. If you think they are going to fall you know what to do."

"You mean… " The Decurion looked appalled at the very thought, "I couldn't kill one of our own."

"Would you rather they were captured? You have seen enough captives to know what that means. Or do you want to leave them to be killed in their way?" The look on Decurion Demetrius' face showed that he had understood. "It isn't right but it is the way it is. Sometimes we have to make decisions as officers that as men we wouldn't."

Julius glanced back down the line where unwounded Batavians were half carrying the wounded. "I know what to do sir and thank you for trusting me with the rearguard. I won't let you down."

"I know Julius."

Riding to the rear Julius came up with an idea. He shouted to his men. "I want one man in two to dismount, and put a wounded soldier on the back of your horse. The rest of you come with me." There was no surprise or dissent from his men. They followed orders. The relief from those wounded men as they sat on the trooper's horses made the discomfort of walking palatable. "We are going to make sure we aren't being tracked. We are going back along the trail. You two go thirty paces to the right, you two, thirty paces to the left." He detailed off the four men and then led them back along the trail they had just followed.

Marius walked over to Decius as he saw what the young man had done. "You have a good officer there."

"I know but he was a prick when he first joined. Just shows what a bit of training can do."

The Centurion laughed. "That's the truth." He dropped his voice and drew closer to the Decurion's horse. "I want to thank you. I know that my wounded are slowing you down. If you want me to…"

Decius shook his head. "No, if it comes to it we will but until we either bump into the main force or the rabble catch us up we'll take it steady. The rest is doing the horses good. Would you like to ride for a while? You can have Snowbird here."

The Centurion laughed. "Thank you for your kind offer but I prefer the earth beneath my feet not a sweaty horse beneath my arse. Besides I am not sure I could stay on."

They both laughed. "Each to his own."

"Prefect Strabo cavalry approaching."

Strabo halted the column as Marcus rode up. "No scouts ahead of you and we found the main force just south of Inchtuthil."

"Crafty buggers. That's really narrow there."

"Should suit your lads shouldn't it?"

The prefect shook his head. "Might suit the legions but my lads like a bit of room. Our shields don't lock together like the legionaries. No, we'll use missiles to annoy them, make them charge us. At least if they are ahead of us and that close it means they aren't slaughtering my cohort."

Marcus looked gravely at his friend. "Unless they are already dead."

"How many did you see?"

"Looked to be two warbands, which normally means four to five thousand warriors."

"In that case either the missing cohorts have killed a lot of men or they are still fighting because two warbands can't take a defended fort. No, they are still alive and you have now given me more reason to pick up the pace. Come on, you shower! Your comrades are waiting for you and you are dragging your heels like recruits on their first day of training." The Centurions picked up the pace as they remembered why they were there.

A sharp-eyed recruit shouted, "Rider!"

Every hand went to a weapon for Marcus had the only cavalry in the area. "It's one of my lads, relax."

Recognising Marcus, the trooper rode straight up to him. "Prefect. Decurion Princeps Flavius sent me sir. He has effected the relief of the fort and he is coming down the trail with the survivors." Those nearest heard the report and the word drifted back like smoke from a fire. Suddenly the column erupted with a cheer and even Prefect Strabo smiled.

"Shut up! Do you want every blue arsed warrior here?" Turning to the trooper he asked, "How many?"

"I think there are over two hundred, sir… I didn't count."

"That's alright lad. You have done well."

"Yes," added Marcus, "and how did we fare?"

"Didn't lose many, sir. We caught them unawares."

"Good. As an experienced trooper take your place at the rear of these recruits." Swelling with pride the trooper galloped swiftly to his place. "That is the best news I have heard in a while."

"I know but it does give us a problem. If they reach the ambush before we do they will be massacred. They are tired, wounded and hungry."

"Let's not waste time then. I'll take my men up onto the ridge to the west and try to skirt the end of their line. When they attack you I will send the trooper back to Decius and then attack their right flank."

"Sounds good to me but Marcus, be careful."

"You know you sound more like Decius every day."

Macro found the ambush and like Marcus recognised its strategic value. He sent a trooper back with the information and then rode the rest of his turma to the top of the hills to the east of the ambush. He drew his men around him. "I realise that we are just one turma and a depleted turma but we are my turma." His men grinned when they heard the pride in his voice. "I am not going to risk us needlessly but there are two vexillations of our friends coming from two directions here. Whichever arrives first will be attacked by those animals down there. When they do I intend to attack this flank and try to draw them off. I am telling you this so that each of you can carry out those orders should I perish." The shock on their faces made him smile; to his men he was indestructible. "We hit them and retreat, hit them and retreat until our horses are too exhausted then we annoy them with arrows, rocks, anything to buy time. After that, we die. Clear?"

"Yes sir."

"Good then let's eat while we wait. I am starving."

Lulach was shocked when over a thousand Batavians filled the valley. Where were his scouts? "To arms. The Romans come. Let us greet them."

The barbarians had been waiting for the battle all morning but they were not prepared for the battle. They had not had time to work themselves up into a battle frenzy. The Batavians stood in three lines with archers in a fourth line; they stood calmly and patiently. Lulach raised his war axe and with a roar of, "Charge!" led the two warbands across the open land. As he raced he hoped that his men would remember that they had to fall back to enable his men to fall on the enemy flanks.

Prefect Strabo stood in the first line calmly chewing on the remains of a wild boar his men had caught. Inside he was a mass of conflicting emotions but to his men, he seemed calmness personified. When the barbarians were two hundred paces away he threw the bone to the ground and shouted, "Archers prepare!" Fifty paces later he yelled, "Loose!" The five hundred arrows stopped the front line in their tracks and the second wave hurdled the dead and dying bodies. They were travelling so quickly that the next salvo of arrows fell behind them and they hit the front line of the auxiliaries like a rock thundering down a mountain. The two lines were locked in a deadly struggle. The narrowness of the valley meant that it was man on man with quarter neither sought nor given. As soon as Lulach saw that they were all engaged he yelled, "Back!" and albeit reluctantly the centre moved inexorably back. The front two lines of the Batavians were drawn forward and a perplexed Prefect Strabo wondered at this. Barbarians normally fought and hit until they won or they were dead. They never retreated and they never pulled back. If his mind had not been so focussed on his lost cohort he might have halted but he knew he had to find them.

Unknown to each other there were two cavalry forces on the flanks about to carry out the same action. Both Marcus and Macro could see, from their vantage point, Lulach's strategy. The Batavians were forcing their way forward but in doing so they were being outflanked. Marcus remembered discussing such a battle with Julius; the battle of Cannae when the Carthaginians destroyed many Roman legions. This time there were cavalrymen behind the flanks. Turning to his raw recruits Marcus addressed them. "We are going to charge their flank. You have never fought before in a battle. Give no mercy. If you see a back then stab it. If you see an unprotected limb then go for it. If you see a comrade about to be attacked unsighted then protect him. Hit them and then withdraw and we will continue to do so. Now let us ride."

Macro saw the Prefect's attack although he did not know it was the prefect. It was the perfect moment for him to charge. "Right lads, change of plan. One volley, then charge in with javelins then withdraw and pepper them with arrows. Should be easy, they have their backs to us."

Lulach was ecstatic for his plan was working. Not only were his men falling back as planned but they were also killing more of the Romans than he had hoped. As the Batavians moved forward into the wider part of the valley they spread out more allowing the superior barbarian numbers to come into play. Prefect Strabo found himself fighting three warriors. Suddenly, out of the corner of his eye, he spied the cavalry charging down the left flank and he heard a roar from the right as Macro hit. It gave him all the encouragement he needed. Roaring, "Halt and hold." He killed one man as the auxiliary next to him stabbed upwards to kill the second. Using his shield the prefect broke the nose and jaw of the third warrior and then disembowelled him in one swift movement. "Thank you, soldier. I owe you a drink."

With no immediate enemies to his front Prefect Strabo scanned the battlefield. The two small cavalry charges had halted the encirclement but they were pin pricks only and the barbarians would soon reform. "Archers! Volley!" The arrows began to fall upon the Caledonii but those at the front had shields and the effect was less than Strabo had hoped. He was contemplating ordering a retreat to the narrow neck when he heard the most beautiful sound he had ever heard, a cavalry buccina. He could see beyond the rear ranks of the Caledonii, Marcus' Horse thundering forward. "Hold them! Hold them! We will yet win!"

The fighting became increasing furious. Despite the respite from the charge of five hundred cavalrymen the Roman forces were still heavily outnumbered. The factor which swung the day in the favour of the Romans was the Caledonii choice of battlefield. The open valley allowed Marcus horse to move at will, avoiding the cumbersome axes and throwing missiles at unprotected bodies. Eventually, however, the horses became blown and the barbarians stood in a shield wall, still too numerous to invite surrender. It was then that Centurion Vestrus marched his depleted cohort to join the dismounted warriors of Marcus Horse and shrink the circle of steel until all that remained were the bloodied mangled bodies of Roman and Caledonii. Centurion Vestrus saluted a bleeding Prefect Strabo and said, "First Cohort reporting for duty. Sir!"

# Chapter 4

High in the hills in the land of the Carvetii, there was a cave cunningly carved into the hillside cleverly disguised by an elder bush. For the past four years, an old woman and her charge had lived there. Inside it was spacious and warm with all that the two had ever needed and it was where the old one, Luigsech, the last of the Mona witches had taught Morwenna her thirteen-year-old charge. She had cared for the child since she had been weaned and she had hidden her high in the hills of the land of the lakes here after the fall of Mona and the destruction of the sacred groves by Agricola and his legions. The child's mother was long dead and had only been with the child for the first two years of her life but the old witch, Luigsech had taught the girl of the power which her mother had held and the legacy she had left her daughter. Now Morwenna was a woman and the teaching would be intensified for the old one knew that her days were numbered and she would not see another spring. The thought of shedding the mortal body did not worry her for she knew that she would join her sisters. She was also proud that she, the last of the Mona witches had been entrusted with the upbringing of the daughter of the greatest Mona witch, Fainch and soon her daughter would wreak revenge on those who had killed her mother.

"Come here and sit by me whilst I tend to your hair."

"Yes, mother."

The old woman paused as she brushed the auburn hair. "You know that I am not your mother."

"I know." The voice was that of the young girl, not the woman she had become.

"It is of your mother I speak for she was a great Druid and a great leader. She fought the Roman invader longer after the rest had died or given up. She died not knowing that she had achieved her aim and defeated the Roman horde."

"My mother defeated the Romans? How? She was but a woman."

"Your mother was more than a woman; as you are my child. She was a powerful witch. She consorted with kings and great warriors. You are the fruit of a liaison between your mother and the man who ruled this land, King Aed."

"Was it he who defeated the Romans? With my mother?"

"No, he was but a stone sent down the hill. Your mother pushed many stones down the hill but she was murdered before she could see the avalanche she had started."

"She was murdered?"

"Aye, and we know the Roman who ordered it."

The young girl's eyes became hard and her voice cold. "Then he shall die at my hands."

"He is a difficult man to kill for your mother had him in her grasp and he escaped. She tried to kill him three times and each time she failed. This warrior has powerful gods on his side do not underestimate him. But I have cast the runes and seen the future and he comes to us. Soon we will begin the training. When the moon's bleeding has ceased then I will give you all the knowledge I possess for at the dawning of the year I will have passed over and you will be alone."

"I will obey you. But what did my mother do?"

"She did what no man had done, not Caractacus, not Venutius not even the mighty Cunebolin; she united the tribes against the Romans and even though the mighty Rome had conquered most of this land the tribes are pushing the Romans back and soon, with your power and your mind, the land will belong, once again, to the tribes. Remember child the charm you wear about your neck is the sign that you are the daughter of Fainch. It will allow you to meet and speak with kings such as Calgathus. Hide it from all others but use it if anyone tests your loyalty."

Morwenna looked at the piece of jet she had worn since birth. It had become so familiar that she had never looked at it. She now did so and saw that it was a cleverly carved raven and its eye was a tiny green stone the colour of her eye and its head was more of a blood-red black than true black."

"Your mother wore that when she spoke with kings and they know of it. Guard it with your life for it may save your life."

And now we must finish your training. We serve the Mother. When I am dead and you are alone you must continue to speak with the dead as I will teach you. Then there will come a time when you will return to Mona and gather around you more women who wish to serve the Mother."

"How will I know them? Will they wear charms as I do?"

"No, child, for you are the only one with the powerful charm. But they will know the charm and they will see you. When you meet a woman look in the eyes. You will see through the eyes into the soul. Touch the hands for when you touch one of the sisters you will know by the touch. Like so." Holding out her hands the old woman gently touched Morwenna's palm. "That is the sign but they will recognise you for your mother's fame spread throughout the land amongst the sisters."

Far to the north, the Romans were mopping up after the battle. Many Caledonii had fled north towards Calgathus and his main army, the rest were being despatched or piled in burial heaps ready for the burning. Marcus, Decius, Prefect Strabo and Centurion Vestrus gathered to discuss their next move.

"I have less than two cohorts left Prefect Maximunius."

"And I have barely four hundred effective riders."

Decius coughed, "With due respect sirs we have had our arses kicked. We cannot do anything up here. We are as far north as any Roman and this wasn't the main force. We," he gestured towards Marius," interrogated a prisoner back at the fort and he couldn't wait to tell us how Calgathus was building a huge army to come south and drive the Romans into the sea. Even allowing for exaggeration this was not the main army. This was the small force to prepare the way. I say let's get back south. If I was making the decision I would take us all the way back to Morbium."

Marius smiled. He and Decius had become friends during the retreat south. They had found they had shared many similar experiences. "The decurion is right. This land is too hostile."

## Roman Retreat

"I agree but I suspect both the Governor and the Emperor might disagree. I think we will head back to the Tava. We have a good line of forts there and now that we know what to expect we can fortify them and make them stronger."

"I agree Furius but I want a better road from the south. We could have been here much sooner with artillery if we had had roads."

"And sir?"

"Yes, Decius?"

"We must recruit more men. Is it right that we are the only cavalry in the north?" The two prefects nodded. "Well unless we get the numbers in the ala up to full strength then the barbarians can surround and attack any fort at will and, with due respect to the infantry, any fort can be taken given enough time."

"Blunt as ever Decius but as usual correct," Prefect Strabo patted the tough cavalryman on the shoulder. "Let us head down the trail. Prefect, will your ala act as a rearguard?"

"Aye and vanguard too."

Governor Sallustius Lucullus was not a happy man. He had been excited when appointed to be Governor of the land once ruled by his father King Cunobelinus but his excitement had been soured as Emperor Domitian stripped the land of troops and money to fund his Dacian adventure. It was as though Britannia was irrelevant. The writing had been on the tablet when the mercurial Agricola had been summoned back to Rome before he could gain even more glory. Perhaps he remembered how his father had become Emperor and was ensuring that he would not be replaced. The latest report was even worse. There had been a catastrophe on the northern borders; three Roman forts destroyed and over fifteen hundred irreplaceable auxiliaries killed. He stroked his chin thoughtfully. He had the beginnings of an idea. "Septimus!"

His clerk had been hovering in the antechamber. "Yes, Governor?"

"How are the provincial coffers?"

The wizened old man looked up a sceptical look on his face. The real question he had been asked was 'How much can I spend without Rome becoming too curious?"

"They are satisfactory."

Sallustius looked hard at the official whom he was certain reported to Domitian's spy chief. "Could I afford to create two more auxiliary units?" The old man quickly glanced up. "To bolster the frontier in light of these Celtic incursions."

"There would be sufficient."

"Good then make the funds available and arrange for the recruitment."

As the man scribbled down some notes onto a wax tablet, Aula Luculla swept into the room. She had been a majestic looking young woman when Sallustius had married her. Her patrician background had made her a real catch. With her long, golden tresses and trim waist, she had been sought after by many suitors. Now, however, she was plumper around the waist and her facial features were becoming pinched, accentuating her sharp nose and deep-set eyes. She glared contemptuously at Septimus as he bobbed his head to her. "I don't know why you don't have the insolent old man flogged. He is far too forward with you."

The Governor shrugged and walked to the doors to slam them shut. "He sends reports to Domitian and I would like to hang on to this post for a little longer than my predecessors."

"Domitian!" She spat the word out as one would a piece of gristle from a poorly made pie. "The Flavians were always opportunists. His father was lucky, for he did not deserve to be Emperor." Aula's father had been a rival to Vespasian and had been eliminated one night leaving the important but poor Aula an orphan. Sallustius was the perfect suitor, rich, not seen as a threat to the Flavians and with the potential to be great. She had leapt upon him like a cat with a mouse. She had plans and would use him. At her father's funeral, she swore that the Flavians would regret the day they ruined her life for she would ruin their dynasty.

"Shush my love. The walls have ears."

"Look what he is doing to Britannia. We now have roving bands of barbarians on our doorstep because he has stripped the land of the legions who would have defended us. We could be butchered in our beds."

"To be fair so far he has only taken one legion and the barbarians are many miles away."

"Remember Boudicca?"

The Governor shuddered. Although he had not been in Britannia at the time, the depredations and horrors had been repeated in Rome. "This is why we have a legion constantly at hand."

"What will you do with these auxiliary units?"

Sallustius looked keenly at his wife. What plans were being fermented in her convoluted mind? "Why? To repel the barbarians. What is on your mind?"

"Britannia is a rich province. If the old goat can find the money for two more units then could you not create more money to fund more?"

The Governor's curiosity was piqued by her train of thought. "We could but what end?"

"Apart from the far north, this province is peaceful. The west is full of savages but if you were to base a legion there and strip the gold mines then that money could be used to build up a bigger army. If you could hold the Caledonii at bay we could begin to make this province civilised."

What she had said made sense but he felt she was leading him further. She had stood behind him and was massaging his shoulders, a sure sign that she wanted something from him. "And then what?"

She sinuously moved around to his front and sat on his knee. "Both Caesar and Claudius had problems crossing the fierce sea which separates us from Gaul. If this land were recaptured by the barbarians do you think that Rome would be able or even bothered to recapture this troublesome little province stuck out on the edge of the world?"

"Well no but they couldn't recapture their land. This incursion is a minor one. The peoples who live south of Caledonia are becoming Romanised."

"True and you are from a fine royal family from this land. Tell me were the warriors good warriors before we Romans arrived?"

He bristled with pride. "We were. We are. Why look what the Iceni, Brigante and Ordovices nearly achieved. It took a genius like Agricola to defeat them and there are not many Agricolas."

"So why don't you use these fine warriors to create even more legions. Celtic legions."

"And repel the Caledonii?"

"The Brigante themselves held off the Caledonii did they not? Imagine if they had been joined by the tribes further south."

Sallustius could imagine himself on a fine white horse leading these warriors north to defeat the old enemy once and for all. "But the money?"

"Surely there are men that you can trust men who could run the mines and the accounts and report to you and not to Septimus?"

Sallustius considered this. He had many family members who were desperate for positions that did not require much work but provided many rewards. "Yes, there are a few."

"Then let us do what Rome should be doing. Let us build up the armies. Endear yourself to the commanders of the auxilia. Reward them give them what they want and they will protect our northern borders. Make them loyal to you."

"Loyal to me eh? An interesting idea. Yes, it will be the auxilia who will have to defend us from the Caledonii horde, not the legions. You are right my love. I will ride to Verulanium and meet with my nephew and then I shall travel north to Coriosopitum and summon my commanders. It is time we sent these barbarians packing."

If the Governor could have seen the sly secret smile which played upon his wife's lips he might have been worried. If he had seen the letter being encrypted by Septimus he would have been terrified.

# Chapter 5

Three of his northern commanders were already meeting. Prefects Maximunius, Strabo and Sura were sat in Prefect's Sura's quarters supping a fine batch of recently acquired wine. Marcus often wondered how the portly prefect kept such a good larder and cellar but it seemed impolite to ask.

"You were both very lucky. The Parcae must have another destiny for you."

"I know Cominius. It does help to have resourceful men like my Decius and Furius' Marius."

"Thank the Allfather that we all have such men. Why does Rome not realise that we could have taken this land in one campaign and we may not lose it in winter?"

"The Emperor is too concerned with Dacia. After all, it is closer to Rome than we are. The Caledonii are no threat to him. Any threat would have to cross the Mare Germanicum which as we all know is terrifying."

Prefect Strabo belched. "Don't I know it. My supplies are sometimes held up for weeks."

"So," continued Marcus, "what do we do? The Governor has summoned us to a meeting in Coriosopitum and I daresay he will expect answers."

Prefect Sura wandered over to the map. "The road to the north is well under way but we need some insurance. We need a stronger fort that is easier to defend. I would suggest here." He poked a finger at a spot on the map. "Alavna. It is at the narrowest part of the valley and there are four forts higher up the valley. We can use the fleet on the Bodotria to keep us supplied and give us an escape route."

"I like it. But it is your decision because cavalrymen do not want to be bottled up in wooden or even stone walls. It is your men who will have to hold them."

Furius waved a hand expansively, "Suits me."

"Right then we can tell the Governor that at the meeting."

"There is one more thing." Both prefects looked at Marcus for his tone was more serious than normal. "I intend to retire."

## Roman Retreat

Even the normally taciturn Strabo was surprised. "But why? You have the finest ala I have ever seen and your men love you. Why Marcus?"

"Simple Cominius I am too old. I have seen almost fifty summers and I can no longer ride with my men as I once did. There are younger men who can lead them. You are right, Marcus' Horse is the finest ala not only in Britannia but also the Empire and I would say that to the Emperor himself." Both men smiled at the pride in his voice. "And that is why I must go. Ulpius was younger than I when he died and I became prefect many years ago. Do I want my successor to be an old man? Marcus' Horse has officers and troopers with courage and brains. There will be a prefect amongst them. And there is another reason." They looked expectantly at him. "Ailis, Gaius' wife is now with their second child. They live close to Stanwyck. I feel a responsibility towards the two of them, Ailis and Gaius. I was not there for my wife when she needed me, nor for my son. I would like to be close at hand."

"Has Gaius asked you this?"

"No, and he never would. He is loyal and loves the ala as I do but I know that he is torn. His wife cannot be here, it is too dangerous but there is still much danger further south. He will be a better soldier if he knows I am close to his family."

"Have you told Decius and the others?"

He shook his head, "I spent the journey north and back arguing with myself about the best course of action. I will tell them tonight. We are having a celebratory dinner. Although we lost some troopers it is the first time our officers all survived a major battle. I have invited them to a feast."

"I cannot deny that they deserve it."

"Would you like some of my supply of wine, Marcus?"

"Why, Furius, I am touched. Your wine is as precious as your life blood."

"I know, Cominius, perhaps I too should retire for I must be becoming senile."

Prefect Sura shook his head and saluted Marcus. "For it has been an honour to serve with such a gallant and fine officer that I would gladly shed some of my blood for you as you have done for us."

Decius and the other decurions had started their drinking early. "Those recruits did well."

"You are right Macro. They were barely half-trained and yet they fought as well as any. It's a pity so many died. We will still be short of recruits. I think it is good that we are recruiting in Britannia. The new recruits are good warriors and understand the land." Decurion Cilo spoke from the heart for he had been born on this island and was one of the first native-born officers.

Decius snorted loudly and wiped his mouth with the back of his hand. "Well if you ask me we should piss off back to Morbium and leave this shit hole to the savages who live here. I can't see any reason to be here. They have more biting insects than Egypt. The beer tastes like piss and the women would as soon castrate you as shag. Leave 'em to it."

All the decurions fell about laughing except for Gaius who was studying a piece of deer hide. Sergeant Cato leaned over and spoke quietly to the newly married decurion. Cato was a quiet leader and preferred the company of horses. Perhaps he had an animal sense which helped him to understand body language. Whatever it was he tuned into Gaius immediately. "Letter from home?"

Gaius looked up, "It is from Ailis. The boy is crawling and the one yet to be born is letting her know he is coming."

Cato nodded. Of all the officers he was the one who understood birth best. "Do not worry. The first birthing was easy as will be this one."

"But I think I should be there."

Cato shrugged, "The stallion does not see his offspring born but he knows them when they gallop alongside him."

"I know. I just wish I was nearer. Decius is right Morbium would be a better posting."

Cato took a long drink from his beaker and then said, "Be careful what you wish for?" Gaius looked up curiously. "If we were at Morbium it means that the enemy would be just over the river. Would you wish that danger on your family?"

Before Gaius could reflect on the appalling idea Marcus entered and they all stood to attention. "Sit, sit. First of all, can I formally thank and praise each and every one of you. Your ride north, your rescue of the Batavians was all that anyone could have expected of Marcus' Horse. The Batavians' thanks are reflected in their generous donations of wines and exotic food which," he added glancing around the empty jugs, "you have enjoyed." Decius belched and they all laughed again. "I have come here with some news, well a couple of pieces of news. Firstly the Governor has summoned all the prefects to a meeting at Coriosopitum. The second is that I won't be returning from that meeting as I intend to retire."

If Marcus had walked around naked or stood on his hands and sang a song he could not have shocked them more. They froze, with mouths open their drinks halfway to their mouths. Once they came to realise what he had said there was a cacophony of noise as they all spoke at once. Finally, Decius managed to get silence. "But why sir? Have we done something wrong?"

"Of course not Decius I could not be prouder of all of you."

"Are you in some sort of trouble then?"

"No, at least, I don't think so. Before I suffer the death of a thousand questions let me explain my thinking. I meant what I said. You are the finest ala in the Empire. Of that, there is no question. Had I had any doubts they would have been removed when you saved the Batavians. You saved them and I wasn't there. You no longer need me."

Macro jumped up. "But sir that's not true you were there at the last battle with the recruits."

"Yes but I only made a small difference. Do not think I am doing this because I am unhappy. I am happy but I would like to spend some time with my family and watch over them."

Decius looked puzzled, "But sir you haven't got a family have you, I mean?" Quartermaster Agrippa nudged Decius in the ribs before he could insensitively blurt out something about Macha and Ulpius, Marcus' murdered wife and child.

"I have Ailis and Ailis' child. Gaius' son." Gaius looked up understanding dawning on him.

"You mean you are going to stay with them?"

Marcus laughed. "I am not sure that your pretty young wife would appreciate an old soldier cluttering up her house. No. Some years ago I purchased a villa between Stanwyck and Morbium. It is not far from Ailis' home. Gaelwyn has been keeping his eye on it. There are slaves farming it, the ones who were formerly at Glanibanta, and I shall become a farmer."

The news was of such import that they all sat and looked at their neighbour. Marcus poured himself a drink and helped himself to the pheasant. Gaius spoke first, "Thank you, sir. You have put my mind at ease." Cato nodded and patted Gaius on the shoulder.

"Have you told the Governor yet sir?"

"No, Decius. I felt I owed it to you, to all of you to do you the courtesy of telling you and explaining my reasons."

"Well, I am going too."

Marcus shook his head. "I know you only promised to stay with the ala until I retired but the new prefect will need your knowledge for a while."

"No sir. I have had enough of this game, besides there are lads here who could give the new prefect the knowledge. Hades any one of these could do my job as Decurion Princeps."

It was obvious that many of them had not thought that far ahead. "Well if you are determined then come with me to Coriosopitum and we will see the Governor together. Gaius would you act as Decurion Princeps in Decius' absence. And now before Bacchus robs me of all senses I had better give you all the information I have. The Batavians are going to strengthen Alavna and we will have a fort built just south of it so your orders, gentlemen, are to build a fort and then patrol the road from the Tava to Alavna."

As soon as they all began their drinking session Gaius sought out the Prefect. "Thank you, sir."

"Thank me? Why Gaius?"

"For going to be close to my wife."

"Ah. When I said to protect my family I did of course mean Ailis, my wife's cousin, but I also mean Ailis' child and the child of the man who has taken the place of my dead son, the man to whom I gave the sword of Cartimandua."

Gaius did not know where to look. "But sir. I did not know. I mean thank you."

"Gaius you have always been as a member of my family as I was with Ulpius. We both knew you had greatness in you. That greatness will come with time. Be all that you can be and fear not for your family for I will do all to protect them."

The new fort at Coriosopitum had only recently been finished and the Governor approved of its cleanliness and space. He also felt far safer there than when he had visited the land of the Caledonii earlier in his rule. The three prefects and Decurion Princeps arrived after the Governor who had taken the opportunity to show them that he respected them. They were shown into their own quarters and washed by slaves. They were then taken into the Governor's dining area where the five of them enjoyed a sumptuous feast. Even Furius Strabo could not complain either with the range or the quality of the food and drink.

"Now then gentlemen. How goes it in Caledonia?"

The four men looked at each other. On the journey south, they had discussed what they would say and had determined that Marcus would speak for all of them. "The problem is Governor that we simply do not have enough troops to control such a vast country. When the general conquered the country he did it so swiftly that many places only saw Roman soldiers for a few weeks. In the south, the people have gradually become Romanised. In the north, there is no Roman civilisation whatsoever. The only presence is that of the military and now that is spread so thinly that they could if they chose, break through and rampage as far south as Eboracum. We have begun to strengthen Alavna which should stop incursions down the east coast."

The other three all nodded. "I agree with you. Your reading of the situation marries exactly with mine. But I am afraid we can expect no more troops from Rome in the foreseeable future. We have to defend Britannia from within the province." Their glum and sour looks told the Governor, without words, that they thought this an impossible task. "I have already found the funds to create two new auxiliary forces. As yet I have not thought of what type. Perhaps you gentlemen could advise me?"

Cominius chose to speak. "The Gauls have some mixed units. They were withdrawn to Dacia. They are part mounted and part foot. They are armed with missiles and conventional weapons. If we were to have only two units to replace all the ones which were taken then they would be the best option."

"I did not say they were the only forces to be created. No, I have plans for many more Britannia cohorts. They are a start. But I like your reasoning Prefect. I think that will suit us nicely. Now as to our course of action; I believe, from what you have said and," he added melodramatically, "what you have not said is that we cannot continue our advance."

"We are saying that we should, if possible, withdraw to a more defensible position. The best place would be between the estuaries of the Clota and the Bodotria."

"I agree Prefect Maximunius but the Emperor would not sanction such a loss of Roman territory."

"We should use the rivers. Morbium was the first such river crossing and has made Eboracum safe from attack. There is now a healthy local population just outside its walls. We should use the rivers. Build strong forts at the Tava, Bodotria, and Tine. Make sure that the forts have good artillery and any Celtic invasion would peter out."

"Where do they get their armies from?"

Prefect Strabo leaned forward. "The winters up there and long and cold. The nights are twice as long as the days. All they have to do is eat drink and fornicate. Every woman of childbearing age is pregnant and dropping their spawn in the autumn. If you want to end the threat then kill every single man woman and child north of the Tava. That way we have a chance to make the rest Roman."

The Governor was shocked. "It is a little savage is it not?"

"The alternative is to spend the next one hundred years fighting off invasions by these children who have nought else to do for the land cannot be farmed. If we were not the common enemy they would fight amongst themselves."

"You say that you have fortified Alavna." Prefect Sura nodded. "Then we must do the same on the west side and I agree with the road building. That is essential. Prefect Sura, find a suitable fort on the west side of Caledonia and make that as strong as Alavna. If you take charge of the auxiliary forces in the west and Prefect Strabo in the east. You will both be given the rank of Tribune to prevent disputes over hierarchy. Now Prefect Maximunius…"

"Before you begin, Governor, the Decurion Princeps and I have come to the end of our terms of enlistment and would both like to retire."

The Governor's reaction was the same as his officers had been. "But you can't. We need you. Britannia needs you."

"Governor we are both getting too old for combat and Marcus' Horse has more than enough excellent officers who can lead the men as we did."

"But they do not have your reputations."

"Not yet but their reputations are growing. Ask the other Prefects, they can tell you the names of my officers and the deeds they have performed. I feel sure that there are not many Prefects who would command officers of such renown."

"He is right Governor. I would have any of his decurions as First Spear in an instant. They are quite simply, the best."

The Governor sank back into his couch and took a large draught from his beaker. "I had counted on you Marcus." He rose on to one elbow. "If there were a role for you outside of combat, one which allows you to be close to your villa how would that suit? And you, er Decius isn't it? If I could find a well-paid role for you out of combat would that suit?"

The two friends looked at each other and said guardedly, "In theory."

The other two prefects were also intrigued and were wracking their brains for the role the Governor had in mind. They had realised that he must be a highly political figure to have survived in Rome so long as a half barbarian.

"Prefect. The area immediately around the Dunum is an important area and needs someone who can take charge. Would you consider being Tribune and overseeing the training of new recruits and the defences? That way you could still spend time with your farms and still manage the defences. It would make me feel safer."

"I suppose that it is a role I might enjoy." As soon as he had been offered the post he knew he wanted it. He would send for Cato and Agrippa and, once again be involved with the young warriors.

"Excellent and as Tribune we could call on you to offer military advice should circumstances dictate."

"Circumstances?"

"Let us say there was an uprising or an invasion you would have the power and authority to control the local forces. I would make you a Legate but that would involve permission from Rome."

Marcus thought about it briefly as he sipped his wine. He knew that in the situation just mentioned, he would not be able to sit idly by. He would want to be involved and this way he would, at least, be able to influence the direction. "Very well Governor."

Grinning from ear to ear Sallustius almost leapt to his feet to shake Marcus by the hand.

A wary Decius spoke up. "And me sir? What have you in mind for me or do I just retire?"

"No Decurion Princeps. You too have many qualities I need," he waved a hand vaguely around the room. "I need a camp prefect for this new fortress. Does that interest you?"

Decius thought about it for an instant. It was a perfect role for him. He would still be close to the people whose company he enjoyed, soldiers and yet he would have a use. "Yes sir. You have a deal."

"Excellent I have a nephew who will liaise with you, Livius Lucullus he is a bright boy but a little lazy. I think that working with you might be the making of him and will take some of the load from your shoulders. Now, all we need to do is to organise a new prefect and Decurion Princeps for Marcus' Horse."

Marcus and Decius suddenly realised that their men might have a brand new commander and second in command. They both had the same thought, 'not another Prefect Demetrius.' "Yes sir. Could we leave that for the morning when we have clear heads?"

"Of course. We haven't even had the entertainment yet."

# Chapter 6

Decius Lucullus was feeling like the prince he felt he should always have been as he rode along the newly made Roman road towards the gold mines at Luentinum. The Gallic cavalry riding in column behind him made him feel quite secure as did the frequent forts guarding this most important resource. The hills were deserted and devoid of people, still recovering from the slaughter of the Ordovices by Frontinus and Agricola. By the time they had repopulated the area, it would be totally Roman with villas, baths and forts. Decius had become a very rich young man since the return of his uncle. Times had been hard for the dispossessed aristocracy of Britannia during the early years of the Roman occupation; they had been particularly hard for Decius' family. His aunt had emphasised, to him, the need for guile and secrecy. She lavished much attention on the handsome young aristocrat. For his part, he had fallen in love with her the minute he had seen her and would have done anything for her. The fact that his uncle had given him such an important task added to the excitement of what he hoped would be a close relationship with his aunt. Their ages were closer than that of Aula and Sallustius.

As he neared the mine he focussed his mind on the task at hand. He knew, quite clearly what he had to do, he had to siphon off as much gold as he could without making the Imperial officials suspicious. To that end, he had sent ahead ten of his own bodyguards disguised as newly appointed clerks and miners and they would replace some of the older miners and clerks. It would also provide him with personal protection for they were all tough mercenaries who had decided that there were easier pickings away from the battlefield and their other option, banditry. This was legal banditry; they would be paid for from the gold he would secure for himself. Life was good.

Luigsech coughed again and Morwenna noticed that, once again, there was blood although the old woman hid it well enough. "We must stop, mother, for you are ill."

Smiling through the pain she said, "I have told you that my time is coming to an end and I must hasten your learning. You have already learned much magic and you have, indeed, your mother's gift and her looks. I can see your mother's soul in your eyes." Morwenna had no mirror and never seen herself. She had no idea what her mother had looked like but the old witch told her that looking at her was like watching a taller Fainch. The long chestnut tresses and the bright green eyes sparkled from a face which entranced, just as her mother's had. Her willowy body belied its strength which had also been part of her training and her mind was as sharp as a piece of flint and as intricate as a spider's web.

"Child, I will soon be leaving you to join your mother and my sisters in the Otherworld. Before I depart I have to set you two tasks; to drive the Romans from this land and to destroy those who killed your mother."

"But I am just a girl."

"No you are a druid and that is more powerful a being than any warrior or king. The only people who are still fighting the Romans are those in the north and the mightiest of those is King Calgathus. He knew your mother and he will recognise you. Seek him out."

"But how will I drive the Romans out?"

The old woman shrugged. "I know not but you are Fainch's daughter and you will find the answer. You will fast and meditate. You will eat the mushrooms and you will dream the dreams. This was as your mother did." The girl resigned herself but it was hard to picture herself coming up with a plan which would work. She had learned, however, to trust the old woman and believe in her teachings.

"And my mother's killers? Do I dream of them also?"

"No. They are closer and easier to destroy for I have taught you all the poisons and potions which can kill or bend men's minds to your will. Even more than your mother knew. The men who killed your mother were the Roman horsemen called Marcus' Horse. They are in the north fighting Calgathus. The one with the sword of Cartimandua is the leader but all of those who wear the red horsehair are guilty. Find them and follow them. Be patient and be cunning. You must visit the places they lived and ask about them. They lived close by here at Glanibanta; over the hills at Stanwyck and Morbium and far to the east at Derventio. You must visit all of these places and discover as much as you can. They do not know you and you will be able to infiltrate their places and their minds. Pretend and feign loyalty; for men always believe women to be the weaker species; you can show them they are wrong."

"I will, I promise."

"And swear that you will be revenged upon them. Swear now and on my bones when I am dead."

"I will swear."

"And Morwenna, you will need a charm when I am gone. You will take the fingers from my dead body and some of my hair. Put them in a bag and keep them with you at all times. That way my spirit will be there to aid you." When Morwenna looked dubious the old woman waved a bony finger at her. "If they had not burned your mother's body after they crucified her we would have had her bones and then you would have been the most powerful witch."

Terrified of having to despoil the body of the woman that she loved but terrified of failing her, the young woman nodded and said, "I swear mother that I will do as you wish."

"Now then prefects, excuse me, Tribunes." Sallustius laughed at his own joke and the four men smiled mirthlessly. "Which officers should we consider?"

Marcus shifted uncomfortably in his chair. "Will not Rome wish to make the appointment?"

Shaking his head he replied, "A legion yes but an auxiliary ala, albeit as famous as Marcus' Horse, I think not. It is part of my role and responsibilities."

"There are then, in my view, three men who could be perfect. The three decurions, Gaius Metellus Aurelius, Macro Annius Barba and Julius Salvius Demetrius."

Cominius sat up. "Julius Demetrius, a fine young man but is he not a little young?"

The Governor sat back, his hands together beneath his chin as though at prayer. He would allow these three to debate and in that way, he would be able to gauge their character. If he were to halt the barbarian invasion he needed to know his leaders.

Decius smiled to himself and waited for his friend's assessment. "That criticism could be aimed at all of them but think what they have achieved in these past few years; the campaigns in the land of the Carvetii, the battles in Mona and the wars under Agricola. They may be young in years but in experience they are ancient."

Strabo nodded. "Let us assess them all individually. Macro?"

Cominius grinned, "The bravest warrior I have ever seen and the best with any weapon."

"He is that," agreed Decius, "and the men adore him. They believe he is a good luck charm."

There was a pause and all eyes swung towards Marcus. Sighing he said, "And yet impetuous. He would lead the ala into a death or glory charge believing he could win. I am not sure that, out of the three, he has the best strategic mind."

"Gaius? I know he is your foster son." Marcus glanced at Decius who shrugged. "Would he be your choice?"

"Probably, Cominius, but not because I am so fond of him. He is the most experienced of the three of them. He is the eldest and, as with Macro, the men adore him."

"Which brings us back to Julius. It seems to me that Gaius would be the sensible and logical choice." Decius, once more sat smiling. In his mind, he knew whom both he and Marcus wanted.

"He is young and he is the least experienced and in his first few months, all I wanted to do was throw him out of the ala. But then a wiser head took him under his wing and made him the soldier he is." He smiled at Decius who nodded and took the compliment gracefully. "He has a sound strategic mind. His knowledge of military history is astounding. In addition, he comes from a patrician family and his father is a senator." The Governor suddenly sat bolt upright. "And I know that it matters not here but it might make the appointment more palatable in Rome if we were to appoint a patrician as prefect."

There was a silence as the two Tribunes and the Governor considered the import of Marcus' assessment. Furius looked over at Decius. "And you Decius what is your opinion?"

"Simple. I only had one name and that was Decurion Demetrius. And that takes nothing away from the other two whom I love like sons. If you want someone to lead the ala as well as Marcus here then there is only one choice."

"That is settled then Decurion Demetrius will be promoted to Prefect and the Decurion Princeps?"

"Bleeding obvious isn't it? Gaius."

"Blunt as ever Decius. Could I apologise for my friend's lack of diplomacy, Governor?"

The Governor smiled. "It is refreshing to hear honesty after the subterfuge of Rome. I will have my clerk write out the orders. Will you deliver them, Marcus?"

"If I could have a few days at my villa Governor then I will gladly do so."

"A few days will not cause a problem. Well gentlemen you all have new roles. I trust you will keep me informed?"

They all nodded and saluted. "Where will you be based, Governor?"

"Good point Cominius. I will be at Viroconium with the Twentieth for the rest of the year. I want to ensure that the gold trains are working at maximum capacity for that will determine how many auxiliary forces we can raise and then I shall return to Verulanium and my wife unless there are problems in the north when I will return to Eboracum."

Marcus felt strange as he rode across the bridge at Morbium. It was so familiar and yet so strange. He had seen the place as a rough little fort and bridge and now it was a powerful fort and thriving settlement. It would make his villa more secure. He had only seen the villa once and that was before he had had the buildings put up. It had been three years since he had set his slaves to build it and he looked forward to seeing it. As he emerged through the trees a couple of miles from the fort he caught his first glimpse of the small one-storied villa Annius and his men had built. Although small it looked quite substantial. Someone must have been keeping watch for, by the time he rode up to the imposing doors, the ten men and women who made up his household were stood at attention, smiles covering their faces.

Whilst one of the boys held his horse Annius, now older and greyer than when he had worked at Glanibanta, bowed. "It is good to see you master. Will you be home for long?"

"Just a week this time Annius but I am home for good soon."

"Excellent. Could I apologise for the bath house is not yet finished?"

Hiding his disappointment Marcus shrugged the apology away. "You have done well old friend to do as much as you have."

The old man looked up. "We did have encouragement from Gaelwyn, your friend."

Marcus laughed. He should have known that his old scout, Gaelwyn would have had something to do with this. "I hope he was not too obtrusive?"

"No sir. Fortunately, his visits were brief but memorable. I suspect he will be calling today for he seems to know instinctively what is going on here."

Marcus remembered the uncanny sixth sense possessed by the fearsome Brigante who had sworn such allegiance to Marcus' Horse and was now the guardian and protector of his niece, Ailis. "Well in that case we have better prepare food and drink.

Marcus had barely had time to wash and change when he was greeted by, not only Gaelwyn but Ailis and her small child, Decius. "Good to see you, Prefect. You should have warned us you were coming."

"You disappoint me old friend. I thought you had second sight and, Ailis, your husband sends his love and felicitations and asked me to do this." He leant forward and kissed her on the forehead.

"Thank you, lord, and how is my husband?"

"He misses you but then most of the decurions miss you. They envy your husband. Let us adjourn to my solar for Annius has prepared some refreshments."

Marcus spent the next hour explaining his new role and his plans for the villa. "I hope to visit with you both often; if only to placate Gaius who worries."

Gaelwyn snorted. "He is a warrior. He is where he should be."

Ailis glanced down at the bump that would soon be a child and catching her eye Marcus inclined his head in sympathy. "How many local warriors remain Gaelwyn?"

"Local warriors?"

"Men who could fight to defend the land of the Brigante."

"Ah. We have ten at Stanwyck. They work the farm and train with me. There are a few at Morbium but they need training. Why do you ask?"

"It is no secret that the legions have departed south. The only army which faces the Caledonii is that commanded by Strabo and Sura. You travelled that land. Do you believe they can stop all the raids and attacks?"

Gaelwyn shook his head. "Then we will spend the winter making our farms stronger."

"Begin with yours Gaelwyn. I will instruct Annius to bring over my workers for I want Gaius to be happy now that he is to be Decurion Princeps."

Gaelwyn grinned, obviously pleased with the decision. "That is good for it means more pay."

Marcus laughed. "Not a great deal of pay." The decurions of Marcus' Horse had done well, not from Roman pay, but from the booty they had looted from defeated foes. One torque alone had paid for Marcus' farm and all the decurions had buried their hordes in the safety of the grounds of Marcus' new villa. "I will be staying a few days and then I will return north to give your husband the news of his promotion. By the end of the month, I will be here with my family, permanently."

By the time Marcus reached Alavna, he could see the work which had already been completed. There was now a double ditch surrounding the fort as well as two extra towers on the valley sides. The lower palisades had been faced with stone and the towers inside the fort strengthened. The ala fort was the largest Marcus had seen except for the huge legionary ones at Deva and Eboracum, and he nodded in approval as he rode up to the porta Decumana. He was pleased when the sentry, whom he recognised shouted down. "Halt! Identify yourself and your business."

"Tribune Marcus Aurelius Maximunius here to speak with the senior officer."

Hiding his surprise at the title the trooper shouted, "Open the gates you may enter."

As a trooper took his horse Marcus was pleased to see an old friend limping towards him. Agrippa had been a weapon trainer and decurion before he was badly wounded in the battles against the Caledonii; as the quartermaster of Marcus' Horse, he could still do a good job and yet remain with his old friends and comrades.

"Good to see you, sir. Did I hear correctly? You are a Tribune now?"

"In a manner of speaking yes but it is purely honorary. Is the ala on patrol?"

The grim look on Agrippa's face told a story without the need for words. "Aye, it takes all the turmae just to keep the road open between here and the north. I fear that the losses may make that impossible soon."

"We have been losing men?"

"Not a great number but every patrol results in injured or dead troopers. We were already under strength and now… But let us not stand here. Come in and I will give you refreshments while I give you the whole story." Agrippa was halfway through his report when Tribune Sura entered. "I am sure the Tribune can carry on with the news sir. If you will excuse me I will arrange your accommodation and have your things put away."

"Thank you, Agrippa."

When they were alone Sura shook his head. "It has only been a few weeks Marcus but things are getting much worse."

"Agrippa was telling me."

"I am not sure how long we can hold on to the northern forts. We are losing too many men and they are indefensible. Until we get more replacements…"

"I know. There is no sign of the Governor's promised troops."

The Tribune shrugged. "It takes time. We have no facilities to train them here. That will be, I am afraid, your job and Decius of course."

"I suspect it will be more Decius' role than mine."

"How is he coping with his new post?"

"Loving it. He knows every trick that soldiers have tried, mainly because he has tried them himself at some time. Before Ulpius Felix took him in hand he was the biggest villain in the ala. The fort is so well run, it is frightening. I never realised how house proud he is."

They both laughed. "I take it you are here to make the promotions?"

"Yes. How has it worked out with Gaius as Decurion Princeps?"

"Very well. It suits him. Macro still races off into danger whenever possible so your decision not to appoint him has been vindicated and I have been watching young Demetrius. The assessment you and Decius made of him was accurate in every way. I am very impressed. He could be the First Spear for me any time. He will make a good prefect. It just depends how the others take it."

"If Decius and I have read the situation aright then they should all be happy." He shrugged. "We will fight it away out later. Will you join us?"

"I would love to. Do you mind if I bring over a couple of my centurions? I would like them to see how well your officers work together. My lads are good soldiers but, and it galls me to say this, not as good as yours."

"Bring as many as you like. I will let Agrippa know. At least he doesn't carp as much about using his precious stores as other quartermasters I have known."

When the patrols returned there was none of the usual banter and, even without seeing his troopers, Marcus knew the patrols had not gone well. He remained in his quarters to allow his officers to begin to work their frustrations out in whichever way it suited. He knew that Macro would hit the exercise yard and begin to work with weights and arms whilst Cato would groom his horse until it shone. Julius would probably sit with Gaius and discuss what went wrong and what went right; probably a good thing bearing in mind the relationship they would need to develop. Galeo and Cilo, old friends that they were would probably open a jug of something alcoholic to take away the sour taste of the day. Within an hour or so they would be less like angry bears awoken from winter sleep and more like the easy-going men he knew and loved. He had no doubt that Agrippa would have told them of his arrival and the plans for dinner. He also knew that no matter how much they wanted to come and speak with him they would respect the closed door.

He had changed his uniform, not for a vain reason but he respected Marcus' Horse too much to gain glory by association. He was now a Tribune and he had to let all know that he was no longer a prefect of just cavalry. For the first time in his life, he was moving beyond the back of a horse. Himli had come a long way since he was captured in a massacred Cantabrian village.

They were all seated when he entered. With a snap, they all stood to attention grins on their faces as they saw him in his new uniform. "Sit down. Sit down. I see that Quarter Master Agrippa has given you the news." Agrippa had the grace to shrug a half-hearted apology. "Luckily for you, it is Tribune Sura who will join us soon who is your commander." He looked across at Gaius. "I am to command the region around the Danum which will allow me time to raise horses and grow fat!" They all laughed and just then the Batavians entered.

"I hope that laugh was the result of a Macro story and not the anticipation of Batavians coming to eat and drink you under the table."

"No Cominius. My old comrades were laughing at the thought of a fat old man raising horses."

The evening went as well as both Tribunes expected and new friendships were formed. After a subtle nod from Marcus, Tribune Sura stood. "Well gentlemen thank you for your hospitality and next time we will raid Tribune Strabo's stores and feast you imperially. Good night."

When they had left Marcus held his hand up for silence. "First of all thank you for making the Batavians so welcome. We are a much-diminished band of brothers now. Secondly, how went the day?"

Gaius spoke. "Much like most of the other days. Arrows from the woods and when we chase them footfalls and traps to break horse's legs and trooper's hearts. Mutilated sentries found hanging from pine trees."

"How many today?"

"Eight troopers dead and five horses lost. Three troopers wounded."

"I have spoken with Agrippa. You shall have the first replacements Decius and I train."

Macro's face broke into a grin. "How is the old bastard?"

"You will be pleased to know that, in his new role as camp prefect, he is making all the lives of the auxiliaries a total misery. He loves it."

Macro nodded. "Tell him I miss him." He looked around the table. "We all do. He was a fair Decurion Princeps."

The unspoken question hung in the air and Marcus steeled himself, took a drink from his wine and then stood up. "As you must have realised you need a new prefect and a new Decurion Princeps. I think you have an excellent Decurion Princeps and I would like to confirm Gaius in the position. Do you accept?" Blushing as everyone patted him on the back he blushed and nodded his thanks. "The role of prefect, as you know is normally an Imperial appointment but the Governor was keen to move forward with the state of affairs here in the north. He has decided to make the appointment himself although I must say in all fairness that Decius, myself and the two Batavian Tribunes all agreed with the appointment." He took another drink from his beaker.

"Oh come on sir. Tell us. I can't stand the suspense. Is it one of the Gauls we worked with last year?"

"No, I bet it is a Batavian. That's why they were here tonight."

"Before you speculate the Emperor himself taking over Decurion Cilo I'll put you out of your misery. The new prefect is Julius Demetrius."

The silence lasted for a heartbeat and then any doubts Marcus may have had were dispelled when every officer in the room rose and patted the shocked Decurion about the shoulders. As they did so Marcus pulled Gaius to one side, "How are you with this?"

Gaius grinned," I am more than happy sir. I know he is a young man but he is the best officer we have and I am happy with my role, thank you, sir." They embraced briefly and then Gaius asked, really quietly, "How are Ailis and Decius?"

"They are both well. Gaelwyn has done a good job. Your new child will probably be a boy from all the activity. I have set men to fortify your home and mine. Not that I fear danger but I wanted your mind to be at rest."

Suddenly they both noticed that all had gone quiet and Marcus turned to see Julius almost tearfully standing behind him. "I would just like to thank you, sir. I am flattered beyond belief and want you to know that I will continue to lead the ala in the tradition of the great prefect I am succeeding."

As they clasped forearms Marcus said, "It is my honour but one more thing, Prefect I would like to steal one object from you and borrow one."

Julius looked puzzled, "It goes without saying you can have anything that is mine but I am intrigued what is it that you want?"

"I would like Decurion Cato to train my horses and men and I would like to borrow Decurion Macro to train up your recruits that is if they both wish to serve with me still?"

Both men grinned and shouted, "Yes sir!"

Julius held his hands out. "It looks like you have your wish sir but Decurion Macro is only a loan! This ala needs its volunteer." The party ended in uproar as the last of the wine was consumed.

In Rome, Emperor Domitian was reading his despatches when his clerk came in holding a sealed tablet. "From Britannia sire."

Domitian knew immediately that it was from his spy. He trusted no one in his Empire and every Governor had a spy. He quickly decoded the message and then sat back. "Well, it looks like Lucullus is taking money from us."

"Do you wish me to despatch your inspectors, sire?"

The inspectors were the group of thugs Domitian retained to eliminate problems. "Not yet. A little fraud is no bad thing, it depends if it becomes treachery or treason. I want a weekly report from now on. That island is too far away to give him a long leash. Let us give him one just long enough to hang himself from, or prove me wrong. Some of my Governors are becoming too greedy. It is bad enough having to fend off political machinations here in Rome without worrying about the men I appointed and trusted stealing from me."

"I will send my clerks over to inspect their transactions sire. We expect some losses, especially with the distances but my clerks are thorough, very thorough." Domitian nodded his approval. The clerks were indeed thorough and were all part of the spy network which kept its finger on the pulse of the Empire.

# Chapter 7

Morwenna laid the body in the grave she had dug the previous day. The lopped grey streaked tresses already lay in the cave and now the young woman, who had bloomed since the autumn, steeled herself to remove the hand as she had promised the dying woman. She extended the hand from the grave and closed her eyes to say a silent prayer to the Earth Mother. The blade was sharp enough to shave with and she began to cut and slice through the scrawny, emaciated grey flesh; she was surprised when no blood came from the wound and she was staggered at the brittleness of the bones. Lifting the hand reverently away from the body she put the arm back in the grave and began to cover it up with soil and then stones. When she had finished she stood and said her goodbyes not only to Luigsech but to the cave which had been her home for so long. This was the day when she would begin the new life; this was the day when she would begin to wreak her revenge on Rome and the soldiers who murdered her mother. Slipping the hand and hair in the leather bag she had prepared she whispered, "Goodbye Luigsech you were as a mother to me here may you protect and watch over me as I go to do the Mother's work.! When she tightened the knot it was as though she was closing a door on her past. She turned and headed east towards Stanwyck and the first stage of her journey.

Tribune Marcus Aurelius Maximunius was a surprisingly happy man. His military duties were not onerous. Macro and Cato were busy building the gyrus and camp with the sixty new recruits leaving Marcus to investigate the fruits of the farm. For the first time since he had been a boy, he was able to forget about military life with barking orders, gleaming metal and creaking leather. At the villa, he could hear the land and feel the peace. He discovered soil and things that grew. He began to recognise his animals as no longer being just a pig or a chicken; he was able to recognise individual animals. Annius had patiently told him all the names of the animals. He enjoyed visiting Ailis and Gaelwyn at their farm and was gratified to see the palisade and ditch surrounding the building growing in strength and height. It would deter all but a large war band. The stone at the base had been Marcus' own suggestion; he remembered too many forts destroyed because the enemy could dig out the posts. No one would dig out these posts. Already his own villa was becoming strengthened.

The winter months had seen him away from the farm for long periods whilst he and Cato bought horses or Macro and he recruited cavalrymen. That part of his role was rewarding, trying to get the funds from the scriveners at Eboracum was not. It wasn't until Macro suggested he take Decius with him that he began to get results. All Decius had said was the Tribune ought to buy some decent wine straight off a ship from Ostia whilst he had a word with the clerks. When Marcus had returned he found a chastened room full of clerks and scriveners who were only too happy to make the funds available. When Marcus asked Decius how he had managed to do this he just said, enigmatically, "You need to know how to talk the right language. I know how to get the best from people."

The other benefit of the winter months was the lack of action in Caledonia. It had been so quiet that Marcus had been able to arrange for Gaius, as Decurion Princeps, to come down to Morbium to choose his new recruits. It was Saturnalia or Yule dependent upon your religion but was neither here nor there as everyone enjoyed the celebration and feasting which was common to both. Marcus felt paternal pride as he watched his young adopted family smiling, oblivious to the woes of the world and enjoying the time together in the depths of the frozen winter of Northern Britannia.

Now as the snows were melting and both recruits and horses were showing signs of improvement Marcus knew he would have to give more thought to the state of the vast region he controlled. Macro had been training not only the recruits but the ex-soldiers who would be taking over his role in the spring. At first, some of these grizzled old veterans had resented the young bull of a trooper but once they saw his deftness with weaponry and his skills as a trainer they were won over. At least the training would go well although Marcus was still less than happy with the number of new recruits. He was not looking forward to his trip the following week down to Eboracum. The Governor would be looking for two mixed auxiliary cohorts and Marcus did not even have one.

The Governor and his wife were at that moment breaking their journey north at the legionary fortress at Lindum. One of the oldest fortresses it was comfortable and warm. Aula still found this land inordinately cold. The fort prefect had given them their own quarters as the legion itself was helping suppress a minor uprising in the west. Aula had ensured that the servants were dismissed; she had put on her most erotic dress and made sure her perfume and make up were of the finest for she wanted her own way. Sallustius had enjoyed the wine and the food and, as he looked over at his wife who appeared more voluptuous than usual, he was looking forward to an exciting night. She curled her elegant finger around his head and played along his cheek with the back of one of her immaculately manicured nails. "The gold has been coming in then my love? In the quantities, we hoped?"

"Yes, Decius has done better than we hope."

"And Rome suspects nothing?"

"My friends in Rome tell me that Domitian looks east not west."

"Would that he continues to do so."

Something in her voice made Sallustius look closer at his wife. She reminded him of a cat which has just stolen a juicy morsel from your table. You know something has gone but you can't work out what it is. "What is going through that devious mind of yours?"

"Nothing really it is just that over the dark dismal winter months when the snow trapped us indoors I began to read through some of the reports about the wonderful resources in this land. It may not have the grapes and olives and farm goods but it is far richer than Rome. There is not only gold there is tin and copper, lead and iron. Why just up the coast there is the precious stone, jet! The man who rules this land could be a very rich man."

"What do you mean rules? I just govern." His sharp ears had picked up the apparent mistake.

"A slip of the tongue but at one time your family did rule did it not?"

"Yes but only one part of this land."

"And now you ru... you control this land. With the use of judiciously chosen men, you could do with the other precious materials what you have done with the gold and think what army you might be able to afford then. An army large enough to…"

Sallustius stood up red-faced. "That is enough. You will get us both crucified. I'll hear no more of it."

Aula smiled the secret smile of a woman who has achieved her ends. The seed was planted. She would let it grow. Later she would trickle more poison in his ear and then? Who knew what might happen?

Marcus felt quite sad as he left his villa for his meeting in Eboracum. Gaelwyn rode over to say goodbye. "I'll keep an eye on your place too but with the ditch and the palisade I think you are safe."

"I may be but I not sure about the wine. Keep Macro away from it."

"He certainly has big appetites but as long as he is staying here it will be safe."

Morwenna arrived at Morbium just as Marcus was heading south and had the Parcae allowed they would have met on the road although mutual recognition might have been slight. Morwenna cleverly hid her stunning features with a hooded cowl and stooped gait as she moved around the busy Brigante settlement. People were happy and prosperous. The new recruits and Roman garrison ensured a ready market for their overpriced wares. They were happy to tell the young visitor, from the land of the Carvetii, of the pleasures of Morbium and the prosperity brought by the ala they all knew, Marcus' Horse. As she played the part of the country girl in a big town for the first time, she was regaled with tales of Macha, Lenta and of course Cartimandua. The Brigante were proud of their heritage. They were so proud that the last relative of the queen had arrived after having married a warrior from the ala, Marcus' Horse and even more proud because her husband now wielded the famed sword of Cartimandua. Even better was the fact that the man who led the ala now lived but a few miles from Morbium. The people of Morbium were indeed blessed.

As she excused herself to use the laundry bowls she came up with her plan. She had arrived at the perfect place to destroy Marcus' Horse and all those associated with it; her mother's killers. She was close to her Nemesis, the wife and children of one of her enemies and close to the training ground. She did not know how but she would find a way to insinuate herself into the ala's fort, and, more than that, to be welcomed. She identified the serving girl who would have to die to enable her to stay. The young girl had seen but thirteen summers and was popular with the young recruits. Morwenna stayed in the background nibbling on a hare leg she had purchased all the time observing what was going on. The young soldiers had only recently arrived at Morbium and decided to impress the pretty young serving girl. They ordered river oysters bantering with each other about the sexual prowess the beasts would bring. Morwenna readied herself for her chance. The young men swallowed the oysters shouting about the power it was giving them. The young girl continued to bring in drink and each time flirted a little more. When the plate had been emptied one young recruit asked for more for the girl and himself. She protested that she had never eaten them but the handsome young man was insistent that she would love them and she relented, her twinkling laugh lighting up the dim room. As the platter was brought in it was just a sleight of hand which enabled Morwenna to sprinkle the deadly poison over the shellfish. She was her mother's daughter and cared not about the incidental deaths she might cause. There were no innocents, they were

Romans and this was a war, a holy war. No one had noticed and she slipped back into the shadows her sharp features accentuated by the shadows and the evil grin which cracked across her face.

The young recruit was adamant that the oysters were a love tryst between the two of them. The girl's father, who owned the tavern, watched on confident that his daughter would resist the charms of the young man but knowing that the club hidden below the counter would ensure she remained a virgin.

Morwenna was becoming almost orgasmic as she watched each oyster descend down the throat of the young man. So far the girl had avoided eating one and Morwenna was not sure which ones would have the poison. Her work would have been undone if only the young recruit died but as long as they ate them all there was a good chance they both would die. At last, the young warrior, a Trinovante, asked the girl to take one as he did. He promised her a taste like no other and she agreed. Time seemed to stand still for Morwenna as they both lifted the oysters to their mouths. There was a charged, sexual feel to the air and almost everyone appeared to have stopped breathing and was silent as the molluscs slipped down their throats. Their first reaction was one of joy for Morwenna had added dried truffles to the poison to make it more palatable. When she saw the ecstasy she knew her plan had worked and she slipped out of the room, ostensibly to thank the hostess for her food. In reality, she was absenting herself from the scene of the crime, and crime it was for there was a sudden pair of screams as the two young people felt the poison work its way down their throats, burning as it went. Their noses began to bleed and they were unable to breathe. Those around them gave them water to assuage the pain but to no avail. As their bowels opened they dropped writhing to the floor dead with two violent judders and their sightless eyes staring at each other. Two young lives snuffed out by a malicious and malignant young woman who held such lives as cheap.

# Roman Retreat

The oysters were blamed; they had obviously been tainted and the distraught parents said prayers to the Allfather. The bodies were removed and the shells of the offending oysters burned as a sacrifice. Morwenna made sure she was still around the settlement for the next few days and, once again feigning poverty, she evoked sympathy as a pleasant young woman thrown on hard times. Her story of raiders from across the western waters, slaughtering her family and enslaving her, fictitious, brothers was a common one. By the time the bodies had been sent onwards and the settlement was back to normal Morwenna was a fixture. She slept where she could and she paid the smallest coins for the barest repasts even though Luigsech had ensured that she was provided with many gold and copper coins. The tavern was just as popular with new recruits arriving daily and it was only three days after the deaths that the hostess approached Morwenna. "Would you like work?"

Morwenna feigned gratitude with eyes as wide as an owl's. "Oh yes please lady."

"I am no lady but I thank you for your manner. You can sleep on the floor and we will feed you. There won't be much money but I daresay if you pretty yourself up you will get tips."

"Oh, I will. Thank you." She kissed the back of the woman's hand and ensured that she was in her good graces.

That evening the tavern was full and Morwenna had shed the dirty look. Her eyes and lips had the subtlest of colours upon them and her hair was brushed and combed. The host and hostess were pleased for it had an immediate effect. The young recruits clamoured for her attention even more than they had for their dead daughter and were happy to buy more and more drinks and food as long as it meant they were served by the enticing Morwenna. By her second night, the tavern was almost bursting and both Morwenna and the landlords were literally raking in the coins. All the time Morwenna was asking subtle questions; interrogating, albeit sweetly, to find out the names of the officers of Marcus' Horse. She had gleaned little until the largest man she had ever seen entered. He was so tall that he had to duck under the lintel to enter and his broad shoulders filled the frame of the door. She knew by the silence as he entered that he was an important Roman but even had he not been she would have sought out his company for she felt s stirring in her loins as he stood erect and beamed across the room.

"So this is where you all waste your evenings. I can see we are not working you hard enough! I can only get here once a month at the most."

"No Decurion Macro, we are only here to discuss the training and how we can become better warriors."

"Metellus Strabo you are a lying little boy lover and for that lie, you can buy me a drink!"

Morwenna could see, in an instant that he was very popular by the way the young recruits crowded around him. She picked up the empty beakers and returned them. As she passed him she brushed next to him. She had created a sweet-smelling fragrance from rose petals and lavender and she knew that it would rise to the huge officer's nose. Sure enough, he turned and she looked up at his face with a smile so sweet and subtle that a man would have had to have a heart of stone not to react and Macro was, above all else, a man. "And who are you my pretty one. I haven't seen you here before?" Macro was smitten. One look at the green eyes, the cascading chestnut tresses and the inviting red lips had done the work of Cupid.

"Why sir, I am Morwenna the new tavern maid."

He lowered his head and his voice so that his words could only be heard by her. "I can see why my boys come here so often, I will have to do so myself."

"You have the advantage, sir. What is your name?"

"I am Decurion Macro Annius Barba. I am, at the moment the trainer at Morbium but next week I return north to my ala for I serve with the famed Marcus' Horse."

Morwenna did not need to feign excitement for she had struck gold. She could ignore all the other recruits as she had found her way into the ala. "Oh, I have heard of them. They are the finest soldiers in Britannia are they not?"

Macro shrugged self consciously, "I don't know about that. But we did defeat all the northern tribes and we would have defeated the Caledonii but…"

"Weren't you the ones who rescued the Queen?"

"Morwenna! Customers are waiting!" the irate tone of the hostess almost made Morwenna decide to kill her there and then but she had a part to play.

"Sorry mistress." She looked up at the huge warrior. "Decurion Macro I would love to hear more about your brave ala. When I have finished I would like to hear more."

Beaming like a child given sweetmeats Macro could not contain himself. "I will await you, princess."

When the tavern had finally emptied Morwenna and Macro were left alone. Morwenna had already made her plans. She could sense that the warrior lusted after her and she had been taught by Luigsech that men were not ruled by their heads when it came to women but by their animal instincts. She knew that she had aroused him. Her mother had used her body and her lovemaking to help defeat the Romans and she was happy to do so. Part of her wondered if this was the right time to give up her innocence but, in truth, she was attracted to this affable young man and was looking forward to discovering what it was like. Her personal preferences were nothing until she had completed her quest.

Macro, for his part, could not believe how beautiful the young girl was. She reminded him of someone but he couldn't quite place her. Perhaps it was his dream, his fantasy. For the first time, he regretted that he would have to leave for Caledonia in the next few days. Now he just wanted to spend every minute he could with this vision of loveliness who seemed to hang on his every word.

"So you rescued Queen Cartimandua?"

"No, for I was but a boy then. No, but it was my ala and my friends Tribune Marcus Aurelius Maximus and Decurion Princeps Gaius Metellus Aurelius who were there. They both wielded the queen's sword. The Tribune has a villa close to here and the Decurion's wife and his young family live close by. If I were here longer I would take you and introduce you for Ailis is a kind Brigante princess and I am sure she would give you better lodgings than this stable."

"Oh, I would love that."

"I could take you to meet her tomorrow if you wish. The training is finished by early afternoon. Should I meet you here?"

Putting her hand on his thigh and giving it a slight squeeze she purred, "Oh yes, please. I would love that and could you tell me more about your ala. I long to know of your brave deeds."

"Of course and now, I suppose I should go?" He stood, towering over her.

Morwenna had decided to use this opening as a way into the heart of those she wished to destroy. She would give him a hint of the pleasures to come which would guarantee his return. "I do not want you to but this is no place for us to spend precious time together." Leaning up she put her arms around his waist and slightly parted her lips showing her immaculate white teeth against the ruby red lips. Macro lowered his head and their lips met; Morwenna opened her mouth and her tongue darted into Macro's mouth. Although she had never kissed a man before she had been taught well. Her tongue flicked into Macro's and he felt his whole body judder with the thrill of it. He felt himself pressing into her and growing. At that moment he wanted her more than he had ever wanted anything in his life. Just as quickly as she had started the kiss, so she ended it. As she lowered herself to the floor she could see that she had succeeded, he wanted more and the words of Luigsech echoed in her head, 'always leave them wanting more for then they will return.' "Until tomorrow," she touched his lips with two fingers, "my love."

Macro almost floated back to the fort unaware that Morwenna was busy planning the deaths of those who had thwarted her mother and ended her life.

Eboracum had grown much since Marcus had last been there. The stone buildings and walls now made the capital of the north much more solid. He reflected as he entered the Porta Praetoria that it was the work of the auxiliaries which meant that it had never been assaulted at all and the guards there had the easiest posting in Britannia. The Optio who stood at the Governor's residence looked down his nose at the auxiliary officer who rode up. Marcus had his heavy cloak around his body disguising his rank. "And what do you want? The auxiliaries have their own fort across the river."

Something about the young officer reminded him of Julius' brother the arrogant patrician who had caused the deaths of many of Marcus' friends. Marcus dismounted and, throwing his cloak over his shoulder to reveal his uniform strode up to the Optio who was already regretting his arrogance. "Listen my fine young Optio," behind him the two legionaries were struggling to hide their smiles. "I was here when this was a wooden fence and it was the auxiliaries who stopped the Brigante from castrating the legionaries who were stationed here so before you begin disparaging auxiliaries thank the Allfather that they are here for otherwise you would be roasting on a Caledonian fire. Now stand to attention and take me to the governor. He is expecting me."

The pale Optio was now quaking. "And who should I announce sir?"

"Tribune Marcus Aurelius Maximunius formerly commander of Marcus' Horse." The two legionaries snapped to attention and the Optio began to wish the ground to open beneath his feet. He was standing before a legend. "And who are you young Optio?"

The Optio stammered his answer, already visualising his military career being washed to the sea. "I am Optio Sextus Cassius Celsus of the eighth cohort, Ninth Legion."

"A fine legion is Decius Brutus still First Spear?"

A voice from behind him bellowed, "Of course he is you old horse shagger!"

Turning with a smile already creasing his face and ignoring the relieved Optio he said, "Decius Brutus! So you haven't retired yet?"

"No, and I can see that promotion has come your way… sir."

As they clasped shoulders Marcus muttered, "Less of the sirs. We are old friends are we not?"

"Aye that we are and there are damned few of us left. Now then Optio Celsus you have learned a valuable lesson today. Never judge a man by what you see and never, especially in my hearing, say anything bad about the auxiliaries they saved my life more than once! Now take us to the governor."

Sallustius Lucullus was sat behind his desk when Marcus and Decius entered. "Ah, Tribune I see you have met Centurion Brutus?"

"We are old friends sir."

"Are you? Excellent then that will make life much easier. Sit down gentlemen my nephew and wife will join us later but I thought we could discuss the broader strategy first. The Tribune here will coordinate the forces south and north of the Danum. As there are elements of the Ninth here that may mean the Tribune will be calling upon their services when necessary."

Decius grinned, his wrinkled face erupting in a myriad of lines. "Were he just a decurion I would answer his call. You need not fear Governor there will be no politics between us two."

Relieved Sallustius leaned back in his chair. "Good that is excellent. Tribune how goes the recruitment and when will they be ready for the field?"

"We have trained those who will be joining my old ala and now we are starting with the Cohortes Equitatae. Before we proceed I will need to know who will be the prefect for these cohorts."

"A good question. Perhaps there are officers amongst the Batavians and Marcus' Horse? After all, they know how the auxiliaries fight do they not?"

Marcus nodded. "That would have been my suggestion too. I would say that by midsummer you will have two more cohorts of auxiliaries and by then Marcus' Horse will be up to full strength."

"Good if you would liaise with Strabo and Sura then I can begin to recruit more forces."

Both Decius and Marcus looked up sharply when this was mentioned. "More forces? How does Rome view this recruitment drive Governor?"

The Governor bristled and coloured slightly. "Centurion I do not need to ask Rome to create new units. Besides which the Emperor is looking east and needs as many men as he can muster."

"Even so Governor this might be seen as a threat by those in Rome."

Waving a hand dismissively Sallustius blustered, "I am no threat to Rome and I think the Emperor knows that. I am Governor of Britannia and I will do everything in my power to maintain it as a thriving and prosperous colony. Do I make myself clear?"

The two soldiers looked at each other and then replied, "Yes sir!"

Just then the door at the rear opened and a waft of expensive perfume entered the room. When it fully opened they could see the Governor's wife, Aula Luculla closely followed by a young man dressed in armour. "Ah allow me to introduce my wife Aula Luculla and my nephew Livius Lucullus who will be working with you Tribune. This is Tribune Marcus Aurelius Maximunius and you already know Centurion Brutus."

Aula's eyes lit up when she saw the handsome scarred warrior standing before her. She had heard much about this hero and all of it appeared justified. She sinuously slid up to him and held out her hand for him to kiss. "At last I have met the hero of the north. Your exploits do you great credit Tribune."

"I was lucky to lead good men, your ladyship."

"I was saying to my husband that it is a lucky thing that we have such leaders in Britannia now that the Emperor has taken our successful generals away."

"Aula!"

"My husband wishes me to curb my tongue but I ask you, gentlemen, would you not wish General Agricola to be in command still?"

Decius and Marcus were at a loss for a reply for this could be a trap with which to end not only their careers but also their lives. "But then your ladyship the Governor would still be in Rome and we would not have had the pleasure of meeting you."

Decius whispered in Marcus' ear, "Cleverly done you, crafty bastard."

Aula laughed, "Not only a hero but a diplomat and a smooth-tongued gentleman. I can see that you have been underestimated Tribune."

Later when Aula and Sallustius were alone they discussed the meeting. "You are right husband he does have charisma. He would make a fine leader."

"When you speak to the tribal leaders, the Brigante, Carvetii and the Novontae he is the one man they respect. With him leading my armies we could defeat the Caledonii."

"Yes, my love but now we need to find out if he will lead them."

As Marcus rode northwards with Livius he wondered what plans and plots were being hatched in the corridors of Eboracum for he had sensed that he was being used. The governor's wife had flirted outrageously with him over their meal and the governor appeared not to mind. He realised that his promotion had moved him from the safe comfortable world of warriors into the murky and dangerous world of politics.

"So Livius, have you any military experience?"

"I trained, along with my cousin Decius, to be a warrior. I can ride and I can use a sword."

"Good. When we reach Morbium you can meet Macro. He is my weapon trainer and we will see how well you learned."

"None of my family's warriors could defeat me, sir."

There was a hurt tone in the boy's voice and Marcus smiled. "No offence intended son but Macro has defeated not only every man in the ala but every Brigante, Carvetii, Caledonii, Pictii and Novontae that he has met. I just need to gauge your strengths and weakness for you will be dealing with warriors much older than you are. Have you ever fought?"

"In a battle?" Marcus nodded. "No."

"It might be that a short time with the ala might help. Would you mind that?"

Livius' face lit up. "A chance to fight, to prove myself a warrior? Yes sir!"

"Good. Then when Macro and I go north you can accompany us."

# Chapter 8

Cato scrutinised Macro carefully, there was something different about him; they had finished training about an hour earlier, sooner than Cato had expected and Macro had washed from head to toe in the river. He then shaved for the second time that day and amazed the sergeant by putting on a clean tunic. Cato had not been in the tavern the previous night but he had heard the recruits whispering about Macro and a pretty girl called Morwenna. "I suspect, Decurion, that a woman is involved in all this preparation?"

Macro was going to deny it but one look at Cato told him that it would be fruitless. He nodded vigorously, looking about ten years younger in the process. "You are right. It is a new girl in the village. Cato she smells, she smells like springtime and she looks, well I have never seen anything more beautiful in my life."

"Be careful Decurion. The last thing you need is an irate parent with a pitchfork aimed at your behind."

"She is an orphan."

"Ah, well in that case be even more careful for she may be looking for a husband."

"She can have one." The seriousness in his tone convinced Cato that this would be more than a tumble in the hayfields for the affable warrior.

Macro had been waiting for almost an hour by the time Morwenna arrived. She too had spent some time making herself look as attractive as possible but in her case, it was to make a trap that would be attractive to her prey.

"You are beautiful."

"And you are handsome." She pecked him on the cheek; he could be tantalised a little more yet. "You were telling me about your deeds and exploits." Macro needed no encouragement to talk of the battles, the friends, the campaigns and the places he had known. Morwenna was an avid listener and, although she did not write down a word, her memory, trained by Luigsech ensured that she would remember every detail. Macro finished with his tale of the rescue of the Batavians and Morwenna lay on his lap, her face looking adoringly at the young Adonis. "How brave and how frightening it must have been. Someone in the village told me of a witch. That would have scared me."

Macro's face darkened. "Aye Fainch. That was a dark time. She murdered the Queen and tried to burn alive the Tribune, although he was just a prefect then."

"What happened to her?"

"We finally found her when we raided Calgathus' village and she was crucified. She was a brave, although ultimately an evil woman. She never cried out, right until the moment she died."

Morwenna kept smiling but her hand gripped the bag with Luigsech's bones and hair and in her head, she was saying a prayer. She reached up with her other hand and pulled his head down to meet hers. "I am the luckiest woman in the world to have such a man as you." She kissed him hard on the mouth and in an instant he became aroused. He rolled over until he was lying on top of her and his hand crept up to cup the small pert breast whose nipple was hard and erect. When he found no resistance he went further and suddenly Morwenna opened her legs. She was as aroused as he and, regardless of his name or her plan she would have carried on as she did.

As they lay on the grass Macro propped himself up on one elbow. "I was your first then?"

"You will be my only for I love you and wish you to be mine forever." Macro did not realise the significance of the word forever. In Morwenna's convoluted and complex mind this was a far more sinister word than the romantic one pictured by Macro.

"And I love you and I am yours. When I return to the fort I will ask the Prefect for permission to marry."

"I thought you had to be of Centurion rank?"

"We will go now and see Ailis. She and Gaius are married; she will know a way. Come you will like her." Like two children they gambolled across the fields.

It was close to dusk when they approached the farm. Gaelwyn's keen eyes had spotted them from afar and he waited by the gate. "Decurion. It is late to be visiting is it not? The gates would have been closed upon you soon."

"I just had to come and show Ailis, my newfound love."

The old warrior gave a half-smile. "Indeed then let us go indoors. She is with the bairn."

Ailis quickly smoothed down her dress as they entered. "Gaelwyn you should have warned me… oh it is you Macro do come in." She threw her arms around him and they embraced as brother and sister. "And who is this pretty young thing? You have beautiful hair, my dear."

Morwenna bobbed and Macro put his arm around her saying proudly, "This is Morwenna and we would like to be married."

Gaelwyn and Ailis burst out laughing. "Do I look like a holy man?"

Blushing Macro said, "No Gaelwyn, I meant we are going to be married and I wanted to tell someone and to ask how you do it?"

Ailis said mischievously, "How you do it? You surprise me I thought every trooper in the ala knows how to do it."

"No, I mean how to get married with me being a decurion and you and Gaius well.."

"Sit down the two of you I am just teasing. I am pleased for you both. Morwenna you don't know just what a fine man you have. And you Macro I am delighted. Let me see how did Gaius do it? He just asked the prefect and the prefect gave permission."

"That's it then? Well, that is easy. We'll just keep this quiet until I have had the chance to speak with him. Do you think I could ask a favour of you Ailis?"

"Ask anything for you know what I owe you."

"Morwenna sleeps on the floor in the tavern and it is not seemly. Could she sleep here on the farm with you?"

Ailis liked the look of the young girl with her innocent smile and the way her lovelorn eyes never left Macro. And as for Macro, the giant had been humbled. She would gladly look after the girl. "Gladly and I am sure she can work here rather than at the tavern. I am sure you would not want the other recruits ogling her while you were gone eh?"

"You are right. Thank you."

"And now let us celebrate." Gaelwyn pulled a jug and the four of them drank while the child played. Morwenna was mentally dancing as she contemplated her position. She would be protected and sheltered by the very people she would ultimately kill and destroy. The Mother and Luigsech were indeed watching over her.

By the time Marcus returned Macro had almost finished training the recruits. He decided not to tell the Tribune his news before he had spoken with Julius partly because he did not want to jinx the relationship and partly because he was intrigued by the young man who trailed in the Tribune's wake.

"This is Livius and I want you to give him a workout in the gyrus."

Macro grinned, "Do you like him sir or shall I give him a real workout?"

Marcus grinned but Livius blushed. "Do not hold back on my account Decurion. I have yet to be beaten." Laughing Macro threw him one of the wooden training swords. Livius shouted scornfully, "I use a real blade not a piece of wood."

Macro's face darkened. "In my gyrus, you follow my rules. Is that clear?"

Nodding, Livius went into a defensive stance. Macro stood like a chimpanzee, his arms hanging down loosely at his side. Livius smiled to himself this would be easy; he would have the ape on his back in two strokes. He brought the wooden sword above his head to slice down at the unprotected neck of the decurion. Almost in an instant, the huge man pivoted on his right foot so that the blow came down into an empty space and then smacked the blade of the sword against Livius posterior. The blow was so hard that he found himself face down on the ground.

"Now then have we finished being a dickhead? Can we try again but this time, do not assume because I look like a Greek Temple I will move as slowly as one?"

Marcus covered his mouth to hide the grin erupting from his face. Livius stood on guard once more but this time the blade was held lower and his centre of gravity was lower.

"That's better, son, now you are thinking. You will still end up on your arse but that is a better starting position."

After two or three parries and thrusts, Livius was wiping the blood from the back of his head. "Better but you still let me get under your skin. Now come on or shall I get a serving girl from the tavern to fight me?" Livius forced himself to calm down and outthink this huge brute who moved like a butterfly.

The last time the bout went on much longer but Macro still emerged triumphant. He walked over to a Livius who was breathing as heavily as if he had climbed Etna. "Good lad. He'll do Tribune. Just needs a bit of work."

Marcus glanced over at Livius who nodded and smiled a wry smile. "I'll learn Tribune. I promise."

"Good. He is coming with us. We go North tomorrow and he can join a turma for a week or so."

Macro looked at Livius and shook his head. "You want to thank your gods that Decius isn't there. He would have your arse between two pieces of bread old son."

That night Macro slipped away to Ailis' farm. He and Morwenna spent an hour enjoying each other's company. "I have to leave in the morning but as soon as I can I will return and we will be married."

"I know my love. I trust you and I believe you. Thank you for putting me with such good people. "

"I know and I will sleep happier each evening knowing that Ailis and Gaelwyn are keeping watch over you."

"Come back soon."

"I shall."

Inside the farm, Gaelwyn was drinking his evening special, as he liked to call it. He looked at Ailis thoughtfully. "That girl reminds me of someone but I can't quite place her."

"She is beautiful, uncle. Perhaps she is the woman you always wanted."

Gaelwyn snorted. "She is pretty but there is something about her. It is the eyes and the hair. There is something. Something about the girl reminds me. That is the trouble with getting old…"

The next day Macro, Livius and the Tribune began their journey north. They had with them the last one hundred trainees for the ala. As Livius nursed his bruises he reflected how lucky he had been. From the conversations he overheard, Macro was the greatest warrior in Britannia and he had had the audacity to think he could defeat him. As they headed to Coriosopitum he determined to learn from the mercurial Macro and become a better warrior.

The change in Livius had not gone unnoticed by Marcus. It reminded him of the change in Julius Demetrius once Decius had effected the changes. Perhaps his legacy was greater than he thought. Perhaps Ulpius Felix had changed them all in some mysterious way that only the Allfather could understand. He looked forward to sharing an amphora of Gaulish wine with Decius and discussing the philosophy of leadership. He laughed to himself. He knew what Decius' reaction would be. 'Bollocks!"

Coriosopitum was one of the largest establishments Macro had seen. Decius snorted. "You want to see what the Tribune is building further north. There are forts and a town. Tribunes Sura and Furius have big ideas for this land."

Marcus nodded. Although just beyond the area of his influence it would provide a buffer should the Caledonii and Pictii move south. "And what of your role Decius? Is it what you envisaged?"

"No! But then I never really saw the role. I couldn't have done this job ten years ago but now? I think I have grown into it. I won't say I don't miss the fighting but then again I don't have some hairy arsed barbarians trying to make a necklace of my bollocks do I?" Marcus and Macro burst out laughing whilst Livius stood shocked. "Besides which you and I were getting too old for fighting. You slow up and that is the problem with barbarians, there are always younger ones coming through. And speaking of young warriors, who is this?"

"Prefect Flavius this is Livius Lucullus my aide, the Governor's nephew."

"Pleased to meet you sunshine."

"Don't worry Livius this is as bad as it gets. The rest are pussycats by comparison."

"Too right Macro. They broke the mould when they made me. I don't know about you but I could do with a skinful."

"Livius we will now test your ability to drink and I hope it is better than your ability with a sword."

Marcus shook his head, "Macro I now know why we never made you Prefect. You have the diplomatic skill of Venutius on a bad day!"

"And I second that Tribune. Give him a barbarian at the end of his sword and he is the best man you could have; anything else and he is fucked."

Macro beamed, "I won't argue with you two older men. All I can say is … you are right. Now let us get pissed."

Livius found a smile creeping across his face. It looked like he was going to get the adventure he had always desired.

On the ride, north Macro told the Tribune about Morwenna. As soon as he began to tell of their courtship Marcus knew that the young man was smitten. "And where does she come from?"

"Her family are Carvetii and lived in the lands to the north of Glanibanta."

"And she with red hair? I suspect she has some of the raiders from the islands in her blood."

Macro nodded, "Her family were killed and her brothers enslaved by the wild men."

Livius looked perplexed. "The wild men? The islands?"

"Ah yes, Livius you would not know of these things coming from the south-east. There are islands to the west and the people's there have never fought Rome. They love to fight either amongst themselves or in the odd time of peace they raid the west coast of Britannia and Caledonia."

"Does Rome not have forts to the west?"

Marcus shook his head. "No. We had one at Glanibanta but that one was abandoned. There is one fort at Luguvalium but that is there mainly to stop Caledonii raids."

"Are we close to Caledonia?" the young aide peered around nervously.

Macro smiled. "No this is the land of the Votadini but the people around here have not been pacified long. The Tribune and I fought many battles against them."

"Are we safe?"

Marcus shook his head. "Once you cross the Dunum you are in danger. Luckily we can now move from fort to fort otherwise you would have the pleasure of building a camp each night."

"And believe me Livius that would soon give you muscles like these." Macro flexed his arm which to Livius looked as big as a leg.

"Where is the next fort then?"

Macro looked at Marcus, "Isn't there one eight miles or so north of here. I think it is a small one."

"Yes. I came south on a ship last time but I believe there is a century fort on the Alavunus estuary."

"Good they have nice fish there."

"Always thinking of your stomach eh Macro."

"If I don't who will?"

All thoughts of food disappeared as they emerged from the forest south of the fort. They could see the spirals of smoke drifting up in the clear late winter evening. Macro gave the order as soon as they saw it. "Stand to."

Livius looked around as he heard the young recruits slide their javelins out and shoulder their shields. "What is it Tribune?"

"Danger Livius. That is the fort and it is burning or burnt." He nodded at Macro who was waiting to take charge. Marcus deferred to the Decurion for the recruits would follow better the man who had trained them.

"Right lads it looks like we are going to get a little action earlier than I had hoped. The first four troopers," he pointed at them to ensure they knew who they were, "you will ride parallel to us about half a mile to our right. For those who are confused that is the bit nearest the sea." The humour slightly relaxed the tension. "The next four do the same to our left. You will ride in single file and your job is to warn us of an ambush. If you see or hear anything then return to us. We are the mother hen, right? And mother does not want

## Roman Retreat

to lose her chicks. Now get into position and remember anyone who is not one of us is an enemy. Strike first and ask questions later." As they rode away Macro addressed the rest. "We are going to ride in a column of fours. When I signal the fours will join up so that we have three lines. That clear?" They nodded nervously. "Listen for me or the Tribune to give orders and whatever we say do it. That way you might live. Now follow us. Livius you ride with the Tribune."

Macro led them out. Livius leaned over to Marcus as they rode. "Don't you outrank him, sir?"

"Not on a battlefield. You will learn that rank means nothing out here. What is more important is ability and Macro has that. Now you watch to your left. You see anything untoward you yell."

The closer to the fort that they got the more the damage was apparent. The small fort had been burned to the ground. The grisly remains of the garrison could be seen spread-eagled against the trees or mounted on spears. Behind him, Livius heard a trooper vomit and he fought to keep down the last meal he had eaten. Macro held up his hand and shouted over his shoulder, "First four follow me." As the five men entered Marcus glanced to the left and right and was happy to see the eight outriders heading for them. "See anything. The eight men shook their heads.

"We could see where they had left sir. Over that way." One of the troopers pointed west.

"Good that helps. You eight form a picket line a mile up the trail. We'll send for you when we have stabilised the situation."

As they rode off Livius asked, "Stabilised the situation?"

"Buried the bodies and cleared the fort."

Macro came out and waved them forward. Inside the scene was even worse. The eighty auxiliaries were all accounted for but their bodies were not whole. Each soldier had been tortured if alive or desecrated if dead. "Looks like they got in over the walls sir, either that or someone let them in for the gate was open."

"Any of their dead?"

"Not a sign."

"So it could have been anybody."

"Looks like it."

"They left west. I sent eight of your lads as a picket line."

"If I had my turma we could find the bastards and… but as it is…"

"As it is we will bury our dead, secure the fort and give our recruits," he emphasised the word, "the chance to learn how to survive in hostile territory."

"Yes sir."

It was a sombre group of recruits who went to sleep that night. The palisade had been rebuilt and a third of them were on duty. Marcus and Macro had drawn Livius to one side. "We will each take a turn at sentry duty. The most dangerous time will be in the dark hours of the night. You Livius will take charge while the Decurion and I sleep. You will awake me in three hours. I have given you one-third of the men as your watch."

Livius looked confused. "Three hours but how…"

Macro pointed to the skyline. "When the moon is there. Listen you will have to watch over these men carefully. They will jump at shadows. Look for movement. Keep the fire tended but tell your men not to look at it and stay in the shadows so that they are not illuminated in its light."

"Do you think they will come?"

"Oh they will come but they will probably wait until the dark hours of the night when they think we are at our least vigilant."

"When you and the Tribune will be on guard." Macro nodded. "Good for there will come a time when I will take the dangerous watch and you will be able to sleep."

Macro ruffled the boy's hair. "That's the spirit."

Macro was right. They came an hour after Macro had fallen asleep. The young recruit came over to the Tribune. "Sir I thought I saw something over there."

Marcus went with him and peered into the bloom of the undergrowth. Despite the warrior's attempt to hide there was just enough white for Marcus to identify him. "Good man. Alert the other sentries." Marcus crept over to Macro who was awake in an instant. The Tribune did not need to say a word and the Decurion went around his watch waking them. Livius took two shakes to awaken him and Marcus held his hand over his mouth. "Wake your watch. They are here." His eyes wide with fear and excitement the aide nodded.

Marcus noted that Macro already had his bow ready and the fire arrow was ready for ignition. "I've been around the lads and told them to be on guard. I have four men holding the horses. Wouldn't do to be afoot here." Marcus slid his blade from its scabbard and hefted the borrowed shield on his left. It was some time since he had fought in such a small action he wondered if he would be up to it. His reflexes had not been tested for some time. This could be the night he went to the Allfather and spoke again with Ulpius. He kissed the hilt of his sword. It was not the sword of Cartimandua but it was a good blade, a spatha and he would use it well.

The arrow slammed into his shield and almost made the seasoned soldier jump. "Here they come." He nodded to Macro who ignited the arrow and shot it into the air. It plummeted down in the dead wood and brush the men had placed fifty paces from the perimeter. Suddenly it was as though it was daylight. Some eight or ten warriors were caught on the wood and were burning. There were others between the fire and the wall.

One in two recruits had bows and Macro yelled, "Loose!" Although their aim was not as good as experienced auxiliaries they still brought down some warriors and soon they were loading and shooting as fast as they could. Macro was choosing his targets carefully, aiming for any sign of leadership or armour. Even so, the enraged warriors made the palisade and the bows were laid down. The first javelins were hurled at ten paces and the second held by the besieged young troopers to stab down at the barbarians now baying for blood. Their lack of training showed itself as some of them exposed too much of their bodies in their desperation to get to grips with their enemies and died as the Votadini took advantage of the mistake.

"Protect yourselves with shields! Do not give them an opening."

# Roman Retreat

Livius was terrified with fear. He had not anticipated a battle would be like this. He had pictured himself in hand to hand combat with an enemy and using his skill to kill him. Here he could not see where the enemy was coming from and they appeared so quickly.

Suddenly two warriors boosted one of their fellows over the palisade. Although the two died, an enemy was in the camp. He quickly killed one startled recruit and then hacked down another. Marcus was on him in a moment. Years of training took over and he punched him with the boss of the shield and then sliced diagonally down to hit the unprotected neck. Soon there were more warriors inside the camp and it became a series of hand to hand combats. Macro was a Colossus and seemed to bring death wherever he strode. Livius found himself facing a powerful warrior who was using a short hand axe and a short sword. Livius was like a frightened hare and he glanced from axe to sword and back. The warrior sensed his indecision and grinned evilly. He feinted with the axe and when Livius reacted sliced upwards with his sword. The trick nearly worked and, were it not for his youth and quick reactions, he would have died. As it was the razor-sharp blade sliced across his shield arm and Livius saw with horror his own blood. He almost panicked and then he heard the Tribune. "Hit him with the shield and then go for the gut!"

Without thinking Livius obeyed. The Votadini warrior had been going in for the kill and the blow with the shield made him spin, lose his balance and fall to the ground. Livius almost tripped over him but managed, somehow to bring the blade down and into the man's guts. The force was so hard that the blade became embedded in the ground.

"Look out!"

Livius rolled away as the sword from behind hit into empty air. The bearded warrior was just about to finish off the helpless aide when Marcus sliced his head off in one movement. That was the last action of the short but fiercely fought battle. The remaining warriors fled to the west as the first rays of dawn peeped over the sea from the east. Macro went to his horse and picked three uninjured recruits to go with him. They galloped off after the warriors; Macro firing arrows as soon as he left the palisade.

"Any enemy left alive?"

A voice shouted, "Here is one."

"One in two keep watch, the other check the wounded and help them. Livius keep watch."

As Livius pulled his sword from the body of the dead warrior he watched in amazement as the young recruits followed orders. For himself he would have sat down and cried or tend to his wound but, seeing the young men doing their duty and ignoring their own hurts, he felt he had to uphold the honour of his tribe. Out of the corner of his eye, he saw the Tribune and a recruit go to the wounded warrior.

"You will die for it is a bad wound." The warrior looked at the intestines spreading out over his lap and nodded. "I can make it quick, give you a sword and send you to the Allfather. One question."

The man looked up, suspicion on his face. "I will not betray my people, Roman."

"I know. Who is your chief?"

There was almost relief on the man's face as he realised he could divulge that information and keep his honour. "Ryan and he has sworn to rid his land of the Roman filth."

Marcus nodded, "Give him his sword." The recruit looked in horror at the Tribune who nodded. When the sword was in his hand the warrior smiled and nodded at Marcus who slipped his own blade into the dying warrior's throat ending his life instantly.

Macro rode up. "We killed another eight of them. They won't be back today but we had better get while the going is good."

Marcus rose wearily. "Place our dead in a row, cover them with the palisade and we will burn them."

Livius looked appalled. "We should honour them with burial."

"We should but then the Votadini would dig them up and despoil them would you want that?"

"No sir."

## Roman Retreat

Macro came up to him. "You have had two good lessons today, son. One is that this is a hard place to live and die and secondly when you fight to use the edge of the blade, not the tip that way it doesn't get stuck, but you did well tonight and you will learn and get better."

When the depleted column left there were twelve empty saddles and the ala would not get all the recruits they expected but as Macro said, philosophically, the thirty-eight they were getting were better trained and prepared.

# Chapter 9

Tribune Sura looked thinner, greyer and totally drained when he greeted Marcus and Macro. "It is good to see you but I fear the handful of men you have brought cannot begin to make up the losses."

Even the once youthful Prefect Demetrius now looked a little greyer and older. "The Tribune is right sir. We need those recruits but, if I am to speak honestly, we need infantry more than cavalry."

"The young man is right Marcus. And if what you say about the Votadini is correct then we may be in danger of having insurrection in our rear."

Marcus looked at his old friends. "The good news is that there will be two complete cohorts of mixed infantry and cavalry ready by summer. Can you hold on until then?"

"If the threat from the Votadini can be negated."

"I think we can but it will mean using the ala to do so. Can you spare them?"

With a grim smile, Cominius said, "They are the best force I have but they are wasted in these woods. They have spent more time fighting on foot than they have mounted. The country of the Votadini is more suited to horses and cavalry. If you can eliminate the threat of the Votadini then we will hold. This fort is now the frontier and Tribune Strabo is as stretched in the west."

"Prefect, shall we give the ala the chance to ride a little freer in the hills of the Votadini?"

The smile came back on Julius' face. "I think the men would appreciate that sir but Tribune Sura, we will return. I promise."

"I know Prefect. I know."

Livius stayed close to the Tribune as they headed south. As he looked around at the troopers of Marcus' Horse he felt intimidated. They were a scarred and battle-hardened group of men and their eyes had the look of men who have seen the worst that war can bring about them. He also chose the position just behind the Tribune as it enabled him to listen to the Tribune talking with such ease to the Prefect and Decurion Princeps. It seemed to the outsider that they were brothers talking of their family.

"So Julius how does command suit?"

"Not as easy as you made it look, sir."

Marcus laughed. "That is the trick. It is like a swan swimming on a lake."

"A swan sir?"

"Yes on the surface all appears calm but beneath his legs are flailing about at great speed."

"I'll have to remember that sir. Keep a calm exterior."

"If you can manage that Julius you will have done well. And you Gaius are you happy in your post?"

"Yes sir, it was easier for me than Julius. I had Ulpius, you and Decius to model myself upon."

"Everyone is happy then."

Julius turned to look back towards Macro. "We have missed Macro. He is such a huge presence in every sense of the word."

"I know. The recruits all look to him as though he is Julius Caesar and Horatius rolled into one. But he may change soon."

"Change how so?"

"You remember Julius that he requested a meeting with you when time permitted?"

"Yes, I don't think I have ever seen him so serious."

"Well," Marcus lowered his voice, "he has met a girl and seeks to emulate the Decurion Princeps."

"Me!" said a startled Gaius.

"Aye, he wishes to marry."

"Macro married! I never thought I would see the day."

"Have you met her yet sir?"

Marcus shook his head, "No Gaius but she lives with your wife and Gaelwyn which is good for them both for Ailis has help with the bairn and Ailis will help Morwenna to understand the ways of the ala."

"I will, of course, give him permission but that means I will have two officers yearning for a posting home."

Gaius and Marcus laughed. "I suspect Julius that Marcus' Horse will be more like to be based closer to Coriosopitum anyway. Once Sura and Strabo get the mixed cohorts they will be in a better position to defend against the incursions and I need a force that can be rapidly deployed against minor rebellions. I fear that this Votadini rebellion is but one of a number. Our Novontae tribesmen are complaining of raids by the Irish and Pictii for slaves and Macro's betrothed was orphaned by one such a raid. The trouble is we did not bring the Pax Romana we promised them. All they see of Rome is the soldiers. At Eboracum and Stanwyck, why even Morbium, there is no sign of unrest. I will have to base the Classis Britannica on the west coast."

"They did a good job the last time we used them."

"Aye Julius but they cannot react as swiftly as you can. No, this campaign will be a long one. The Votadini will need a lesson teaching to them which will make them think twice about rebelling. I intend to build a series of forts west from Coriosopitum as a barrier and a place where we can base troops. I have an idea for using the ala as smaller units perhaps four turmae."

"That would work."

"I would not suggest it with any other ala but you have officers who can work together. Even the new ones you used to replace yourself and Gaius."

"They have learned quickly."

"They have had to."

"I intend for us to camp at the site of the burnt fort tonight as we know that is close to the rebels and we can rebuild the fort. I will send to Decius and ask him for a century of his Gauls to garrison it."

"That will please the old goat! How is he?"

"Enjoying the role rather more than I thought he would."

Livius felt like a spare part as the ala busied themselves building the fort, clearing the lines and preparing food. Gaius took the opportunity to speak to him. "It must seem strange to you the way this ala operates."

"It feels like some sort of closed order elite. Everyone knows what to do I feel like an outsider."

"We all feel like the first time. Remember Livius you did not train with the recruits, you are an outsider. They will get to know you. Marcus has told me that he wishes you to ride with a turma. That is the best way to learn what it is like to be one of us for when you fight you have to rely on the man next to you and behind you as he relies on you. If one man does not do his job then we all suffer."

"That is a high standard."

"Yes, and it was not achieved easily. We have had our bad apples who would have spoiled the barrel. The Prefect's own brother nearly caused the ala to be massacred."

"And yet he is Prefect."

"Yes because he deserves it and is a good leader. Marcus' Horse made him so. This ala is like a test for good warriors. If you are a good warrior it will make you a great warrior. If you are not then you will leave or die."

"What will I be?"

Gaius looked at the nervous young man. "Macro told me of your first fight. You did not run; you stood against a better opponent and you won."

"Only just and that was because the Tribune shouted a warning."

Gaius gave Livius a knowing glance. "One of your comrades helped you out?"

"Ah. Now I get it."

"No, you begin to get it. It is a long journey but, believe me, it is worth it."

Livius was even more impressed when he saw how the ala took to building the fort. The brush and woods were cut further back. As the troopers laboured Macro confided in Livius, "I don't like to speak ill of the dead but the soldiers who built this originally did a half-arsed job. The ditches weren't deep enough, the palisade not high enough and they allowed the undergrowth to grow back. That's the trouble with garrison duty; you get lazy."

Livius nodded. "Will the ala become lazy?"

Macro shot a disparaging look at the boy. "The short answer is no but if you want to know the reason why then I suppose it is because we have a reputation to uphold.

Everyone is proud of the honours we have received and no one wants to be the one to bring disgrace. Besides, the leaders wouldn't allow it: Ulpius, Marcus, Decius and now Julius, all want this to be the best, and it is. Anyway, we have had our rest and it's time we dug a ditch or two."

Livius looked shocked; he was the son of a noble, the nephew of the Governor. "But I thought only troopers did that sort of work."

Laughing, Macro slapped him on the back, "Well first old son at the moment you are a trooper but secondly, every man you can see here was a trooper at one time or another and if you look closely you will see the Tribune with a mattock in his hand."

Livius saw, for the first time that the whole of the ala was working. "This will take some getting used to."

Macro glanced down at the soft hands of the young noble. "Well look on it this way, the calluses and the extra muscles will help you fight a little better and don't forget that when the fort is finished you and the other recruits have combat training." Livius groaned. This was a harder posting than he had expected.

By the time the drizzle had arrived with the tide and the fall of evening every single man was tired. Livius was exhausted and all he wanted to do was to sleep. He saw the Tribune and Macro approaching, bows slung over their shoulders. "Ah Livius we thought you had worked hard enough today and the Prefect has excused you the evening duties. We thought you might like to come with us to hunt up some venison."

Livius paled at the thought. He had envisaged falling into a deep sleep as soon as he reached his tent. "Yes sir but I am not a very good shot."

"You have the finest teacher here. Macro could pluck an eagle from the sky."

"But I wouldn't." They both looked at the Decurion who looked very serious.

"Why not Decurion?"

"They taste awful, all plucking and bones." Grinning at his own humour he handed a bow and quiver to the aide.

"Do as we do, hold the bow in your left hand with an arrow notched, put a second one between your teeth. You go behind me to my left and watch for my hand signals. You are to hit anything which comes past me and goes left. The Tribune will do the same to the right."

Livius found he could barely see Macro as the big man slid silently into the woods. He had to keep looking down to avoid the twigs and branches which littered the ground. He looked up to see the right hand of Macro ordering a halt. He watched as the mighty Decurion drew back the string. He did the same but he had no idea what he was aiming at. He saw the arrow release and then suddenly a huge stag leapt towards him. He had no time to aim and he just reacted. His arrow flew but he had no idea if it hit or not as he took cover to avoid being hit by the dying beast. When he found his feet he followed the other two who were running down the wounded animal. Livius could see the blood trail before him. This was not how he had hunted with his noble friends, then they had had beaters who had forced the animals into the open where they had bravely thrown their spears at the beasts and, while the slaves cut up the meat they had supped and drunk fine wines.

A few paces further on he found Macro and the Tribune standing over the huge animal. Macro was pulling an arrow from the rump of the beast. "Here is your arrow. Well done you hit it but remember next time that you must lead the animal. This barely wounded it. If that had been an enemy you would now be dead."

"But it came too quickly. I did not have time to prepare and aim."

The Tribune smiled, "In battle, you have no time to prepare. It is the quick that live and the slow that die. You did well."

Macro had cut down a young sapling and was sharpening the point. "You will also learn not to look down when walking quietly." He began to slide the sapling through the animal's body. The Tribune held its head.

"Then how do you avoid making a noise?"

The Tribune began pulling the sapling from the deer's throat. Macro looked at Livius. "I am a big man?" Livius nodded. "Did you hear me? No, and why because I put each step down slowly and I feel the ground beneath me; if I feel something I move my foot. My eyes are always looking around me for that is where the game is or the danger. You need to practise. For me this was a childhood game, stalking my friends in the woods. Did you not have such games?"

Livius shook his head. His games had been dice and throwing sticks. "No, it seems I had a poor upbringing. I was playing the wrong games."

The two officers laughed. "Well, you have come to the right place then. We will teach you real games."

As they walked back to camp the sapling between the Tribune and Livius, the aide reflected that he was no longer tired and also he marvelled that the most senior officer did the menial work while Macro walked behind. He now knew why. Macro had the better ears, eyes and was the better shot; in this ala, the best man did the job not the most senior.

When the fort was finished Marcus called together the officers. "Julius and I have spent many hours devising a new way of operating. Gaius will remember how we operated in this way with Ulpius Felix after we rescued the Queen." Gaius nodded. "We will divide into three vexillations. The prefect will lead four turmae, Gaius another four and Macro with the last four. Each party will have a different sector to patrol. We are trying to find the camp of this Ryan. The fact that there are one hundred troopers in each patrol means that you should be able to deal with anything other than the main warband. Regard each Votadini as an enemy."

Livius held up his hand, "Sir what about the fort. Will we leave it empty?"

The other decurions all laughed and Marcus held up his hand for silence. "No Livius the Quartermaster and Sergeant Cato will remain with one trooper from each turma. The troopers are rotated on a daily basis. Good question though Livius, it shows you are beginning to think. We will make a cavalryman of you yet. I will ride with Gaius and you Livius will go with Decurion Macro for he has the other recruits with him."

Whilst the Prefect headed north and Gaius south, Macro and his vexillation headed west. "There is a fort guarding the main north-south road. I intend to get there today and then circle back southeast."

Decurion Cilo nodded, "We had some trouble south-east of that fort the last time we were in this area. They are sneaky bastards."

Macro had ordered Livius to ride at the rear with Decurion Cilo and he had wondered why. As they rode he found out why. "The Decurion thinks you have the potential to become a good officer." Livius beamed at the compliment. "I am your test because I can sniff out a bad officer. Decurion Galeo and I suffered at the hands of an arrogant patrician, Decurion Demetrius." He saw Livius start and shook his head. "Not the Prefect but the little shit who was his brother. I am not saying you will be the same but I will tell you when I think you are going down that road. Right? Plain enough for you?"

Livius smiled a wry smile. "I am learning that men in this ala speak their minds whether you want or no."

Cilo laughed and slapped the young man's shoulder. "Good you are learning."

The first part of the day was uneventful and then, just before noon Macro held up his hand and the vexillation halted. A trooper rode back. "Decurion Macro has spotted something ahead. He wants you to take your turma southwest and then head north."

Without a word, Cilo led the turma at a canter across the trackless moor land. Livius turned to the trooper next to him. "What are we looking for?"

"The enemy."

"But where?"

"If Decurion Macro says they are ahead then believe me that is where they will be. I would loosen your shield because when we go into battle you will have no time and loosen your sword in its scabbard. It was a cold night you don't want it sticking."

Livius heed the advice and suddenly they stopped and the Decurion wheeled them into line. Livius still couldn't see an enemy but he noticed, high in the air crows and magpies circling. The Decurion drew his sword and Livius followed when he saw the other thirty troopers do so. When they moved forward they did so at a steady pace, gradually increasing their speed. Suddenly Livius could see the enemy. A small detachment of auxiliaries were fighting desperately against a Votadini horde. The Decurion lowered his sword and the line leapt forward, silently. The Roman auxiliaries could see the wave of death approaching their enemies and hope entered their hearts but the Votadini were too intent on finishing off this detachment. Out of the corner of his eye, Livius could see Macro and another turma approaching from the east, he assumed the last turma was heading south. Almost in an instant he saw a Votadini turn in shock and he remembered his hunting lesson, he sliced down on the bare flesh of the man's throat. The blade slid through flesh and the man's throat erupted with blood; withdrawing his blade he looked for his next opponent. He saw a warrior holding a spear in two hands attacking the unprotected side of the trooper who had given him advice. Livius headed his horse towards the man and just bowled him over. The trooper looked in alarm as he heard the dying warrior's scream and nodded his thanks to Livius who halted to look for another enemy. There were none. The surprise had been complete and the remaining eight auxiliaries were grateful that the turmae had turned up when they did.

The remaining Optio reported to Macro. "The First Spear sent us to investigate the fort at Alavna. They hadn't been heard of in a few weeks. He thought a half-century would do it. We were ambushed and were trying to get back to the fort when you arrived. Thank you."

"The bad news is that the fort and its garrison have been destroyed but Marcus' Horse is there now. The other news is that the Votadini are rebelling."

"That is bad news but I am glad that Marcus' Horse is here."

"Well we will escort you back to your fort and I will have a talk with your First Spear."

The fort had a good position with clear lines of fire. Macro nodded in appreciation as they entered the Porta Praetorium. The Centurion who greeted them was an enormous soldier, almost as big as Macro. The two men went inside while the troopers watered and fed their horses. The trooper whose life had been saved by Livius wandered over. "Annius Salvus is my name and I am in your debt. " He clasped Livius' forearm and the aide saw the rest of the turma nod their thanks. He had been accepted. He was now a member of the turma and nothing he had received so far in his life, riches, position meant as much and he felt himself swell with pride.

Macro emerged from the headquarters and spoke to the vexillation. "It seems the Votadini have not been as far west as this so we will head south-east and make our way back to the fort. Well done for today."

Over the next month, the ala scoured the land seeking out and destroying the rebellious bands of Votadini. Not all of the Votadini had revolted and Livius learned another valuable lesson about handling tribes who could become disaffected with the wrong approach. All of the officers from the Tribune down seemed to know when to be firm and when to make concessions. His fighting skills improved and he knew he had been accepted when the turma began to banter with him.

Finally, the campaign came to an end and Ryan was captured and brought in chains to the fort and brought before Marcus. "Tell me, King Ryan, why did you rebel? When we came to your land we promised you all the benefits of Rome; the education, the buildings and the security."

"Yes Roman you did but when the Caledonii came south to raid our cattle where were you? When the raiders came across the sea from the north where were you? Where are the buildings? Where is the education? All that my people saw were Roman soldiers strutting along their new roads and taking animals to feed themselves. When my people went hungry I chose to take back what was ours. Now enough talk. Kill me."

Marcus shook his head. "No, for this is not the old tribal ways. This is the Roman way and, despite what you think, Rome is fair and just. You have suffered injustice and I understand why you did what you did. It is our fault that there was no one to whom you could address your complaints. I will remedy that. Free him!" The only two who were surprised by Marcus' action were Livius and Ryan himself. "Go back to your people. I will instruct the soldiers to protect you and I will punish any soldier who takes goods or services without payment. But that in itself is not enough for we are both old enough, king, to know that there are always people in your tribe and mine who will not walk the straight way. If you have complaints then take them to the fort at Coriosopitum and I promise you that they will be dealt with."

He held his arm out and Ryan clasped it. "I will trust you Roman for I see no lie in your eye and your warriors are brave and honourable. I feel no shame in our defeat."

One night, when the handover of the rebuilt fort to the auxiliaries was nearly complete and the summer days were lengthening the Tribune asked Livius to walk with him by the sea and the sand dunes. "Over there Livius is Rome and here, although we are part of Rome that water makes us separate. We are the only part of Rome that cannot be visited on foot alone. That will be the downfall, perhaps, of this province, for we are the only chance that Rome has of sustaining a presence in Britannia and you, Livius, and other native-born Britons are the only chance the province has to survive the day that Rome leaves."

"But will Rome leave?"

Marcus shook his head. Not in my lifetime but one day it may. Alexander's Empire did not last a generation past his death. The Pharaohs ruled their land for hundreds of years. Empires come and go. History will judge the success of the Roman Empire, not us. You have done well Livius. Do you see why I wanted you to spend time with the ala?"

"Yes, Tribune and believe me I have learned."

"Good, for your apprenticeship, is over and you will now have to leave the ala and become my aide and emissary. You know the way I think and you know how we operate. That must become part of you for you will be giving commands, orders and suggestions to soldiers who are older than you. Can you handle that?"

"Yes, Tribune. I am ready."

"Good."

# Chapter 10

Morwenna sought out Ailis after they had put the child to bed. Ailis was about to birth herself and welcomed the chance just to sit and chat. "Yes, Morwenna what is it?"

"My moons have passed without bleeding."

Ailis smiled. "I sensed it, my love. You are with child." Ailis threw her arms around the child. She liked the young girl and felt that she was part of the family already.

"I feel it inside."

"Good, for Macro needs a son as Gaius needed his own son. They are returning to Morbium soon. We can make preparations for the wedding."

"Will it be allowed?"

"Gaius wrote that the Prefect has given permission. You will be wed by midsummer."

Morwenna's smile was spontaneous and real but the thoughts hidden in her head were dark, sinister and evil. She would be able to do what her mother had never managed to do she would be able to do her work from the heart of the enemy and the enemy would help to raise her child; the viper in the bosom.

The sentry at the gates of Eboracum watched as the caravan headed ponderously along the newly built road. "Who in Hades is this?"

The Centurion peered at the finely dressed figure with the embossed cuirass, flanked by the column of heavily armed warriors. "That, my son, is Decius Lucullus' the Governor's nephew and he is rapidly becoming a powerful man. He is still a little arrogant shit but now a rich and powerful one. You see the mules he has behind him?" The newly arrived sentry nodded. "They are laden with gold, copper and tin. Our Governor is becoming a rich man."

"Does it not go to Rome?"

The Centurion laughed, "Of course it does." He glanced down at the naïve young legionary. "But not as much as is dug out of the ground."

The Governor and his wife were watching from the solar of the palace. "Decius has done well husband."

Sallustius said sourly, "He could be a little more subtle. He arrives in broad daylight with shiny armour and mules that are so heavily laden that they can barely walk. It will not take long for Rome to realise that her profits are not as great as they should be."

"But that is why we base ourselves here in this northern hell hole, far away from spying eyes."

"We are a port and there are clerks and officials here who would as soon inform as breathe."

"A little longer my love, just a little longer and we will be safe here from any attack, from any quarter." She began stroking his brow with her soft manicured hand and he closed his eyes in pleasure. "Have you given thought to the soldiers in your province?"

"I have promoted the leaders is that not enough?"

"It is a start but you need to win over the men. You could lead the army to a great victory over the barbarians and become a hero."

"If my able and competent commanders in the north cannot do so then I doubt that I will be able to manage to do so."

"In that case then you should increase their pay."

"Above that of the rest of the Empire? It would not be sanctioned."

"Call it a frontier bonus and let it be known that you pay it from your personal coffers. I believe Julius Caesar did so."

"I know and look what happened to him."

"We must take chances to achieve greatness. If you increase the pay by a little then more men will join, why you may even find soldiers coming from the mainland for the greater pay."

"I will consider that."

Just then there was a knock on the door and the sentry entered, "Decius Lucullus to see the Governor."

Sallustius would just as happily have continued the conversation with his shrewd and cunning consort for she had ideas which meant greater power and profit for them all but he knew he would have to meet with his nephew sometime. As the door closed Aula embraced Decius, "Good to see you nephew. Your laden mules tell us that your endeavours were successful."

"They were and the miners found another rich seam as I left."

The Governor looked shrewdly at the impeccably dressed and armoured young man. "I hope that I am seeing all the profits. I would hate to think that someone was creaming a little off before I saw it."

Decius hand went to his sword, "Are you impugning my name?"

Aula came between them but the Governor lowered his voice and said threateningly. "Nephew remember this, I rule here and you work for me. I took you from your little village where you strutted around the farm yard like a cockerel and gave you this opportunity. Do not throw it away in such a cavalier fashion."

Aula's eyes pleaded with the boy to back off and Decius registered the word rule not govern. "I am sorry sir that you doubt me but all that is yours you receive."

"Then who pays for your fine armour and increasingly numerous bodyguards?"

"The armour and the bodyguards are needed uncle for the land through which we travel is wild."

Mollified the Governor waved his nephew to a seat. "I am glad that Tribune Maximunius is coming today for I would have his advice about these wild parts of Britannia."

"Is my cousin still his aide?" Decius was not over-fond of his cousin. Where Decius needed to bully and buy friends, Livius managed to make all like him. Decius also knew that Livius was a better warrior, and he resented it.

"Yes, they have been busy putting down an insurrection in the north."

"There is always an insurrection in the north."

"Yes, my dear but I believe the last letter from the Tribune suggested he had a solution to that particular problem. If he can solve that one then we can really begin to make the southern half of the province as prosperous as we would hope."

"Well, Livius we will see today if your uncle has found the gold to pay for the troops he promised us."
"To be truthful sir I do not know my uncle well. He lived in Rome whilst I was growing up but I do know that he wants the best for Britannia. He believes that the province can be great."
"Good for I have come to love Britannia and its peoples too."
"Sir, can I ask you a question?"
"Ask away Livius and I will give as honest an answer as I can."
"Why did you let the rebel king live?"
"A good question; had he rebelled against Rome's rule he would have died but he did not; he rebelled because we, no it was I, who failed him. I gave the tribes my word. Rome promised safety and prosperity and delivered neither. If I had executed him, as was my right, then the Votadini would have been an ulcer for years. They may become one yet but I have bought Rome time until we can bring to the Votadini what the legions brought to your people."

Sallustius greeted Marcus like a long lost friend. "How good to see you. I see from the reports that you have managed to quell a rebellion. I feel that your appointment was a timely one. And my nephew is he learning?"
Livius felt himself blushing. His uncle was talking about him as though he were not there. He felt a surge of pleasure when the Tribune put his arm around his shoulder. "I would like to thank the Governor for appointing such an intelligent, hard-working and resourceful young man as my aide. My task has been made much easier."
"Good, good. Now then what are we to do about the Caledonii?"
"Sir, Livius and I have a map and if we could find a quiet place we will explain the strategy we propose."

Livius could not help but notice the contrast between his uncle and the cavalry commander. One included whilst one excluded. The irony was that it was his family who was excluding him. He thought back to the way the officers of the ala had been with each and he saw that his first family was now the ala. When they put the map on the table Livius took the pointer while Marcus strode around the table explaining.

"The rebellions of the Votadini and the problems we have had in the past with the Brigante have convinced me that we need to make the land either side of Dunum into Rome in every sense of the word. Just as it is south of the Dunum. The people need roads, schools and education so that they feel Roman. The land between the Dunum and the Tine and Ituna rivers should be the next area we civilise. To do so we need two barriers one along the line of the Bodotria and Clota and the second along the Ituna, Tine border. North of the Bodotria should be abandoned."

The Governor sat up in his seat his eyes boring into Marcus'. "That would be tantamount to telling the world that we have failed."

"No Governor. Between the landing of Claudius and the defeat of Venutius, almost forty years elapsed. We only crossed the Bodotria less than ten years ago. We are not withdrawing we are consolidating. Besides we have not the manpower to defeat the Caledonii. The land is almost as big as the rest of Britannia and we have a handful of auxiliary cohorts. We need a barrier."

"What do you mean by a barrier?"

"A series of self-supporting forts; the Northern one garrisoned by the Batavians under the two tribunes and the Southern one garrisoned by the new mixed cohorts. The two sets of forts were built in Agricola's time and were only temporary wooden structures. We can build better defensive features and use more stone to make them both substantial and defensible. The land between the two lines suits cavalry whilst the land north of the Bodotria can only be conquered by the legions."

"And where would you place your old ala, Marcus' Horse?"

"Veluniate on the shores of the Bodotria."

"Interesting. Why there?"

"They can move south and west easily and, if needs be could be moved by sea further distances. The auxiliary's role would be to stop the raids and incursions. But no matter how well they patrol, determined warriors can still evade a static fort and the ala would be in a good position to pursue and catch a warband. The watchtowers we are building would enable signals to be sent to the Cohortes Equitatae and they could move up for the south. The cavalry would be able to ensure that the trade routes stayed open while the infantry could make sure the roads were well built."

The Governor pondered for a while and then darted a question at Livius. "And you, nephew? What is your view?"

"I have seen the land north of the Tine. It does suit cavalry but we must make it Roman. The Tribune's plan is a good one."

"I know and I applaud it. It also suits my larger plan. The other four auxiliary forces could be based here at Eboracum ready to support the legions retake Caledonia in the future." Livius and Marcus exchanged looks but did not say anything. "And now Tribune I have something to show you." He opened the door and a soldier came in holding a long object in sackcloth. "Put it on the table and leave."

When the man had gone Sallustius opened it up to reveal a lance. Marcus looked at it and the Governor inclined his head to show that Marcus could touch it. He held it in his hand, raised it up, felt the weight and then tossed it from hand to hand. "I have not seen this design before."

Beaming widely Sallustius said, "It is of my own design. I call it a Lucullus. Notice how it has a tapered guard to protect the hand and can be tucked beneath the arm. I wanted to show it to you before I ordered some to be made for your ala. Could they learn to use it?"

Marcus picked it up again and then Livius grinned, "I bet Macro would love to have a go with this."

Marcus laughed, "The problem would be to stop him throwing it."

"No, no, it is not for throwing."

"I know Governor but the Decurion we are talking about is so strong he would believe he could throw it. Yes, I can see how it could be useful. I will certainly talk to Prefect Demetrius about it."

As they rode North Livius said, "I thought the extra cohorts were to be for north of the Dunum?"

"They will be. At the moment they are still being trained at Derventio and Cataractonium. I will see they are deployed where necessary when they are trained. We will after all station ourselves at Morbium. And that is closer to the training camps than Eboracum. I suspect your uncle is playing a game and he has not told us the rules."

Lucius Antoninus Saturninus was the Governor of Germania Superior. Like his counterpart in Britannia, he was becoming increasingly alarmed by the removal of forces from his province. Like Sallustius, he too was contemplating moves to make his own position much more secure, however, he had gone one stage further; he was planning to leave the Empire and set up his own country. "So tell me Rufius would this Governor of Britannia join us in our endeavour?"

The furtive looking man peered over his shoulder, even though they were alone and then said, "I have spoken with his nephew and the man is lining his pockets at the Empire's expense. If he would not do so willingly we could coerce him."

Lucius shook his head. "No, I need whole hearted support, not grudging subservience. What else."

"My spies tell me that his wife is ambitious and he is building auxiliary units loyal only to him. He recently gave all his troops a pay rise."

"Now that sounds like a good idea. How could he afford that?"

"He has gold mines in the west."

"This sounds like just the man for us then."

"Why, sir, do we need him?"

"Britannia is an island and, as such, more secure than we are. If our endeavour failed here we would have a bolt hole especially if your information about the gold is true. In addition, it would make it more difficult for Domitian to attack if he had two enemies raising forces. Go to this man and gauge how he might react to such an offer but do not use my name and do not give him any details, just the concept."

The ala reached Morbium just as Marcus was briefing the Governor. Marcus and Gaius were obviously keen to leave for the villa but they were both professional enough to build the camp and await permission from the prefect. Julius Demetrius appeared, to Gaius and those who knew him well, to have become older suddenly. He no longer looked like the little boy in a uniform two sizes too big and he had a demeanour that commanded respect. Only Macro knew of the hours the prefect had spent with the weapon's trainer building up his body and exercising to the point of exhaustion just to fill out his frame. This was one of the many reasons why the prefect could not deny Macro's request. As for Gaius, even though Julius had served a shorter period, Gaius had shown no resentment at having a junior officer promoted above him. In fact, Gaius had gone out of the way to make life easier for his superior and to support him at every turn. Therefore when they both arrived at the headquarters' building with their request for a two-day furlough the prefect handed over the tablet already signed and sealed giving them a five-day furlough. "The Tribune won't be back for five days and this gives the other decurions time to assess the new recruits who are waiting for us. It just means Decurion that you will have a shorter time to train them as we head back north."

"Don't worry sir it will be worth it to see Morwenna and to marry her."

"Go on then be off with you."

Riding through the familiar country in high summer was a delight for the two officers. Both wanted to gallop as though it were a race but rode gently along sharing their hopes and dreams for the future. It was Gaelwyn who greeted them. "About time you two reprobates showed up. When I was a scout we defeated our enemies quicker than now."

Waving an acknowledgement the two men leapt from their horses and raced to the brick-built farm. Gaius enfolded both his son and his wife and the new baby in both his arms while Macro literally swept Morwenna off her feet. "You had best be careful Gaius."

"Why is that Ailis? I am just so happy to see the woman who is to be my wife."

"Which is good but do be careful with your unborn child."

Macro almost dropped Morwenna and Gaius' jaw dropped. "You wasted no time did you, Gaius?"

Ailis nudged Gaius in the ribs, "Gaius, outside, let them alone."

As he was dragged outside he protested, "But what did I do?"

Macro held the diminutive Morwenna at arm's length. "How long have you known? When is ..."

Morwenna held her hand to Macro's lips. "I have known for three weeks and the child will be born in six months just after the Yule festival."

"Enfolding her in his bear-like arms he said, "Then we shall be married at once."

Ailis had correctly predicted Macro's reaction and a pig had already been slaughtered. There was beer and mead and the farm looked as clean as when it was built. There were few guests but that, in itself, made it a more memorable occasion.

Gaelwyn and Gaius sat off to one side as Ailis put the children to bed. "She is a pretty girl."

"She is that but do not be fooled she works hard and she is a great help to Ailis. Your wife cannot have her husband and she needs the company of women. A gruff old uncle who can only talk of war and hunting is no compensation."

"I am sorry uncle but I am pleased that Morwenna has come." He took a draught from the jug of spirit which

Gaelwyn had produced. "She reminds me of someone or I have seen her before."

"That was my thought but I cannot think who. Perhaps she looks like every pretty woman we ever saw. Not that we saw many."

"No, the Caledonii women could only be separated from the men by the shortness of their beards." They both fell to the floor laughing at the mental image they both had.

Macro nestled Morwenna's head on his shoulder. "I am happy that you get on so well with Ailis and Gaelwyn. They are good people."

"They are lovely. Gaelwyn can be a bit gruff but he is so helpful and Ailis is the kindest person in the world."

"Good for I fear that this break will be too short and soon I will return North."

"To Morbium?"

"No Alavna in the land of the Caledonii, at least that is my guess but if not there then Coriosopitum."

"I wish to be with you."

Shaking his head he said vehemently, "It is no place for a young mother with a child."

"Ailis could look after my child until he is older and as we are married I could live near the fort."

"It is a wild land Morwenna and we hold on to it by our very fingertips. We could have to move very quickly and I would not be able to look after you."

Sensing his weakening resolve she pursued her point. "I travelled here alone, Macro. I can look after myself. I could travel up to the fort with supplies. I would be safer."

Relenting he said, "We'll see., but first we need my son to be born!"

The smile which erupted on her face made Macro's heart melt. Inside Morwenna sensed victory. She would become ensconced in the heart of the ala, in the perfect place to poison men's minds and bodies and finally eradicate the curse that had destroyed her mother.

Marcus and Livius reached Morbium just as the ala was due to head north, first to Coriosopitum and then on to Alavna. "Livius the first task, working on your own is to await the next batch of recruits and bring them north." Livius looked apprehensive but before he could speak Marcus went on, "You have completed the journey before. You take them to Coriosopitum first, then Trimontium and finally Alavna. It is a three-day journey. Remember you know more than the recruits."

"But sir, am I ready?"

"The problem is Livius that the ala will need all its experienced officers with the ala if we are to enable the Batavians and Gauls to build their forts. Passengers are a luxury we can't afford. The days are growing shorter; we have to make the forts as defensible as possible as soon as we can."

Macro spoke up, "I don't mind waiting with him."

Marcus threw him the same look he had when Macro had been a young trooper trying to pull the wool over his eyes. "Decurion Macro I think the Prefect was more than generous with the furlough he gave you. Your pretty wife, who, incidentally, I have still to meet, will have to have the baby without you. I believe women have been doing successfully that for some time."

Sheepishly the affable giant put his head down and mumbled, "Yes sir."

The next month saw the whole of the Roman Army in the north busy building roads, strengthening forts and defences and training men as rapidly as possible. Livius soon became adept at escorting the recruits to their new postings. He got to know Camp Prefect Decius very well and Livius suspected that the Tribune had had something to do with his warm reception. He found that Decius was like a familiar uncle, prone to saying the wrong thing but eminently trustworthy and reliable. He also had a way with the recruits which made Livius' job easier. On his journeys south, he began to spend an extra night with the ex-cavalryman listening to the stories of the ala when they were still the Pannonians.

Tribune Sura was pleased with the new strategy. "Alavna is a nightmare to hold Marcus. There is but one wall where they are unlikely to attack and they are constantly slipping over the palisade and slitting throats. We have to do double guard duty which exhausts the men. The sooner we can withdraw to a defensible line the better."

"Aye Decius is busy with the southern forts. We are using the fort at Coriosopitum as the anchor and the forts go east and west from the secure base. Furius is strengthening the forts to the west. By Spring we should have finished."

"I am glad that the governor made good with his promise for more troops and the pay rise has made the men happier."

"I am not so sure Cominius. He asked for the last four cohorts to be sent south to Eboracum. Luckily I had already garrisoned Morbium and Coriosopitum with the first recruits so the south is safer now."

"But why? The land is safe there and they have the legions a stone's throw away."

"I am not sure but I think the Governor has some different ideas but at least we now have two spare cohorts. Young Livius is bringing them north as soon as they are trained."

"Macro is going around with a face as long as a cow's behind."

"Yes he got married and he moons after her. She is with child. It should be due next month by which time he will be even worse."

"I hope he takes out his frustration on the Caledonii."

"Don't worry. He will."

# Chapter 11

In Rome, the Emperor summoned three men to a secret meeting. One of them was his spymaster. His true identity was a closely guarded secret and only Domitian was privy to it. All in the palace knew of his existence and had even seen him flitting in and around its corridors but even the Praetorian Guard did not question him. He was known as the Cowl for he always had his face covered with a hood. In each meeting, he sat in the shadows with the hood over his head hiding his features. He was the one man Domitian trusted. The other two were also trusted by the Emperor. They were soldiers who had served his father well as Tribunes.

"I have brought you two to this meeting today because I need both of you to be Legates for me. Before I outline your mission do you accept?" They both nodded for they both knew that refusal would see their dead bodies in the Tiber before dawn. "Good. Cornelius Furcus you are to go to Britannia. Julius Verinus you are to go to Germania Superior. You are to take charge of the legions and auxiliaries in those areas. In Britannia, the peoples in the north are causing problems and in Germania, it is the tribes near to the river. However, you need to know that I do not trust the two Governors. They appear to be hiding facts and money from me. When it is time to act I will but I need you two to be my eyes and ears. You will see far more than the spies we have." He handed both men a seal. "Use this to seal your despatches and mark them for my eyes only. Is that clear?"

"Yes, Caesar."

"Good and if you need to take drastic action then do so."

The two old soldiers looked at each other. Cornelius said, "Drastic action Caesar?"

"You are both blunt warriors; let me also be blunt, if you have to rid the province of your Governors then do so. I have many more governors. "He gestured to his spymaster and added, with a smile, "My friend here will brief you on the personnel and forces at your disposal."

Rufius Agrippa was a cautious man. He knew his activities were treasonous but he longed for the riches promised to him by his employer. He had been in Eboracum for a few days to acclimatise himself not only to the bizarre weather but also to the views and opinions of its inhabitants. Eboracum was quite a prosperous place and Rufius knew that the rest of the country might not hold the same opinions but as the Governor had spent some time in the city this might give him a better picture of his popularity. He visited as many taverns as possible and he eavesdropped on every conversation from the merchants complaining about the city taxes to the soldiers extolling the virtues of the man who had raised their pay. He found himself in agreement with Lucius Antoninus Saturninus, the man was taking chances, and if the Emperor found out he would soon find himself in the Imperial dungeons. He also discovered that the Governor's nephew was involved in his schemes. It had not been hard to elicit that information. In the second tavern, he heard the name of Decius Lucullus as a man who was powerful and becoming more powerful by the day a man it was wise to stay the good side of. He found Decius Lucullus in the most expensive tavern. Even had he not known his identity he would have recognised him by his entourage. The bodyguards looked like thugs and were powerfully built and armed. The sycophants who pandered to him were all tricksters and con men. Rufius decided to make the young man's acquaintance for he would be the best way to get the Governor's confidence.
    He waited until Decius was about to leave and, while he was bidding farewell to his new best friends, Rufius went outside where he slipped the guard a large enough bribe to ensure that he would be allowed to speak to Decius.
    "Decius Lucullus? If I could have a word." Rufius had developed a voice that sounded both pathetic and wheedling. He had found it useful to convince others that he was no

threat. In reality, he was an accomplished assassin but this mission required diplomacy and he could be diplomatic.

"I have bought enough drinks and friends for one night. Go away."

"Oh, no fine sir it is I who wish to bring better fortune to your good self."

Decius paused, mid-stride. "Good fortune eh? I am incredibly rich already how could you add to that?"

"The man I serve is even richer believe me and an association could bring even more reward and, more importantly, power for both you and your uncle."

"My uncle? What do you know of my uncle?" Decius was on his guard for he wondered if Rufius was an Imperial spy sent to trap him.

"I know that he too is a rich man and has become richer since the gold mines opened."

Decius Lucullus put one hand around Rufius' neck. "If this is an attempt to get money from me…"

"I told you before sir that I wished to make you richer. I have no interest in how you and your uncle make your money but it does, perhaps, tell me that you may be interested in a scheme which would make the gold mine seem like small change."

Releasing him Decius smiled a mirthless smile. "Carry on then benefactor. How can we make such Croesian sums?" He straightened his uniform and ran his hands over his long, oiled hair.

"If you can arrange a private audience with your uncle then I can, perhaps, tell you both at the same time." Although his remit had been to involve the Governor only Rufius was astute enough to see the potential of involving the preening, peacock parading before him.

"Are you staying nearby?" Rufius nodded, he would be changing his accommodation as soon as Decius left; he was taking no chances of a blade in the night. "Then meet me here tomorrow at noon."

Rufius knew that the Governor had taken the bait when Decius was waiting for him in the tavern. "Come with me." He was taken quickly to an unguarded rear entrance of the

Governor's quarters. Decius left him at a large plain door. "Just knock and you will be seen."

Rufius smiled to himself. The Governor was a careful man. He wanted no witnesses to the conversation. "Come in." Rufius found himself facing the window which faced south. The late autumnal sunshine made it difficult to see. The Governor was using every trick he could to gain an advantage. "How are you going to make me rich?"

"To be honest Governor the rich part was for your nephew, he appeared to like money and I thought it would gain me an audience." He heard a reassuring chuckle from the Governor who appreciated Rufius' accurate assessment of his greedy nephew. "You will become richer but my proposal, our proposal, will make you more powerful; in fact the most powerful man in Britannia."

"I am already the most powerful man in Britannia."

Dropping his voice Rufius said, "The man you serve has all the power. You and I know Governor, that should we have another Emperor you could lose that power in an instant."

"Go on."

"I serve a number of men as powerful as you."

"Governors."

"I did not say that. Do not jump to conclusions. Let us say they are men who wield a certain amount of power and would like more power. I have been sent as an emissary to see if you too would like more power; the ultimate power; the power which your grandfather had before he was betrayed." The quick glance told Rufius that he had scored a point. "At the moment this would involve nothing more from you other than your word that you would not interfere should there be a change of power close by and secondly your views on joining such a venture."

"You give me much to think on. I can say that there would be no interference from Britannia because we have too many enemies at home. I cannot be sending my armies to fight across the sea. As for the other, I think I need to reflect and sleep upon it. I would like to meet with some of those who wish to increase their power, without of course any commitment on either side."

Rufius smiled his obsequious smile. He had him; the bait had been duly swallowed. "I will return to the interested parties and bring you an answer by the end of the month."

"He is close then?"

"Perhaps I just know some shortcuts."

"You are a resourceful man er…"

"Just call me the Broker and that way no one will suffer any indiscretions eh?"

"The Broker it is."

Calgathus was a patient warrior. He sometimes found it hard to control some of his wild and headstrong warriors but, the Swordsman as he was known, was still the finest warrior in Northern Britannia and the young cubs soon learned who was master. Since the defeat of his army by Agricola, he had avoided another pitched battle. His warrior numbers were still being built up and the young boys who had now become men had to be blooded in smaller ambushes. This suited the wily king for he was slowly bleeding the Roman behemoth to death. Their supply lines were constantly attacked and, were it not for the fleet, they would have had to withdraw even further.

The next nut he needed to crack was Alavna and he was finding it hard. The Romans had extended the walls so that they filled the valley and the gates were protected by towers filled with scorpions and ballistae. Behind the wall, they maintained mobile patrols that travelled the valley sides all day. Once he cracked this nut he knew he could roll up the rest of the Romans north of the Bodotria. His younger warriors were itching to tackle the fort but Calgathus had seen the effect of their artillery and he would not risk such slaughter.

He was sat one evening enjoying the music and the fire when one of his oath brothers who had lost an arm at Mons Graupius leaned over to him. "When my arm was hurt in the battle the healers wrapped tight bandages around the top of the arm and stopped all blood and life from entering the dead arm. The arm still lived a little, I could feel it but when the blood stopped the life died and the arm was sliced off as easily as you might cut an apple from a tree."

One of Calgathus' other drinking companions who had had far more to drink and was not renowned for his quick wit, more his mighty arm looked at him strangely. "Is this another way to get us to ask about the battle in which you lost your arm?"

Calgathus smiled and patted the one armed man on the shoulder. "No, he has given me an idea. The fort is like the arm we want to remove so we need to stop the blood from reaching it." The one armed man smiled and nodded.

"The blood?"

"Aye food, water, ammunition and men. We will close around the fort and starve them out. Winter will be upon us soon and the weather will be our ally. It is at the end of their lines and the other forts are smaller. When we have destroyed Alavna, the rest will fall like wheat to the scythe. Tell the warriors. Tomorrow we begin our preparations for war. We summon the fighters from the far north. When they are here then winter will be upon us and we can strangle this monster."

Morwenna's waters broke in the early hours of the morning. They had not expected the birth for another three weeks but Morwenna had been helping Ailis to move some tables. Ailis had objected but Morwenna had said that she was becoming lazy. As soon as the waters broke Ailis gathered the other women in the house and they put Morwenna to bed and then began to boil water. "Will it hurt?"

Before Ailis could answer Megan, one of the older women known for her bawdy humour broke in, "After that giant of a man has been between your legs I don't think a wee bairn will give you any trouble."

While the other women laughed Ailis scolded the older woman. "Megan! Behave yourself. There will be pain child but it will soon be gone."

Morwenna was not concerned with pain but she was playing a part; she needed to convince Ailis that she was not going to be a good mother. Once the baby was born she had no desire to feed the little beast. As soon as she could, she needed to be in the north beginning her plan. "Thank you, Ailis. It is good that you are here."

Her labour was relatively short, a mere five hours and when the child was born he was a boy, his green eyes identifying his mother for all to see. He was also hungry and began to suckle as soon as Megan had cleaned him up. Morwenna looked up in alarm as Ailis began to move towards the fire with the afterbirth. "No Ailis!"

"What is it, child?"

"In my clan we bury it. I know it is silly but it would make me happier knowing we did things the way my mother did."

Ailis smiled, pleased to be able to accommodate the young mother for she had become very fond of the child. "Of course Morwenna. Any special place?"

"On the west side of the house and if you could mark the place for me then I would be grateful."

The nights were longer than the days when the Caledonii began their assault. Two huge warbands slipped through the hills and positioned themselves close to the fort ten miles from Alavna. The daily patrols between the forts were ambushed and slaughtered. They had begun to become complacent as the Caledonii stopped their attacks and some of the men began to think the fighting was over until the spring. Their corpses littered the newly made road but, unusually for the Caledonii, the bodies were not mutilated. They had other plans. Waiting until just before sunset on one of the colder, darker nights, they began their attack on the walls. Calgathus only threw a thousand or so men against the walls but it was enough for the garrison to light the signal fires. The attack was only half-hearted, the warriors just making their presence known without risking their lives.

In Alavna the Camp Prefect, who was in command whilst Tribune Sura was working on the new forts, immediately ordered four centuries to double-time down the road and find out what the alarm was. With Alavna's attention south the other Caledonii warbands north of the fort went into action. It was a cold moonless night and the thousands of warriors were able to move the huge tree trunks within one hundred and fifty paces of the walls. Although not a permanent fixture they quickly built five walls each eight logs high across the valley. As Calgathus had explained to his men; they needed to be close enough to attack with arrows and yet be protected from the deadly scorpion bolts which could penetrate shields and armour alike.

When the four centuries were half a mile from the attackers they went into three-line formation. The Centurion addressed his men. "There are barely one thousand warriors there and we have them pinned against the fort. No cheering or shouting we just double time and give them a couple of volleys of javelins." Laughing he added, "We'll be back home before they have turned stiff."

So intent were they on achieving surprise that they failed to notice the woods on either side filling with warriors. The first they knew of their danger was when they heard the unintelligible screech from the forest. Suddenly the warriors attacking the fort turned and charged towards the Batavians. At the same time, two huge warbands attacked their flanks. The Romans stood no chance. The first century, who were moving forward behind First Spear, managed to hack their way through and found themselves, much depleted at the Prima Porta.

First Spear turned around to see his men being massacred and had no option but to enter the fort. The garrison's commander greeted him. "Well, that was a nasty little trap we fell into. How many men did you bring?"

"Four centuries."

Looking at the survivors the camp prefect said, "Almost three hundred men killed in the blink of an eye. And Alavna is now cut off."

"Aye and with less than a thousand men."

"Send a messenger south to the tribune. Tell him the Caledonii have attacked in force and Alavna is cut off."

"Sir come and look here." First Spear pointed over the palisade where they could see men erecting log barriers as they had north of Alavna. Before the scorpion and ballista crews could fire any weapons the walls were finished and arrows began to rain down from the barriers.

"See if you can destroy those log walls. The rest of you take cover."

Behind the walls, the Caledonii were bracing smaller logs against the long ones and putting deer skins filled with soil and rocks behind them. As the crews found out they would not be easily destroyed.

In Alavna the situation was even worse for they were assaulted on two sides and, as the chief engineer said, "We have limited bolts. We will need to save them for their attack."

The camp prefect agreed. "I just hope they have sent for reinforcements because we only have food and water for three weeks at the most."

The young leader of the raid ran up to Calgathus as he arrived to view the fort. "We should attack now while they are weak."

Calgathus shook his head. I would not throw away any of my warriors uselessly. Time, winter and the land is on our side. Use fire arrows. Have half your warband attack at night and half during the day. Do not give them the time to rest. We will wear them out as water wears down the rock, not quickly but inevitably and, more importantly, successfully."

"They will put out the fires oh king."

"With what?"

"With water."

"And that is water they could use for drinking. Be patient. This is their most powerful fort when this one falls they will have to run all the way back to the river."

Tribune Sura was meeting with Tribune Strabo when the riders reached them. "There it is. We knew the day was coming. I just expected it next year."

"What will you do Cominius?"

"Send word to Marcus. We could use the ala and then I will take, with your permission, the two Cohortes Equitatae."

"Of course. I will continue to build up the forts' defences and I think I will add an extra ditch."

"I think we will need it."

Marcus was at Coriosopitum when the news reached him three days later. He and Decius had been enjoying a pleasant evening of powerful drink and fine food when the rider burst in.

"Haven't you heard of knocking!"

"Sorry camp prefect. We have just had a messenger from Tribune Sura. The Caledonii have surrounded Alavna it is cut off and the other forts are being attacked."

"Did the messenger say if Prefect Demetrius had reached Alavna yet?"

"No sir he didn't say." Saluting, the sentry left.

"I doubt it, sir. They only left yesterday. They are probably at Trimontium by now."

"You are right Livius. Decius, you had better send warnings to all the forts and put them on alert. Livius send a messenger to Eboracum and then bring all the recruits we have from Morbium. Do not waste time. I want you up there in three days."

"But sir it is just one fort."

"No Livius, it is the last fort. If that falls then we fall back to the Clota and the Bodotria and there the forts aren't ready, we still have much work to do on them. We have to defeat Calgathus at Alavna. We will still abandon the fort but we will do it when we are ready. Now go."

Marcus caught up with the ala just as they were approaching the Bodotria and the fort at Veluniate. "Do you think this is significant then sir?"

"Yes Prefect Demetrius. Winter is approaching and this is deliberate. They have never besieged before. When they took the forts last year they used the tactic of surprise."

"And took many casualties."

"Yes, I wondered about that. This Calgathus seems to protect his warriors more than other barbarian leaders like Venutius and Maeve. More worryingly he is learning how to fight us. He evaded Agricola and he was the first enemy to do that."

"The problem is sir this is not cavalry country. I have looked at the maps. The valley sides are wooded and it is very narrow. The reports you showed me indicate that they have erected barriers to protect their archers from missiles. Our armour cannot deal with arrows."

"Unfortunately Julius you are the only trained unit we have. We are still making up the losses from last year. Perhaps we don't use the horses."

"Pardon?" The normally quick Prefect seemed confused by the tribune's suggestion.

"We both know that using horses in winter means having to use a lot of forage, forage we don't have. It also means greater losses amongst horses. If we don't use the horses but use the ala as infantry we still have a thousand men we can use and, when we defeat them, we will have a thousand horses to pursue them."

Nodding he replied, "Makes sense and Decurion Macro has been training the men that way using foot tactics. Yes, I think it will work and it will take his mind off his wife and unborn child. Have you seen her yet?"

"Who? Morwenna? Macro's wife? No, not yet but she is supposed to be very pretty. Right, Prefect let's get the ala sorted out. We can leave the horses here and march the men up the road. It is just twenty miles to the fort which the tribune is using as his base."

"How many men does he have?"

"About fifteen hundred. If he stripped the forts he could double that and if Tribune Strabo added his then we could quadruple it but I don't want to strip the forts of their defenders that may be just what Calgathus wants. If Livius gets the extra cohorts from the Governor we might have enough men but, unless they come by sea, it would take weeks."

"And the winter storms will be on us soon. No, you are right sir. It is us or nothing." He smiled grimly. "I suspect the men will be less than happy with the thought of a twenty-mile march before bed."

"A twenty-mile march carrying the camp they have to erect."

"Better and better. This will be a good test of my leadership then won't it sir?"

# Chapter 12

Morwenna's plan was succeeding. She had fed the baby but made sure she was tearful. She had overheard Megan say that she knew other mothers who were sad after a birth. When Ailis was busy feeding her child Morwenna smeared wormwood on her nipples. The baby, called Marcus at the moment, began to scream so loudly that Megan and Ailis both burst into the room.

"Why child what is it?"

Morwenna sobbed. "I am an evil mother! My child will not take my milk! The gods do not want me to be a mother!"

Megan put her arm around Morwenna. "Don't be like that child, the bairn is probably not hungry. Here give him to me." The baby continued to cry and Megan looked over to Ailis. "He looks hungry."

Ailis bared her other breast. "Let me try with my milk."

As soon as Marcus felt Ailis' nipple he began to suck hungrily and was soon contentedly drinking.

"You can both see, it is me!"

"I have heard of this. It is nought to be afraid of, child. Ailis has more than enough milk for both of them."

"But I am bad for my child. Look he only cries when near me. Ailis," she dropped to her knee. "I plead with you. Let me go to my husband. If I cannot be a good mother at least let me be a good wife."

"Oh, I don't know Morwenna. Gaius would not like it."

"I have only been with my husband for a few days. Can I not just go to Morbium and tell him he is a father."

"He may have moved to Coriosopitum."

"I can follow. I promise I will return when I have seen him. Please."

"Well…."

"Oh thank you."

"But only in the morning and Gaelwyn will take you."

Livius was at the fort when Gaelwyn and Morwenna arrived. They were both admitted to the Praetorium.

"Decurion Macro has left with the ala. They are going to Caledonia. I am afraid you have missed him."

Morwenna had been ready for all such problems and she began to cry quiet, deep sobs. Gaelwyn, who knew the workings of the military inside out said, "Are there no troops going to Alavna or Coriosopitum? I am sure the young woman could ride."

Between sobs, Morwenna nodded her quick eyes taking in every movement and gesture. "Well, "the camp prefect began, "the Tribune's aide is taking fifty troopers with him to Alavna but I can't ask him to take you."

Gaelwyn stood up. "We can ask him then can't we?"

"You can ask him." The Camp Prefect knew of Gaelwyn's reputation as a warrior and also knew of his truculent nature. He also understood how fond everyone in the ala was of the old man and he would do anything to appease him.

Livius did not know what to say and Morwenna sensed this. She opened her eyes as wide as they would go and looked up at him through her long eyelashes. In a moment his heart melted. "If the lady would not mind riding with us then I would happily take her to Decurion Macro. But you should know that I am charged with getting the recruits to the Bodotria in three days." Later Livius would regret his generosity as would Gaelwyn and the Camp Prefect, but at that moment they were all happy at the successful outcome.

Livius was surprised at the ease of the journey. It was helped by the fact that Morwenna never complained about any of the privations or the difficult conditions and did not slow them up. That she was in discomfort was obvious when Livius saw the bloodstains on the saddle cloth. However, a young man brought up in the world of men was not going to ask an indelicate question and all he knew was that she had had a baby. His constant question," Are you comfortable?" always brought a smile and a reply in the affirmative. The recruits were also desperate to please the wife of the legendary Macro. They had all trained with him and would have done anything for his wife. The caravan made good time to Trimontium only to discover that the ala had moved on. Morwenna just smiled and the hearts of the garrison were also won over.

"Good to see you, Marcus. You were wise not to bring the horses we have neither food nor stabling. Good to see you Julius; you look leaner."

"All this walking sir."

As the three of them warmed themselves around the brazier in the fort's Praetorium the wind howled outside. "What is the situation then Cominius? And how can we help?"

"The woods on either side are filled with warriors. The road is blocked by log barriers, I will show you them in a moment when you are warmer. Until we clear those we cannot move up to relieve Alavna. I daresay they have the log barriers around those too."

"Hmm. Much as I am enjoying the warm, it does my aged bones good, I fear we must view the field for ourselves."

As soon as they stepped outside, the wind, which howled and cursed from the north chilled and cut them to their very bones. Julius glanced up at the walls. He did not envy the sentries. They had to stand out suffering all that this wild and desolate land had to throw at them; snow and rain like needles and cold which seeped up from the ground making feet feel like stone. At the bottom of the ladder, a sentry handed each of them a shield.

Marcus looked questioningly at the Tribune. "They watch from the woods and the barrier. As soon as they see a head, flurries of arrows fly in. We lost a great number of men before we adapted."

Holding the shield above their heads they mounted the tower from where they could see the road snaking north and the barrier of logs. "There are four sets of these?"

"Yes, Marcus." Suddenly their shields were peppered with arrows, some bouncing off and some sticking in the leather coverings. "Annoying aren't they? Yes, they are using the barriers as small forts from which to attack us. We at least can fire back, as for the other fort… they had limited ammunition at the start and now I dread to think what they have left. The barriers are as high as a man and the gaps between them mean that they can support each other should we attempt to attack them."

Julius peered out at the tree line. "The tree line is what? A hundred paces from the barriers?"

"Nearer one hundred and fifty. Why Julius, do you have a plan?"

"Just the beginnings of one. If we go back to the headquarters and warm the Tribune's bones I will outline it."

Once back in the warmth Julius used the three men's pugeos and gladii to show his plan. "When they put up the barriers it was at night was it not?"

"Yes, we could see nothing."

"That is how we will defeat them. We attack at night. We will use a mixture of your men and mine. Macro will take half the ala into the woods to the left. Gaius and I will take the rest to the barrier. We will slip out of the Porta Decumana and slither along the ground so that the guards do not detect our approach as you did not detect theirs. Our aim is to take out the two log barriers on the left and neutralise the warriors in the woods to the left. Once we have done that you send out a cohort with a couple of bolt throwers and we should be able to take out the other two barriers. We then hold until morning."

"Will Macro be able to deal with the warriors in the woods?"

"Have you tried a night attack yet?" The Tribune shook his head. "Then they won't be expecting it. Macro will take the best archers and all he has to do is stop them from interfering with our attack."

"Yours is the harder role, Julius. For if you are seen as you make your way across that killing ground there will be no escape."

"We will manage."

Tribune Sura shrugged his shoulders. "If you are willing to do that then we will support you. What happens if and when we take the log barriers?"

"I assume that the Caledonii will attack from the right for we will have eliminated those on the left. Your artillery should be able to deal with them when they are in the open. They will not have the barriers to protect them from your bolt throwers and I assume you have plenty of ammunition."

"And then Tribune we need to reinforce this fort to enable us to take a force and rescue your lost cohorts."

"That sounds simple in words but it will be hard in deeds."

"It also begs the question about Alavna. What do we do? Rebuild and reinforce or abandon?"

"While you two tribunes discuss the strategy I had better brief my officers."

"Thank you, Julius."

When he had left Cominius turned to Marcus. "That was a good appointment. It is an old head on young shoulders. Returning to our dilemma; it is not merely a problem of abandoning Alavna. That would mean we would have to, eventually, abandon every fort down to the Clota."

"I think it will come to that but it is your decision. The question you need to ask yourself is this; what is gained by maintaining these forts along this valley?"

"I am not sure what you mean."

"Whom do we control by using these forts?"

"The Caledonii."

"And how are they controlled?"

"They cannot use the lower part of the valley."

"True but they do not need to. They use neither wagons nor trade. They can use the trails over hills, as they have so ably demonstrated, in their ambush and siege. If you were to make your fort line along the Clota solid then you would be protecting the whole of the south of the province."

"Convincing argument and in truth, we have not the men to maintain this tiny artery."

The only Decurion who looked pleased with the orders was Macro. The rest did not question the orders but their faces betrayed their thoughts. "Do I get to use my men first, Prefect?"

"Yes, Macro. Choose the best archers and those who are swift and light of foot for they will be opposed by more warriors than you will be taking."

Turning to the others Macro pointed to their faces. "Get your men to put mud or charcoal on their faces, hands and arms. Dull your blades so that they do not reflect and remove the crests from your helmets or they will stand out."

"There is heavy cloud tonight and I believe it will rain."

Decurion Cilo murmured, "It always rains here. I could be a soothsayer."

They all laughed and Julius knew that they would cope with whatever hardships they had to face. "Only one man in two will carry a shield in our half of the ala and they will follow those who are armed with gladii and pugeo."

"The lads won't like leaving their spathas behind."

"I know but this will be close work and we need to use the right weapon. Once we eliminate the guards we go defensive until the Batavians join us with their men and the bolt throwers. I suspect that will be a hard time for those behind the other barriers will be on us quickly. Decurion Macro will need to disrupt those in the woods until supported too."

"Hopefully their main camp will be some way away. We have not got enough men to hold up the main warband."

"Right. Go and brief your turmae. Make sure they are all fed and if any are sporting injuries leave them at the fort for speed is the watchword."

Because Macro had chosen his men from all the turmae they felt special. In the ala, every man was equal and equally valued but Macro's choice made them feel like an elite. "Now our job is to be hidden. We take out the sentries with arrows if they are in a clearing or with a knife otherwise. We need to kill every warrior we see. No prisoners and no one left wounded. Once we have eliminated them we then have to support our comrades and stop them being flanked."

One of the recruits who had been chosen said nervously, "Will we be outnumbered?"

The more experienced troopers all laughed. "We are always outnumbered but as one trooper is worth four hairy arsed barbarians, apologies to those of you who were until recently hairy arsed barbarians," everyone laughed at this, "I don't think we have a problem. Seriously though if I think we are in danger of being overrun I will order the recall. If you hear my first shout run back to the fort for there won't be a second."

The ala made a rare sight as they waited by the gate. Macro's men had removed their helmets and all of the troopers were blackened up. Tribune Sura came up to Julius and clasped his arm. "I will await your signal."

Marcus opened the gate. "Good luck my brothers. I will join the Batavians when we charge." Saluting them he stood back. Within moments they had left the fort. One third went around the eastern side whilst the remainder headed west. As Gaius dropped to the floor Macro led the rest of his turmae in a halting half crouch half run to the safety of the undergrowth. When Macro waved his bow Gaius signalled his men forward. The ground was hard and slippery after the recent rain. By morning it would be frozen. Gaius suddenly remembered he had not warned the men about stones. Metal rasping over a stone would be like an alarm bell. It was too late to worry about that and instead, as he crept past the corner of the fort, he glanced over to where the Prefect should be doing the same. He saw nothing, which either meant he had not reached there yet or he could not be seen. Gaius hoped it was the latter.

In the woods, Macro led the way like the point of an arrow. He held his hand up and the three hundred wraiths stopped like statues. Drawing his arrow back he released it with a soft whoosh. He noted, with satisfaction, that the sentry had been struck in the throat and pinned in to the tree. His eyes were now accustomed to the dark and he gestured for Decurions Cilo and Galeo to creep forward with their men and eliminate any other sentries. As they disappeared into the darkness and gloom he and the other turmae notched arrows in their bows and scanned the forest. Macro almost jumped when the trooper next to him released his arrow but he nodded with satisfaction when the missile took out the sentry who had appeared from behind a tree. It seemed like hours later but in fact, it was merely minutes when he saw Cilo wave him forward. The line moved inexorably forward through the woods. Glancing to his right Macro could see that they were beyond the log barriers and he could only see two guards on the barriers. His comrades should achieve their first objective.

Julius' arms were bleeding and scratched from the stones and rocks beneath him but, as yet he had not heard a sound neither from his men nor the enemy. As they approached the barrier he held up one hand and the assigned men went around the edge of the barrier. Julius followed. When he looked to his left he was surprised to see two Caledonii whispering to each other. They had been doing so very quietly for Julius had not heard them. He began to rise to his knees praying to the gods that they would not turn. Out of the corner of his eye, he saw two other troopers doing the same. Almost in an instant, both men rose and the throats of the two negligent sentries were slit. Julius quickly took in the scene. There were thirty warriors asleep; nodding to his men he reached down, put his hand over the nearest man's mouth and plunged the sword through his eye into his brain. There was only one man who made a noise and, while it sounded loud to them, the fact that no one else reacted meant it had been unheard. Julius hoped that Gaius was having as much luck. He whispered, "Make the bodies into two barriers around the side."

Gaius had not been as lucky for his sentries were more vigilant but, as they peered over the top of the barrier four men took them silently down and the rest were killed just as Julius'. Gratius, one of the new Decurions said, "I saw the sentries go down over there."

"Thanks." Gaius knew it was now or never. He went to the western end and waved his arm. If Julius had failed he would know it by the arrow plunging into his body. Julius' arm waved and Gaius went to the other end of the barrier. Once again he had to rely upon a comrade. Had Macro achieved his objective? Gaius waved and he saw the returned wave. He then left the safety of the barrier and walked twenty paces in front where he had left the pot of fire. He lifted the lid and blew gently. The flames came up lighting his face and Gaius heard the gates swing open. Unfortunately

# Roman Retreat

so did the sentries to the east and suddenly they heard the alarm being sounded. "Right lads now we hold."

Glancing over the barrier Julius saw the recognisable figures of Tribunes Sura and Maximunius leading the cohorts in two columns with the bolt throwers between them. Arrows began to erratically fall on the eastern column and Julius saw auxiliaries fall. "Get the Caledonii bows and keep their heads down."

The defenders of the next barrier got a real shock when arrows began to descend upon them from their own lines and the auxiliaries managed to reach the barriers without further losses. "Well done Julius. Put your bolt thrower behind this barrier. Auxiliaries! Two lines on either side. Julius, you form the third line."

On the western side Tribune Sura was doing the same. The forests seemed very quiet and Gaius wondered where Macro was. Suddenly a figure burst from the trees and an auxiliary was going to drop him with an arrow when he quickly gave the watchword, "Ulpius! Sir. Decurion Macro says the sentries are all dead and the forest is quiet."

"By the gods, Gaius, that is a bit of luck. You four take the other bolt thrower to Tribune Maximunius he will need it." They could hear the sound of warriors screaming their war cries as they hurled themselves at Marcus and Julius. The first grey of dawn was spreading behind the warriors and Gaius could see there were thousands of them. "Permission to take my troops to assist sir?"

"Permission granted. If you hear the buccina then come running." More troops were coming from the fort to reinforce the advance party. The barbarians were enraged; Calgathus' plan had been working successfully and suddenly they were being attacked. As the bolts scythed through them, taking files of men down, the warriors hurled themselves onto the auxiliaries' spears. By the time the sky was brighter and the forest could be discerned the field was littered with the dead and dying.

Suddenly Gaius heard the buccina. "The Tribune! He is being attacked."

Marcus shouted, "Batavians defend this flank. Marcus' Horse in two lines, follow me!"

The warband had heard the noise and flooded down the valley. All that they could see was a small force of auxiliaries defending their log barrier. They ran headlong in a wedge to cut through and massacre the Romans before them. In their haste they did not see the trees fill with Macro's men nor did they see the six turmae form line to their left flank. They did, however, feel the effect as volley after volley flew into their unprotected side and javelins crashed into thin shields. Tribune Sura had had time to form lines and, by the time the front of the wedge had reached the barrier, it was a fraction of the force it had been.

The sun seemed to take forever to drag itself above the horizon and bring a little warmth to this icy battlefield but by the time it did the battle was over. Hundreds of Caledonii lay dying while the few survivors limped off into the woods to take their disastrous news to Calgathus.

The Tribunes met in the centre of the battlefield as the buccina sounded the recall. Macro's men began to filter from the woods and cheers began erupting from the fort. "Part one complete. I would suggest Tribune that you take your men down the road before the barriers near the other fort know what is happening."

"Thank you, Marcus. If your men could hold this fort for us we'll see what we can do."

Although tired the Batavians were elated by their victory and keen to avenge themselves on the enemies who had tormented them for so long. As the cohorts began marching double-quick time up the road Julius gave his orders. "Decurion Macro, well done. Keep one turma in the woods as pickets. Decurion Princeps get these barriers demolished. Put the logs inside the fort. Er Tribune Marcus could I ask you to take Gaius' turma and move the wounded inside the fort."

Smiling at the Prefect's embarrassment Marcus gave a slight bow, "Delighted Prefect and well done yourself. It looks like you have fewer casualties than we thought."

"Yes, sir we were lucky."

## Roman Retreat

"In my view, Julius, good luck normally follows good planning."

# Chapter 13

Dusk came and there was no sign of the Tribune. Marcus sent Gaius and some of his turma to Alavna. "Just find out what has happened. Take no chances. There are only five of you because there are only five horses here but I need to know if Tribune Sura has succeeded otherwise I will have to send for Tribune Strabo."

"You can rely on me, sir."

Marcus had withdrawn Macro's men from the woods and lit a huge fire two hundred paces from the fort to illuminate any sneak attack when he heard the shout from the walls. "Decurion Princeps returning sir."

Marcus breathed a sigh of relief when he saw the five troopers. Had Gaius not returned he would not have enjoyed telling Ailis that he had sent her husband to his death.

"He relieved the fort sir but he lost many men. He intends to withdraw tomorrow morning. He wants the prefect to meet him halfway."

"Will he have to fight his way out do you think?"

"I don't think so. The two walls going from the fort to the woods are still in place and the barbarians can only use the wooded hillsides. He is going to fire the fort and that should stop any pursuit. He is more worried about being cut off."

"Very well. I will tell the prefect. Go and get some rest."

Livius and the recruits could smell the sea and hear the gulls long before they could see the Bodotria. The men were reluctant for the journey to end but Morwenna was desperate to reach her destination. The sooner she reached the fort the sooner she could contact Calgathus and plan the removal of the Roman blight.

Livius turned to Morwenna. "I am concerned, lady, that we have seen little traffic on the road."

"Why would that be a problem?"

"Normally there would be mule trains and wagons moving regularly between the northern forts and those in the south. I hope this does not mean that there are difficulties ahead."

"You would not be worried were it not for me would you?"

'How astute,' thought Livius. "Yes, lady. My men and I are prepared to fight but if we were attacked whilst protecting you we would be distracted."

She turned and looked him straight in the eye. "Do not worry for me Livius. I lived on my own for some time. I am not the innocent little flower you take me to be."

Livius realised that there was far more to the diminutive girl than met the eye. It was fortunate he could not see into her soul for he would have seen pure evil which hoped for nothing more than to be attacked by Calgathus' men and her erstwhile protectors slaughtered.

Julius and the ala saw the smoke in the distance. They readied their arms for they knew that Tribune Sura would not be far behind and their role as escorts would begin. "Macro, take your turma into the woods on the left and Gaius do the same in the woods to the right. When we fall back, return here."

The Batavians showed the battering they had received as they slowly trudged and limped painfully along the road. "The fire halted them Prefect but thank you for waiting."

As they fell back Julius turned to Cominius noticing how drained and exhausted he looked. "I take it you did not sleep?"

Cominius nodded, "The garrison was almost ready to surrender although I did point out that they would have received no mercy from Calgathus and his barbarians had they done so. They were, however, at the end of their strength. We must get the wounded away and then work out how to destroy the other forts without being harassed by the enemy."

"It would help if we had our mounts. We could deter the enemy much more effectively."

"Then you escort the wounded back to Veluniate and return with your mounts. That will give us the chance to empty the fort of all that is valuable."

Marcus looked with dismay at the small number of troops who passed between the gates. As soon as they were through Marcus ordered the logs to be braced against the gates. Gaius looked at Marcus curiously. "We won't be using this gate again and when we fire the fort the logs will add to the fire and slow down the pursuit."

Julius explained to the tribune the plan to bring back the horses. "An excellent idea. I don't know about you Julius but I felt very vulnerable without a horse."

"Me too. Luckily there was little threat."

"But if you look at the casualties the Batavians have suffered it could have been very different."

"Will the new forts be finished?"

Marcus shook his head. "Those in the west are in a much better state and almost ready to resist attacks but the ones on this side are still weak. Were it not for Veluniate it would be an open door. When you have escorted the wounded back and returned to aid the tribune I shall take Livius and we will bring the fleet around to the Clota. It should make it easier to defend the east. Had Livius arrived?"

"No, he would be three days behind. I suspect he knows nothing about this."

"He is getting a rapid education is he not?"

"That he is."

At that moment Livius was regretting his decision to bring Morwenna into the hornet's nest that was Caledonia. The Camp Prefect pointed at the ala's horses. "The young lady won't be going anywhere. The ala is somewhere up there," he pointed vaguely north, "I received a message yesterday to say that they would be returning for their mounts in the next few days so if the recruits and the lady want to wait here I am sure that would be for the best." The Camp Prefect was pleased to have the extra fifty troopers as many of his men had been sent north to fortify the forts along the route to Alavna.

Livius bowed his head to Morwenna. "And here we must part. For I need to report to the Tribune and you will be awaiting your husband. He is a very lucky man and I envy him."

Morwenna became quite coquettish and held her hand out for the young aide to kiss. The Camp Prefect disguised a smile and half turned away. "You are a real gentleman and the girl who wins your heart will be lucky indeed."

Not daring to speak further Livius bowed and fled red-faced. "Now if you would like to come with me young lady we have spare quarters we reserve for visiting tribunes and Legates I am sure you will be comfortable."

Livius made good time riding up the road which had only recently been completed. He was barely a mile from the last fort when he met the ala. Macro greeted him with a huge smile. "Livius! Come to join us?"

"No Decurion I am looking for the Tribune."

"He awaits you at the fort Livius."

"Thank you, Prefect. Did you manage to rescue the Batavians?"

"The ones who were left, yes."

"Safe journey gentlemen. Oh, by the way, Decurion Macro."

"Yes, Livius?"

"I think you will have a surprise when you reach the fort."

"Is it news of my child?"

"I won't spoil the surprise." Livius enjoyed the confused look on the big Decurion's face.

Livius and the Tribune wasted no time in greetings and partings for speed was of the essence and Livius did not even get to dismount his horse. They swiftly rode along the coastal path towards the signal tower on the estuary. It was a place Livius had never visited.

"Morwenna came here? She came to Caledonia?" he shook his head in disbelief.

"Yes, Tribune. She left the child with Ailis and Gaelwyn brought her to Morbium. It was Gaelwyn who persuaded me to bring her. I hope I did right?"

"If Gaelwyn willed it then it would take a stronger man than you to resist him. Do not chastise yourself. It is, however, a dangerous place for a young woman; she has courage I grant her that if not common sense. Perhaps she and Macro are really meant for each other. I cannot wait to meet her."

"Are we not going to Veluniate?"

"No, we ride to the coast. I need to contact the fleet. We need close support until the forts are completed. We will leave in the morning by which time the ala should have returned to escort the Batavians."

"The ala was escorting many wounded men."

"Aye and many bodies left in the fortress. This has been costly. Our next task must be to go to Coriosopitum and see how Decius progresses with the new forts. My worry is that we may need them sooner rather than later."

When they reached the signal station the contubernium stationed there were surprised to be visited by a Tribune, especially by one as famous as Marcus Maximunius. "I need a signal to the fleet. I wish to speak with the commander here. My name is Tribune Marcus Maximunius."

"Sir! Er, this may take some time. The fleet may be out of sight of a tower."

"We have slept on the ground before now Optio. Just let us know when you have received the reply."

"These towers, Livius could be the salvation of this frontier. Light travels much faster than men or even ships. Signals could save lives. The sooner the line is completed to Coriosopitum the better for it would save you and me many hours in the saddle."

As it turned out they merely had to wait hours not days. Part of the fleet had been taking on water and three ships hove into view. Whilst they were pulling into the shore Marcus drew Livius to one side. "I have been thinking Livius; the Governor made you my aide so that I could be in two places at once. Ride to Coriosopitum and ask Decius to send the garrison to Veluniate. I will then send the ala back to Coriosopitum for the winter. "

"You want it stripped of defenders?"

"No, tell him to use the recruits who will be waiting to travel north. And if your uncle has not sent the cohorts yet let me know for I will then sail to Eboracum with the fleet."

The reunion at Veluniate between husband and wife touched everyone, including the normally dour Cilo. Morwenna burst into tears, cleverly fabricated, as she embraced her husband apologising for leaving their child, his son, and foisting herself upon the ala. Before Macro had time to respond Prefect Demetrius put her mind at rest. "You are the wife of a member of Marcus' Horse. It is right that you are here. We make you welcome. Gentlemen let us leave the Decurion and his wife. I daresay they have much to speak on."

As they left Sergeant Cato said to Gaius, "Did she not look familiar? She reminds me of someone."

"Me also but I cannot place her. Perhaps she is the personification of all that we would wish Macro."

Prefect Demetrius overheard this. "I agree she reminds me of someone but there is another matter far more urgent which we need to discuss. She cannot stay in the fort. It not only goes against every military covenant it is asking for trouble with such a pretty girl and so many men."

"I agree sir perhaps we could lodge her in the town? I will ask the Camp Prefect to ascertain where she might stay whilst we are returning to the Tribune."

"Excellent and I must say I am looking forward to a good night's sleep tonight."

"I think the only one who will not be thinking of sleep is Decurion Macro."

Once they were alone Morwenna nestled her head in Macro's chest. "Do not be angry with me husband."

"Why should I be angry?"

"For leaving our child but honestly he cried so much when I fed him and yet when Ailis suckled him he was content and happy. Ailis is a much better mother."

"You will be a good mother, it takes time and you are yet young, but you cannot stay long here on the frontier, it is too dangerous."

"But I want to be with you."

"We may not be here very long. The ala is moved around the frontier wherever danger threatens."

"Then I will move with you."

"We will see." Macro had already made the decision that he would send her back to Decius at Coriosopitum as soon as possible. He might miss her but she would be far safer and he knew that Decius would look after her far better than anyone else.

The next day whilst the ala was riding north to support Tribune Sura, the Camp Prefect took Morwenna to the local settlement which had sprung up next to the military road and the fort. As with all Roman forts, settlements grew quickly around the perimeter, its occupants keen to make money from the soldiers. This in turn meant that, generally, the people there supported the Romans. Mairi was an old widow who would have died long ago if left alone but she had found that the officers liked their laundry done for them and profited from the relationship. It provided her with a good living and she had a wattle and daub round hut. "I spoke with Mairi this morning and she is willing to put you up. The Decurion has arranged payment."

As Morwenna looked at the old woman and saw the toothless smile she realised that Macro had been charged an exorbitant amount. That suited Morwenna for she needed to be out of the fort to meet with those people who could pass messages to Calgathus. It also meant that she had a certain amount of control over the old woman who would not wish to lose such a lucrative tenant. Putting on her most endearing smile she cooed, "It is fine. Thank you mistress for taking me in."

The Camp Prefect breathed a sigh of relief. Morwenna was a headache he could do without. "I will send a soldier with your things."

As she inspected her surroundings Morwenna was already planning her next move. How to make contact? "Lady if you would excuse me I need to get the night water from the fort and begin my laundry."

"Do not worry about me I shall look around the settlement."

"Be careful lady for there are some around here who might wish harm to the Romans and their ladies."

Those were the very people she sought. "Thank you for the warning. I shall be careful."

The settlement was crude but lively. The two taverns were being cleaned as she wandered along and the owners viewed her suspiciously. She smiled and nodded, playing the part of the young girl exploring the village. She headed west along the well-worn track to where it met the military road. She did not know what she was looking for but she was certain she would know when she found it. She had sharp eyes and a slight movement in the undergrowth grabbed her attention. Someone was hiding thirty paces from the road. If they were hiding from those who used the roads, the Romans, then they were the very people she sought. She moved along the road some distance and then saw a lonely tree struggling to survive in this hostile environment. She wandered over to it and, lifting her shift, she squatted as though passing water. As she did so she glanced down the road and confirmed that there were indeed warriors watching the road. They had ignored her as a girl and their eyes were locked on the road to the fort.

Instead of moving back along the road, she headed directly for the warriors, hiding in the undergrowth. She was but twenty paces from them when they saw her and their dilemma was obvious. If they stood then the guards in the tower might see them; if she were a Roman or a Roman sympathiser then she might alert the sentries. Addis was the younger warrior and he pulled out his knife. Lulach, Calgathus' son, hissed a warning. "Be still you fool it is but a girl. Come here, child."

Her calm demeanour and confidence took both warriors aback. When she was close enough Lulach pulled her to her knees. "Now then my little wanderer tell me why I should not slit your throat here and now and leave your body for the crows?"

"Because your king, Calgathus, would not be pleased that you had rejected a spy in the Roman camp and the daughter of Fainch."

Addis looked at the king's son in surprise for it was as though he had been struck in the face. "You are Fainch's child?"

"I am."

"Your face, your eyes, your hair they say you are but you could be a Roman spy."

"True, for a Roman would know that it was Marcus' Horse who murdered my mother but they would not know that I will be revenged on the whole ala."

"Fine words but meaningless and as empty as the air which whistles around us. Why did you seek us? Do you wish to die?" She shook her head. " What would you have us do then?"

"Pass a message to the king that Fainch's daughter has returned and would speak with him."

Lulach snorted in derision. "Do you take me for a fool? Bring Calgathus here so that he may be captured by Romans!"

"Take me to him then. Blindfold me if you feel it necessary and fear a stripling girl but you will need to be swift and he would need to be close by for if I am missed then the Romans would come looking for me."

"And why would the Romans seek a slip of a girl?"

"For I am married to one of the officers of Marcus' Horse."

Lulach could not believe his ears. He was a cunning warrior but he could not see a lie in the girl's story. She looked like her mother. At first, there was a resemblance but once you knew who her mother was then the family traits were obvious. "Calgathus is too far away and you would be missed. How else could you help?"

She shrugged, "If I could meet with one of his chiefs or a member of his family I could prove who I was."

"I am Calgathus' son, Lulach; prove it to me."

Addis growled, "If she is a spy then she will shout now and the Romans will have a fine catch." He glared up at

# Roman Retreat

Morwenna. "Consider your next actions carefully wench or my sax will rest in your heart."

Lulach put his hand to stay Addis. "You speak of proof. What is that proof?"

Morwenna removed the raven charm from beneath her shift and Lulach turned it over in his hands. "You are indeed Fainch's daughter. I am Lulach and this is Addis."

"I am Morwenna and I am living in the settlement beside the fort."

"I would know how you came to marry a Roman but time presses and we have tarried here too long. You can have valuable information for us."

"The first I can give you is this; the Romans intend to withdraw to this line of forts."

Addis and Lulach exchanged a look of joy. "When?"

"The ala has ridden north to escort the Batavians south and as they come they will burn the forts."

"Excellent and if true proves your story more than a charm. When we wish to contact you where are you staying?"

"With the laundry woman Mairi but if I am moved I will need another means of contacting you. The other forts they may take me to are Morbium in the far south and Coriosopitum. They are the bases the ala uses."

"I will send a man with his laundry to Mairi. She will be silent for we knew her husband and son. She has little love for the Romans but best you play the part of a dutiful wife. Farewell Morwenna today has been a happy day and I hope it bodes well that the witch has returned. I will tell my father of the aid you have given us."

"Lulach, I do it for my mother and until the Roman ala is destroyed, I cannot rest." She strode away and both warriors were struck by her confidence and poise. She looked like a girl but moved, spoke and thought like a full-grown woman.

Rufius Agrippa was admitted straight away to the Governor's private quarters. This time the cat-like Aula was curled up on the couch her eyes assessing the furtive looking man with the shifting eyes. "What did the people you represent have to say?"

"In the next few months, there will be a rising of the legions."

"And where will that be?" Rufius shrugged. "Perhaps Germania?"

Rufius hid his alarm well but both Aula and Sallustius saw that they had, indeed, struck the mark. "Does it matter where? All you need to know is the time so that you can strike here."

"Has your, er leader, the support of the legions?"

"Aye and the tribes."

"Then he has the advantage over me for I only have certain troops and certain tribes who are loyal to me."

"Husband I think you underestimate yourself. You are the grandson of the last king of this land, Cunobelinus. When we raise your standard the tribes will all flock to your side."

Flattered by his wife and encouraged by Rufius he nodded. "In the spring we will rise. You may tell your principal that."

"Late winter would be better."

"I need to summon my Tribunes and Legates if I am to pull off this coup successfully. It will be the spring."

Shrugging Rufius said, "Very well the spring it must be."

None of them heard the door shut with the faintest of noises nor the feet which shuffled off down the corridor.

# Chapter 14

Marcus reached the tribune before the ala. "How goes it Cominius?"

"Slowly I am afraid. There are two more forts on this road and, until your men arrive we cannot move. The valley sides are crawling with barbarians. As soon as you leave the road or the fort you are prey to their arrows and sorties. We have lost two dozen men already."

"The fleet will spend the winter anchored in the estuary. It will give us mobile artillery and, unless the Caledonii get boats in a hurry, they should give us the edge we need."

"I wish the Governor would get his finger out of his arse and send those reinforcements."

"I think our Governor is playing a dangerous game."

Cominius shot a sharp look at his friend. "Dangerous? How so?"

"I take it your men were pleased to receive the increase in pay?"

"Of course. Wouldn't any soldier?"

"Where did it come from? How did the Governor acquire it? He is not a rich man."

"Taxes?"

"That would make sense but he has decreased, not increased the taxes. The people love him, the army loves him."

"So he has bought popularity. Isn't that what Emperors do when they throw many days of games?"

"Precisely. What Emperors also do is keep forces close to them who are loyal to them. The four new cohorts are at Eboracum enjoying a very pleasant, highly paid life far away from barbarians and having to actually fight. Who are they loyal to? If I order them to charge the Caledonii or you order them, will they obey? No Cominius, something about this stinks like last week's fish. I intend to go to Eboracum and demand the cohorts."

"Be careful Marcus. Politics is a dangerous game."

"I am not playing politics; I am serving Rome and Britannia and would that our Governor was doing the same."

"If things were easier here Marcus I would join you."

"No Cominius. Your presence here along with Furius is our only hope. I am confident that the two of you, with the support of Julius, should be able to stem the tide. Winter is coming and the barbarians like to spend it in their huts. I do not think we will need the cohorts urgently but I would like them here and fully trained before the winter snow thaws. I have ordered Decius to strip the garrison from Coriosopitum to reinforce you and when you have finished with the ala I intend for them to winter at Coriosopitum. They will be close enough to aid you and the horses will have better grazing."

"Thank you, Marcus. The extra cohorts might be the difference between success and disaster. I look forward to a quiet if cold winter. It will give the men the chance to recover after this arduous summer."

Cornelius Furcus arrived at Eboracum without any warning. He had left Gaul with his bodyguard of old soldiers who had served with him in Germania. They were extremely tough and experienced; all of them had been centurions, signifiers or aquifers. He had brought them out of retirement for what he hoped would be a sinecure. His authorisation from the Emperor should have been enough but some of these Governors viewed themselves as equals of the Emperor. The information he had been given about Sallustius had been interesting. The first thing which intrigued him was that he was a native of Britannia and a native with no military experience. That meant he was dealing with a politician which, in turn, ensured that Cornelius would only believe one word in two. The Emperor's spymaster had told him the names and identities of his agents as well as the agents of the other rebel Governor.

Leaving two of his men on the quayside to guard his belongings the Legate decided to take a turn around Eboracum before greeting the erstwhile governor. He needed to see the way the land lay and the best way was to wander the stalls and taverns and just listen. He wanted to know what the people thought of Rome and the Roman Governor ruling them.

Two hours later he and his companions sat around a table discussing what they had all gleaned. "He is a very popular man is our Governor. The soldiers think he is their friend and the reduced taxes mean that the people would do anything for him."

"Aye, and I have also heard of gold coming from the west to be shipped to Rome but only a fraction actually makes it."

"What of the army not in Eboracum? Those cohorts fighting in the north and the west?"

"The legions are further west and south of here and they appear to be doing a satisfactory job. It is in the north where the problems lie. The Caledonii are threatening the borders"

"Yes, I heard that he made three Prefects Tribunes and one of them a barbarian."

"The people and the soldiers speak highly of the barbarian. Apparently, he has been fighting for Rome since Vespasian's time. He is in the north now. He fought with Agricola."

"Agricola was a good man. The politicians did for him. Well, it is time we sought out this Governor and showed him our credentials."

His men laughed at the crude joke. "Let us hope he knows that the Emperor has given you the power over him."

"He will soon find out. Cassius, while I am speaking with the Governor find a clerk called Septimus and take him to my quarters."

Cassius gave a quizzical look. "Who is this Septimus? A soldier?"

"No much better, an Imperial spy. He is the reason we are here. He has sent back some interesting reports. Lentius explore the residence; see if there are any hidden and secret little places."

The Governor and Aula had just finished their meeting with Rufius who headed for the back stairs. There was no

## Roman Retreat

knock on the door instead the doors of his private quarters were thrust open and Sallustius found himself looking at eight well-armed and extremely tough-looking legionaries. "What is the meaning of this outrage? Do you know who I am?"

Cornelius almost laughed aloud at the ludicrous nature of the question. "Yes, Governor but you obviously do not know who I am." Cornelius unrolled the scroll and handed it to him. "If you read this you will see that Emperor Domitian has appointed me Legate of all the forces in Britannia. If you read further on you will see that I am answerable only to the Emperor."

Spluttering as he read the orders he shook his head in disbelief. "But I am Governor and…"

"You are still Governor," he paused and grinned, "for the moment. I will not be interfering in the way you run the province merely the way you are conducting military and economic affairs."

Aula felt a chill run down her spine. Her husband had left it too late to revolt and now it would be too late. She had seen the politics in Rome and knew there was a judicious moment to make an exit; this was that moment. "Legate if you will excuse me. The morning has been tiring and I need to lie down for a while."

"Certainly lady for I only need your husband for a short time and then he will join you."

There seemed to be a threat hanging in those innocent words and Aula determined to find refuge elsewhere before this hawk-nosed warrior could uncover their plots. She just hoped that Rufius Agrippa had left unseen.

When they were alone Cornelius asked, "Could you find someone to show my men to my quarters whilst you and I discuss the military situation."

It was many hours later when Sallustius had finished with his interrogation. He got the impression that the Legate knew more than he should have. He could feel the inquisitor's irons already. When he reached his private quarters he thought he had been robbed; clothes were scattered around the room and the chest with the gold in it was open and worse still, empty! It was only when he saw that the clothes which had been spread around with such abandon belonged to his wife and none were his that he knew what had occurred. "Bitch!" She had left him!

Aula and her maid were riding cloaked and hidden through the streets of Eboracum. She had no idea where she could go for she knew no one in Britannia and then she remembered, Decius! He too would be in as much danger as she. She turned the horse around and headed north out of the city. Decius had built himself a villa two miles from the city. Close enough to receive protection but far enough away to enable him to indulge his eccentricities. She just hoped that he would be there. As soon as she saw the guards at the door she knew he was home.

The guards recognised her immediately and allowed her to enter. "Where is he?"

"He is in the solar lady but he is not alone."

Ignoring the guard, she burst in on her naked nephew and the two young girls who looked to be little more than children. "What the…?"

"Believe me Decius you will need to hear what I have to say. Dismiss those girls, get dressed and I will tell you all."

Something in her voice told him to take this seriously. "Get out. I'll join you later." When they had gone and he had put the toga on he added threateningly. "This had better be good."

"Good is not a word I would choose. Domitian has sent a Legate to run the army. He knows about the gold and he may suspect about your uncle's plans."

"Shit! What do you intend?"

"I have left the Governor and Eboracum!" He gave her a shocked look. "What good would it do for me to share a cell with your uncle? At least this way we are both free and with gold, we may affect his escape."

"You have gold?"

"Yes," she replied cynically, "as I am sure you do. The difference between us is that you have guards to protect our gold." She reached over and touched his cheek.

That and the use of the word 'our' told Decius all he needed. "We need to leave and leave quickly. North is no good, too many barbarians. I would head west but if he knows about the gold then our Legate from Domitian will head there. I think we will head south to the civilised lands. We will create an identity as we travel."

"I had been worried Decius but you are so resourceful that I feel safer already."

Decius felt safer too but that was because he knew he had his uncle's gold as well as his own and when he tired of the old hag then he knew how to dispose of her.

Septimus had a smug smile on his old face as he sat opposite the Legate. The news was racing around Eboracum that the Governor's wife had fled and the Legate had ensured that no one else could leave the city which now had all its gates barred and guarded. "So you have compiled facts about the Governor for the Emperor?" Cornelius felt distaste for the spy but he needed the information the man had. "He has been siphoning off Roman gold from the Emperor through his nephew Decius Lucullus. He has four cohorts at Derventio ready to back him if needed and he has met with a representative of the Governor of Germania Superior and planned to rebel in the spring."

Cornelius looked up. The Governor had greater ambitions than he had thought. He was not concerned with Germania Superior for his counterpart was already there but he would take great pleasure in adding this fact to his first report." And why was this not conveyed to the Emperor?"

"It only transpired this morning. The envoy is still in the city."

"Is he? When we have finished you can give his description to my man Cassius. Anything else?"

The old man paused, looking almost embarrassed. "Well, he…"

"Come on man spit it out!"

"He has named a lance after himself."

Even Cornelius was surprised at that and he burst out laughing. "The man has an arrogance I have never seen before. I do not think the Governor would approve. You are dismissed."

Unless Cassius could apprehend the envoy there would be little evidence of his treachery but he had enough to warrant an arrest. He decided he would send him to the Emperor who was in Germania Inferior along with his report. He had the authority and the Emperor could make the judgement call. Little evidence or not he was sure that Sallustius Lucullus would die.

Marcus was delighted when the ala finally arrived. The Caledonii attacks had become more intense over the past day. "Prefect you will have your work cut out to extract the Batavians without too many casualties. When you have succeeded I want you to take the ala to Coriosopitum and winter there with Decius. I fear that in the spring the Caledonii will mount far more serious attacks on our forts."

"I agree and where will you be sir?"

"I will visit with the Governor and ask about the cohorts he is hanging on to. We need them here not lounging about in Eboracum. Good luck there then sir."

"And good luck to you." Clasping hands he turned his horse and headed south.

Julius looked at the Batavian, Tribune Sura appeared to have aged ten years in the past few days. "You need rest, sir."

"I know Julius but unfortunately the Caledonii don't know that. They seemed to have intensified their efforts in the last day, whilst you were away. All the forts down to Veluniate have been attacked. We cannot do anything about destroying the forts."

Julius looked at the map. "There are three forts including this one right sir?"

"Agreed."

"And we don't want to leave anything which they might be able to use. I assume that you have buried anything which can be buried as the legion did at Inchtuthil?"

"Yes, but we have javelins and arrows that cannot be buried as well as forge equipment."

"Have you any wagons?"

"Yes, a couple. Why?"

"I could get a couple of my turmae to empty this fort and take the surplus down to Veluniate leaving just the men. My other turmae will harry the enemy."

"How? "

"Half on foot using bows the other half mounted to pursue if necessary."

"Sounds risky to me."

"No riskier than trying to move without doing so. When we have engaged the enemy you can move your men to the next fort and fire this one. We repeat the action."

"Sounds easy but won't they learn what you are about?"

"Oh yes. This first decamp will be the easiest; then it will become harder. If you'll excuse me I'll get the ala organised."

"Decurion Galeo, go and find a wagon and hitch it to horses."

"Where will I get horses from sir?"

"Any you can find. Use ours if you have to." The raised eyebrows from the Decurion were the only sign that he found the order strange.

"Decurion Cilo, find the Camp Prefect when we have the wagon, I want everything putting in it that we can't bury; shields, forges, anvils, spears; anything that the barbarians can use we take. Whatever can't be put in the wagon goes on spare horses and before you ask use ours. We will have some spare."

"Gaius! Macro!"

"Sir!"

"We are going to make life harder for these barbarians. We are going to attack them whilst the Tribune marches his men the five miles to the next fort. As soon as the fort is fired we will withdraw. But we will need to buy them some time. They are exhausted. We will have to hold off any attacks. We will attack those barbarians in the tees with mounted archers. That way we can escape quickly."

Gaius looked up at the hillsides. "If they decide to attack us from both sides we will be in trouble."

"Yes, but they won't be expecting this. You, Gaius, will have three turmae as a mobile reserve. Attack anything which comes at you. Next time we will have to come up with something else."

"Next time?"

"Yes, Macro. Tomorrow we do the same and the day after, for the last time, hopefully."

Gaius looked at the crestfallen young Decurion. "Yes Macro, your lovely wife will be alone again."

"In that case the sooner we start, the sooner I sleep better."

The men all worked urgently realising that speed was of the essence. They needed to be in their winter forts soon otherwise the decamp would prove impossible. The ala proved highly resourceful and even found a few spare horses.

"Ready Julius."

"As ready as we will ever be. Decurion Princeps begin your attack. Decurions take the wagons south."

The Tribune's voice rang out. "Fire the fort!"

In the wooded sides of the valley, the barbarians were taken by surprise. Lulach had told them that the Romans would be leaving and they had been prepared to fall upon them as they left the fort. Suddenly they found themselves having to shelter from the rain of arrows. The chief blew on the ram's horn and, from the other side of the valley a horde of barbarians raced across the open ground. Before they were halfway, the three mounted turmae reserve had crashed into them causing many casualties. Gaius was at the point of the wedge the Sword of Cartimandua cleaving a path for his troopers close behind. As they emerged they wheeled and fell upon those who still stood. "Reform!" The one hundred troopers reformed into two immaculate lines.

Decurion Marcus Saurius was on the extreme right and he saw the archers who had emerged behind the warband draw their bows back. "Shields! Arrows!"

The well-disciplined ala put up their shields and whilst they were protected three horses fell to the ground. There

# Roman Retreat

was little point in waiting for more casualties. Archers could not catch them. "Withdraw!"

The dismounted men doubled up and the three turmae trotted down the road after the Batavians, Macro had kept an eye on the skirmish and when he saw Gaius move out he yelled, "Time to go lads, one last volley and then mount up."

By the time the Caledonii knew what was going on and their tormentors were disengaging the ala had formed a defensive circle around the Batavians and they lurched into the fort exhausted by their double march.

That evening the Tribune and the Prefect treated the decurions to a fine feast. "We might as well eat well. We would only have to leave it for the barbarians."

"Did Galeo and Cilo get away with the wagon?"

"Yes, they should be back before night."

"Good," said Julius between mouthfuls of stew. "Quintus and Pontius tomorrow you do the wagon run. Leave before dawn. They will be expecting us to do everything the same way."

"And won't we sir?"

"No. I expect that this time they will send men ahead of us to attack the Batavians before they can be protected by our protective circle. Macro when the wagons move out I want you to take two turmae, archers only and set up an ambush in the woods. When they try to attack the Batavians you can attack them."

"With two turmae sir? I am good but not that good."

They all laughed and Julius smiled. "No one could accuse you of modesty Macro. No, you will not just attack with two turmae. The Decurion Princeps will also attack from this flank and Galeo and Cilo will form the rearguard. Give their men the chance to fight."

The Tribune smiled. "I will have to remember these tactics when I get my Cohortes Equitatae."

"I think they would do the job even better sir. We are just cavalrymen adapting. And tomorrow night we will have to adapt even more."

The next day's action was not as successful and resulted in the first loss of officers that the ala had suffered in a while. Decurion Gratius Agrippa had been leading his turma in open order in the woods. He was on the extreme right flank and the Caledonii had managed to get around his flank. He heard the screams of two of his men and turned to see fifty warriors streaming down the hillside. "Fall back!" As he yelled his last command he calmly turned to face the horde. The first warrior ran onto his blade and the second he punched with his shield and then stabbed him in the neck. The chief who faced him had a war axe which he swung at the Decurion's head. He ducked beneath the whirling blade and stabbed up at the unprotected chest of the chief. When he fell, his enraged warriors descended on Gratius. Despite his heroism, he could not hold them all off and he died with a dozen wounds. His bravery allowed not only the rest of his turma to escape but the rest of the ala.

It was a sombre group who saluted their dead comrade that evening. The losses amongst the ala had been higher than the first day. "Tomorrow could be interesting."

"Yes, Tribune but at least we are close to Veluniate."

"Yes, which gives me an idea. If we brought a cohort up from Veluniate we could catch the Caledonii between three large forces."

"Then why don't we send off the wagons tonight; they can ask the Prefect to do as you suggest."

"I will write the orders now."

The next morning was a shock to both Romans and barbarians. The blizzard which hit was a vicious white-out storm that reduced visibility to the length of a spear. "I am glad that we sent the wagon last night. I think that today we keep the ala closer to my men Prefect."

"I agree and we will just be using swords, the snow means that the bows will not be effective."

The day was a bloodbath. The barbarians were able to get closer to the Romans and cause greater casualties. For their part, the Romans were able to cause huge casualties with the sudden appearance of the garrison of Veluniate which appeared out of the grey and white murk like an avenging monster. By the end of the day the Romans had reached their goal and the white snow was riddled with blood and littered

## Roman Retreat

with bodies. As the gates slammed shut the Romans were behind their ditches and protected by the forts. The barbarians were halted. But as Calgathus viewed the red crests behind the wooden walls he was satisfied. He had reclaimed much of his land and in the spring he would begin to destroy the fortifications. The witch's daughter had done well and might be the key to unlocking the fortress that was Rome.

# Chapter 15

Cornelius summoned the Governor to his office, which had, until recently been his own office. The armed guards at the door now answered to the Legate. His report was already on its way to the Emperor. The Governor had lost all his bluster. "So Sallustius still no news of your wife," he shook his head, "nor your nephew. I do find that interesting, not to say suspicious. It does put you in a very poor light and begs the question, why did they leave in such a hurry and carrying gold too. Gold that came from?" He held his hand up as Sallustius began to rise. "You will be pleased to know that I have finished my preliminary investigations and I am afraid that I find that you have abused your power and as a result, I am removing you from office." He looked sternly at the ex-Governor and his words conveyed a threat like a death sentence. "Before you bluster and complain remember this, I have the Emperor's authority. My orders will be obeyed. The Tribunes and Prefects here and in the south understand that and when the other Tribunes arrive, the ones you appointed then they will be told of the change of command."

"What are these abuses I am accused of?" The question sounded weak in his head and even worse when he heard it echoing around the room.

Cornelius smiled, "You really want them itemising? Let me see, you stole gold from the Emperor, you created cohorts for your own use."

"They were to replace the legions taken by the Emperor."

"You now accuse the Emperor of treachery," he wrote on his tablet, "another charge. If the cohorts were intended to fight the barbarians why are they here and not on the border?" There was a loud silence that filled the room. "I shall carry on. You named a lance after yourself without asking the Emperor's permission." Sallustius' mouth dropped open. "I know it sounds pathetic and, were it your only crime, you might still have a post somewhere in Britannia, probably a clerk somewhere. As it is, this is serious enough to be brought to the Emperor's attention.

And then there are the charges I cannot prove. I have informed the Emperor about these crimes and told him that the evidence is thin."

In a small voice, the ex-Governor murmured, "What crimes?"

"Treason! You were working with the Governor of Germania Superior to jointly rebel against Rome. Had I got my hands on this Rufius Agrippa, his emissary, you would already be dead." He slammed his hand down on the table. "As it is I will send you to the Emperor to allow him to decide upon your sentence."

Sallustius slumped, his shoulders sagging with the weight of his woes. He was already dead.

Macro had to see to his men and his horses before the Prefect would allow him to go to Morwenna. She feigned sympathy very well. "Are you hurt my love? Did the barbarians kill many of your men?"

"Do not worry my sweet, we slaughtered far more of them."

"And your friends? They are all safe?"

"Not a scratch between us. We must bear charmed lives."

Inside Morwenna was seething for she had hoped that, with the warning she had given, the Caledonii would have killed far more of her hated enemies. "Good. I pray to the Allfather for you. When will I get to meet your friends?"

"Tomorrow we are having a farewell dinner and the Prefect has invited you."

"Farewell dinner? Who is leaving?"

"We are. The ala. We go south to winter at Coriosopitum. You will get to meet Decius there, he is camp prefect. They have emptied the fort to make way for us."

"Will I meet the famous Marcus at the dinner?"

"No, he is heading south to Eboracum even as we speak."

Once again she cursed the luck her enemy had. She had hoped he would be close enough to be in her clutches but at least she had some useful information for Lulach. Perhaps they could benefit from the empty fort and, if the Mother permitted, another of her mother's murderers would die.

Marcus and Livius were riding hard south of the Dunum. They were trying to outrun the snowstorm which they could see looming black and threatening behind them. Decius had urged them to stay in the fort but Marcus had too many pressing issues on his mind. "There is something wrong Decius. Why won't the Governor send us his cohorts? Does he want us to fail? We are hanging on by our fingernails and the only force we have to stop an invasion is the small group of auxiliaries trapped in their forts and the ala. We need those men."

"Politicians!" Decius had snorted. "They are useless."

Now as the two men hurried south Marcus couldn't help but agree with Decius' assessment. Give him soldiers any time. You knew where you were with them. "Sir, are we going to stop before Eboracum?"

"No, we will change horses at Cataractonium. The ride will make the beds in Eboracum seem even softer."

Livius was not sure he agreed with the Tribune but if a man twice his age could manage to ride for such long distances then so could he. As they thundered down the vale between the snow-topped hills rising away east and west of them, Livius could not help but reflect on the changes since he had been seconded as an aide. When he had heard that his cousin was to take charge of the gold mines he had been resentful. Now he knew that he had had the better of the arrangements. For he had come to love the life in the ala, the comradeship and if he was honest, the danger. His cousin was a merchant but he, Livius, was a warrior and he could wish for nothing more.

At the fort of Cataractonium, they were warned of wolves in the vale which had descended from the hills and forests. "That is another example, Livius of the problems the Governor is creating. The auxiliaries should be here to protect the people not guard the Governor. The sooner we see him the better."

They arrived at the city after dark and the gates were closed. "Tribune Maximunius and his aide to see the Governor."

The huge doors swung open and when they entered they were greeted by ten grim-faced soldiers. The biggest of them, a Centurion to rival Macro, stepped up to him and said, "Tribune Marcus Aurelius Maximunius and Livius Lucullus by order of Legate Furcus I am placing you under arrest." Before either could react their arms had been taken from them and they were marched away.

"I will have to go to the fort, my love. I will return for you this evening. Remember to pack your things for we leave on the morrow." As he looked outside at the snow-filled hills he asked, "What will you do today? The land is so cold."

"Oh I shall wrap up and look at the hills," she said airily.

"Make sure you do wrap up then." She smiled at his concern and obvious affection. He was like a piece of clay in her hands; he would do everything she asked of him.

As Macro strode away to the fort Morwenna decided that the snow would be a good way to hide her from prying eyes. She intended to find Lulach and tell him of the ala's movements. As she left the hut she heard the tramp of feet as the cohorts from Coriosopitum marched up the military road to reinforce the forts. Lulach and his companion were harder to see in the snow but Morwenna knew where to look. They all squatted down behind a snowbank.

"The ala leaves tomorrow to winter in Coriosopitum." She pointed at the auxiliaries marching west. "Those are the garrison which was stationed at Coriosopitum, the fort is now empty."

"Good. We can attack the fort tonight. There is a warband south of the Bodotria. I will send orders for them to raze it to the ground. My father says you are, indeed, your mother's daughter and he is pleased with your work." Morwenna nodded graciously, pleased by the compliment. The king's praise was unnecessary; all she wanted were her mother's murderers dead and the Romans to be finally, thrown out of Britannia. "Will you go with your husband?"

"I will have to but I can still aid you."

Lulach nodded. "I will send three men south. Aodh here will be your contact and will protect you."

She flashed him an angry look. "I need not your protection!"

He looked at her as a master looks at a slave who has questioned his orders. "You will have it whether you want it or not. You are too valuable an asset to throw away. Now go back to Mairi's. Aodh and his men will follow you and the ala when you travel south. You will need to find some time during each day when you walk and Aodh will meet and contact you."

Decius felt uneasy as the snow hurled itself at the solid walls of the fort. His fifty recruits were strutting the walls as though they were battle-hardened veterans but Decius knew better. Veterans would see in the dark and not be spooked by branches. Battle-hardened veterans would not gossip like girls and giggle at flatulence. Old soldiers knew that a moment's lack of concentration could result in a throat being slit. He yearned for daylight and the arrival of the ala. He had decided he would forego sleep. He had another reason not to risk sleep for the previous night he had had nightmares about Fainch. He was not bothered that he had killed a woman but Fainch had been a witch and his nightmare had been real enough to make him wake in a sweat. The spectre of Fainch with a knife, filleting him like a fish whilst he had been unable to move had made him afraid; his dream had been so real that, when he awoke sweating, he felt his body for the wounds she had inflicted. The walls and the snow were safer for one night than a Fainch filled nightmare.

"Sir?"

"Yes, trooper."

"We have heard many stories about Marcus' Horse. Are they all true?"

"Probably not. It depends which story and who told you."

"Did the Prefect, Marcus fight King Venutius to get the Sword of Cartimandua?"

"No, you pillock! The Queen gave the sword to Ulpius Felix and when he was dying he gave it to the Prefect. He, in turn, gave it to the Decurion Princeps."

"Oh. So you probably didn't kill the Queen of the witches either?"

Suddenly his nightmare became real and he shuddered. "That one is true. We crucified her as far north as any Roman soldier has been and good riddance for she was an evil bitch. Now stop asking stupid questions and watch."

"No one is likely to attack the fort are they?"

"If they know I have a bunch of wet behind the ears recruits they will. Now watch." As Decius glanced around he thought he detected a movement. He focussed on the spot and saw snow fall from the bush. He whispered to the trooper. "Go to the barracks and rouse the men but do it quietly." The young man was going to ask a question but the look in Decius' eyes told him that this was serious. He quickly went around the other sentries. "Stand to!" He whispered. "Enemies out there. Keep your eyes peeled." He made sure each man had javelins. It was then he realised that none of them had bows. That part of their training required Macro. They would have to make do with javelins but in his heart, he knew men would die because the enemy, whoever they were, could get much closer.

The flaming arrow was aimed at the tower but the young sentry walked in front of it and was hit in the chest. His screams seemed to launch the attack for the air was filled with war cries, screams and arrows. "Use your shields over your heads and throw your javelins." Experienced men would have known that but Decius had to make do with what he had. He ran to the dying trooper and put out the flames with the bucket of sand which was placed near the tower for such incendiary attack. Raising his shield he peered over the wall. They were Caledonii. He picked out his target, a leader and hurled his javelin into the warrior's unarmoured chest. His young recruits were making a valiant effort but there were many more Caledonii than recruits.

Cursing himself for his oversight he shouted up at the tower. "Fire the bolt throwers now!"

# Roman Retreat

Suddenly the pendulum swung the Roman's way and the bolts from the two towers caught many Caledonii in the crossfire. Some Caledonii had however made it to the wall, and the recruits were taking too many casualties. Drawing his sword and hefting his shield Decius ran down the walkway. He did not pause when he reached the melee he just punched with his shield and his sword. One warrior fell over the ramparts and was impaled on the spikes thrusting out of the snow-filled ditch. The other warrior fell backwards into the fort and, even with all the noise, Decius heard the crack as the man's back broke. He found himself facing two warriors who had despatched the young troopers guarding that section. Decius lowered his knees and then punched one with his shield whilst slashing down at the other warrior's sword. Seeing the opening Decius head-butted him and, when he instinctively put his hand to his damaged face, he finished him off by slicing through his unprotected midriff. The first warrior took advantage of Decius' distraction and hacked the shield from his left arm. It was now blade to blade and Decius felt his years as the younger man relentlessly forced him back. When Decius tripped over the dead trooper's body the warrior's eyes lit up and he stabbed down. Decius tried to roll out of the way but the sword went through the soft flesh of his upper arm and pinned it to the walkway. Before the warrior could withdraw the blade Decius stabbed upwards between the man's legs and, as he felt the warm arterial blood gush over his arm, he knew that the man was dead.

Two troopers ran over to help Decius. While one removed the sword the other wrapped a cloth around the wound. "Looks like they have gone, sir."

"Well done lads. Go around and check for any of their wounded." He looked each of them in the eye. "Finish them off."

As dawn broke Decius could see how lucky they had been. Forty dead bodies lay outside the fort whilst inside there were eight who had made it over the ramparts. Decius looked at the line of troopers lying in straight lines within the fort. They had lost twenty brave young men. As the surgeon bandaged his arm Decius again wondered how they had known. He deduced that they must have had spies watching who saw the garrison leave but there must have been a warband close by. When the Prefect arrived he would have to be informed. This would not be the easy posting they all hoped for. They were all in danger.

Marcus stood with Livius in the Governor's quarters in Eboracum. The guards surrounding him were unknown to both men and Marcus could see from their decorations that they had fought in many campaigns. From the decorations on his uniform, the Legate was obviously an experienced soldier. Marcus noticed how he had studiously ignored them both as he read the tablet in front of him. Off to the side was a clerk who appeared to be making notes. Eventually, the Legate looked up. "Do you know why you are here Prefect?"

Marcus picked up on the title as Livius glanced up at him. Marcus chose to ignore it. A title was the least of his problems. "No sir I do not."

"You do however know the Governor Sallustius Lucullus do you not?"

"Yes sir."

"And you follow his orders."

"Yes sir."

"And you accept his promotions and pay rises."

Marcus could not see where this was leading but he determined to keep telling the truth. "Yes sir as did all my colleagues."

The smile on the Legate's face was the smile of the wolf as it is about to devour the sheep. "But your colleagues are in the North fighting the barbarians for the Emperor."

Livius could contain himself no longer. "As was the Tribune. Two days ago we fought the Caledonii."

"Ah, another Lucullus. Is Decius Lucullus your cousin?"

"Yes sir."

"And do you know where he is?"

"No sir. He serves the Governor managing the gold mines in the west."

## Roman Retreat

"Indeed he does. Well Prefect," the word was emphasised. "Your military record is exemplary. You were a fine soldier. Tell me, er Marcus isn't it?" Marcus nodded. "Tell me Marcus why did you decide to betray your Emperor?"

If Cornelius had slapped him Marcus could not have looked more shocked. "I have never betrayed the Emperor. I serve the Emperor."

"As you serve the ex-Governor who is now heading across the Mare Germania to meet with the Emperor. The same ex-Governor who stole money from the Emperor, who raised cohorts to fight against the Emperor and who plotted with the Governor of Germania Superior to rebel and revolt against the Emperor Domitian's rule."

"I knew none of that."

"You knew about the cohorts."

"Yes, but I thought that they were for the war in the North."

"Apparently they weren't. And you, young Lucullus did you know that your cousin has disappeared with a large quantity of the Emperor's gold."

"I did not."

"You will forgive me if I do not believe you for the other members of your family have all proved that they are liars and thieves and I have to make that assumption about you." He nodded and the guards produced manacles which they placed on their wrists. "You will be taken from here by sea to Lugdunum Batavorum where the Emperor will decide your fate."

"But..."

For his troubles, Livius was struck about the head by the Centurion's vine staff. "Prisoners have no voice young man. Take them away."

Decurion Macro had been given permission by the Prefect to escort his wife to the civilian settlement of Coria some mile and a half from the fort. "But I want to stay in the fort with you."

"I am afraid that is impossible. No officer is allowed to have his wife in the barracks. Even the Prefect."

Pouting Morwenna sulked as they rode ahead of the ala. Macro's turma smiled at their masterful leader being tortured by his pretty young wife. Macro silenced the few chuckles with a scowl.

Morwenna was working out how she could use this state of affairs to her advantage. She had hoped to be able to ride up to a burnt-out fort with dead and dying soldiers but so far she had seen no smoke and she wondered how her Caledonii brethren had fared.

The Prefect could see the damage to the walls and the piled barbarian bodies. "Looks like Decius has had a little trouble, Gaius."

"Can't understand why sir. The people here are peaceful and they look like Caledonii bodies. How did a warband get past the forts?"

"Yes, I wondered that myself."

As they entered the fort Decius greeted them his face pale and his arm in a sling. "I am so glad to see you lads."

"What happened?"

"Come into the headquarters where it is warmer and I will tell you. I have some warmed wine ready." When they had warmed through Decius told them of the attack. "So you see Julius they must have spies nearby and that warband had to be close or they wouldn't have been able to get here in the time they did."

"Worrying Decius. Worrying. And the Tribune and Livius?"

"Left before the garrison heading for Eboracum."

"Good, then I hope that he managed to convince the Governor to release those cohorts. We need them now, not later."

"Where is Macro? I had expected his bulk to be filling the room."

Gaius smiled. "Decurion Macro is a changed man. He now runs around after that pretty young wife of his. He is busy arranging accommodation in the town."

"I will have to go and pay my respects when we have got the men billeted."

By the time all of the turmae had found their barracks and Sergeant Cato had seen to the horses, Decurion Macro tramped into the headquarters. "What's up with you then?"

"Women Decius. They are complicated. They don't understand military rules."

"That's why we don't let them fight. That's why the barbarians are barbarians, they let their women fight. So when do I get to meet the woman who has changed the mighty Macro for all time?"

"We have found her a hut and she will have it sorted by tomorrow. She was busy getting the slaves organised when I left. She shooed me away." He sounded indignant.

Decius laughed. "I will go and find her tomorrow. Where is the hut then?"

"It is the last one in the settlement, just past the smiths. She wasn't happy about that either."

Decius now knew why he had never married. No matter how pretty they were, they all ended up as shrews or worse, witches. Just thinking the thought made Decius think once again of Fainch and his nightmare and he shuddered.

"Someone walking over your grave Decius?"

"Something like that. Let me show you your quarters and your turma."

Morwenna left the hut as soon as she could. The three slaves Macro had purchased for her were busy making it habitable but she needed to meet with Aodh. She left the settlement and walked down the new military road as though she was exploring the neighbourhood. She heard a whistle and she left the road as though she was going to make water. As she squatted Aodh crawled along the ground next to her.

"What happened at the fort? I expected a burning ruin."

"They put up more resistance than we expected and we lost many men."

"I am going to the fort tomorrow night. Meet me in the morning at my hut and I will send the slaves away. I should have more information then about the patrols and how we can destroy them."

"Good."

Livius and Marcus were in the deepest and darkest part of the ship as it lurched and wallowed its way across the Mare Germania. They had both emptied their stomachs and it was now merely dry retching. The smell from the bottom of the ship testifying to its previous occupants.

"But we are innocent."

"I know we are but that counts for nothing. The Emperor could have us executed, knowing that we were innocent merely to make a lesson for others."

"But it is so unfair."

"Life is unfair. I am lucky I have lived longer than you."

"Surely you are not giving up?"

"No, but I am not going to beg either. If we are given the chance I will give the Emperor the evidence which should prove our innocence but it may be a summary trial and execution. Be prepared my young friend. We do not know what your uncle has said or what lies have been told. We are not Romans in their eyes. We are barbarians fighting for Rome and that is the difference."

As the ship gave another lurch Livius tried to retch again but the bile in his mouth seemed to reflect the bile in his mind and he began to silently weep.

The snow started to melt slightly turning the well-worn paths and roads into a slushy slippery morass. Prefect Demetrius ordered all the turmae to patrol and discover if there were any more warbands in the area. "Go as far as you can, ensuring that you can be back before dark and look for any sign. Leave those whose mounts need rest or are carrying a wound to defend the fort with the recruits."

Decius decided he would take the opportunity of visiting Morwenna. He was not much use with one hand and he felt that the walk into Corio would do him good. Besides he was looking forward to the opportunity of meeting with the lovely Morwenna. The word amongst the Decurions and troopers was that she was a beauty who could entrap any man. He stopped at one of the stalls to buy her a jug for the house. He had no idea what sort of presents a girl would like and he had never bought a present for a woman but he felt a practical present would be the best. He walked cautiously for carrying the jug in one hand and with his injured arm if he fell on the slippery, snow-covered path it could be a disaster.

Julius took the opportunity of taking his mount for a gallop. On his way back to the fort he noticed Decius in the distance walking to the settlement. He remembered that he had said he would visit Morwenna. On a whim, he decided to join him.

Aodh and his men squatted in the hut. Morwenna told them what Macro had told her the previous night. "They know a warband is in the vicinity and they are looking for them today."

The warriors looked at each other. "We must hide."

"No first we must warn our brothers for they are close by. We will leave now and contact you later."

Decius saw the three men leave the hut and he wondered if this were the right one when Morwenna emerged. He saw her arm first and called. "Is that Morwenna, Macro's wife?"

The three warriors disappeared around the corner and Morwenna turned on her most radiant smile. Whether it was a trick of the light or Decius' dream, he would never know but suddenly he stopped five paces away from the young woman, his face drained of all colour. "Fainch it cannot be you are dead!"

Stepping towards him Morwenna's hand went to the dagger she had hidden in the folds of her shift. "No I am Morwenna, Macro's wife."

Decius' face became a mask of fury as he saw what no one else had seen, this was Fainch's daughter. "You are the witch's daughter and you are…"

Before he could get another word out she had slipped the blade up between his ribs. He smashed the jug against the side of her head causing her to fall but the wound he had received was mortal and he fell in a bloody heap. At the end of the road, Julius saw what had happened and could not believe what he was witnessing. He galloped his horse as hard as he could. Morwenna knew that the game was up and she raced away as fast as she could. Aodh and his men were barely round the corner. "I am undone. Help me! A Roman is pursuing me."

The three men took their slings from beneath their cloaks and hid as best they could. Julius' mount slithered and slipped around the corner. The three stones hit the horse on the head causing him to fall and throwing the prefect against a hut. The four of them ran away as fast as they could for people were coming out to see what the noise was. By the time he came to, Julius could see nothing of them and he remembered Decius lying bleeding. By the time he reached him the Camp Prefect's breathing was laboured. "Decius I'll take you to the fort."

"No Julius I am done for." A rivulet of blood ran from his mouth. He struggled to make his words clear. "It was Morwenna. She is Fainch's daughter. She is a spy. Tell Macro..." with a splutter of blood Decius Flavius once time Decurion Princeps of Marcus' Horse died; not killed in battle but murdered by a young girl. Morwenna had finally had her first taste of revenge. She had killed one of her mother's murderers.

# Chapter 16

It was Gaius who picked up the trail of the warband. They were moving northeastwards towards the land of their allies the Selgovae. Although the Selgovae were at peace with the Romans, it was an uneasy peace. Gaius turned to his turma. "There is a warband ahead. Looking at the spatters of blood some of them are wounded but we take no chances. I want an extended line. When you see them raise your hand. I do not want them warned."

At the same time as Gaius was on their trail Macro had moved his turma north. The river cut across his route and he led his men west to find a crossing higher up. His deviation brought him, unknowingly, across the line of retreat of the warband. The last seventy-five survivors were exhausted; a night in the cold with no hot food after a fierce and fruitless battle meant that they were not as alert as they might have been. One of the younger warriors with keener eyes spotted Gaius' turma and the warband immediately changed direction and headed north. If they could reach the river they would have a chance of evading their pursuers for the river banks were rocky and would not suit the horses of the ala. Gaius saw that they had been seen and his turma galloped hard after the fleeing men. As the warband glanced over their shoulders they failed to notice Macro's turma appear over a low rise. The two turmae and the warband collided in a bloody tangle of horses, blades and spears. It was all over in moments.

Macro grinned like a child, happy to be doing what he loved. "The Allfather was with us today Decurion Princeps."

"That he was. Let us remove their arms and get our wounded back to the fort. I think that this is the last of Decius' foes."

"Aye, the old goat should be happy."

"You never know Macro; he may even buy some wine."

The younger troopers were very excited after such a one-sided victory. Gaius listened with a paternal smile on his face as they asked Macro about his skills. "Sir, how did you manage to kill two of them on opposite sides of the horse?"

"Easy. You need to gauge which is the closer; hit that one and then continue the blade's arc. Don't fight it. Let it come around in a loop."

"But you got another one with your shield."

"Yes, that was because I used my mount. I guided him with my knees and used the angle to sweep down low."

"I'll never be as good as you, sir."

"It's just practice but you need to work out. Build up the muscles."

The hero worship was apparent in all of them. Gaius couldn't help but smile. His gigantic friend had it all; the adulation of his men, the approval of his peers, a fine son and a wife who adored him. Who would not envy Macro?

They knew something was amiss when they trooped through the Porta Praetorium. Prefect Julius was waiting for them and every face was sombre and dark. Gaius was convinced that one of the other turma had had a disaster but, as he looked around, he could see that all of the other decurions were present and there did not appear to be too many men missing. Every eye was fixed upon Gaius and Macro. Macro whooped as he slid off his mount. "One warband destroyed. Tell Decius he can sleep safe tonight." When every face but the prefect's looked to the ground Macro asked, "Where is the old goat? Sulking because he couldn't join us? Deciuuuuuus! Come out and play."

Julius walked over to Macro and put his hand on his shoulder. "Decius is dead. He was murdered earlier on today."

The two turmae paled as a man. They felt so guilty having been so happy while the whole time the popular Decius had been dead. Gaius dismounted and put his arm around Macro. "You couldn't have known Macro. Decius would have understood."

Julius said, very quietly, "It is worse than that come to my quarters, this needs a little privacy."

When they were in the headquarters with all the Decurions stood to the side Gaius noticed that they looked not at him but solely at Macro. "There is no easy way to tell you this Macro so I will have to come out with it. Morwenna murdered Decius." He paused to let that world-shattering news be absorbed, then he added the other, equally terrifying news. "She is the daughter of Fainch the witch and she has fled with three Caledonii warriors."

Afterwards, Gaius went over Macro's reaction in his head; he curled up in a ball and began, very slowly to cry, his sobs becoming louder and louder. No one knew what to do. These were warriors and tears were for women but they all understood the big man's pain. They looked away, at the ground, at Julius, in fact anywhere but at Macro. It was Gaius himself who put the arm around his friend's shoulder and allowed his tears to course down his cheeks. As he cried Julius explained what had happened. He had expected Macro to question the story but the death of Decius appeared to have sucked the spirit from him.

"Decius thought she must have been a spy. It makes sense. It would explain how they attacked this fort so quickly and how their attacks intensified when we began to withdraw from Alavna."

"What now, Prefect?"

"I will have to send a report to Eboracum for the Tribune and the Governor. After that…" he shrugged his shoulders.

"Macro I promise you that Ailis and I will raise your son as though he were our own."

Macro looked up his eyes cold and dead. "What son? I have no son. He died with Decius."

The Legate, when he arrived, brought with him the four cohorts raised by the Governor. He arrived unexpectedly at Coriosopitum and, were it not for the forces he brought with him, Julius might have been tempted to think they were Caledonii in disguise. Even the calm and studious Prefect was shocked at the disclosures. "But sir, Marcus Aurelius Maximunius is the most loyal soldier in Britannia. If it were not for him then the Caledonii would now be here."

"You have a high opinion of him but he has been implicated in a plot."

"You are a soldier Legate. Do you think Marcus is a traitor?"

"What I think is irrelevant. It is the Emperor's decision."

Julius looked into the Legate's eyes and said coldly, "You are wrong!"

"Do you question me, sir? Be careful or you will join your friend." The Legate looked at the Prefect and saw an over-promoted young man. He was insubordinate!

Julius felt his fellow officer's presence behind him. "Do not threaten me with your empty gestures. You are in a land you know not. You have thrown the finest warrior in the land to the wolves and there is not an auxiliary unit in Britannia which does not love and respect Marcus Aurelius Maximunius. Until you present me with proof neither I nor my men will believe these lies."

For the first time in his life, the Legate was worried. The decurions behind the Prefect looked every bit as determined as their leader. The young pup had appeared to him to be a soft patrician with no backbone but suddenly he felt threatened and his ten Centurions would be of no use if this ala took it into their heads to end his life now. "Are you threatening a Legate of Rome?"

Julius stepped very close to the Legate and spoke very quietly. "Rome is many miles away from here sir and the Emperor a vague memory. Marcus Aurelius Maximunius is not and you have made a grave error. When you lead these men into battle will you be looking over your shoulder or will you lead from the rear? You have yet to fight the Caledonii. Yesterday two of my turmae destroyed a large warband, not ten miles from here so do not talk to me of threats. I ask you again; do you think him a traitor?"

At that moment Cornelius would gladly have struck down the arrogant young pup but the battle-hardened officers in front of him left him in no doubt that he would have died in an instant had he done so. "No, I do not."

"Then will you write to the Emperor and tell him so?"

"It will not make a difference."

"Then it will cause you no harm to do so and might win the loyalty of the very men you are to lead into battle for believe me Tribune Sura and Tribune Strabo love and honour Marcus Maximunius as much as we do."

There was a pause and the Centurions looked nervously around. These barbarians were not the soft garrison troops they had seen before and, in a fight, the Centurions were no longer confident of victory. The tension in the room was almost palpable and the only one who seemed calm was the Prefect. "My men sir, are but a step away from barbarians." He smiled. "To them, there is no greater honour than to die with a sword in their hand and to die for their king. Marcus Aurelius Maximunius is their king. Think on that, Legate."

"Very well I will write the letter but I will not forget this meeting."

"I hope not Legate for until Marcus is returned to us, you will find that the auxiliaries of Britannia will be, "he paused dramatically, "unpredictable."

The next day the Legate demanded an escort to take him to the border. As Julius scanned the faces of his decurions he could see that none of them relished escorting a man they despised, a man, in their view without honour. "Decurion Septimus you will escort the Legate with your turma." Julius lowered his voice, "And Septimus, cooperate." The decurion looked quizzically at the Prefect. "Take him along the road, not the back trails and protect him. The last thing the ala needs is for the Legate to come to harm whilst under its protection."

As the Legate left Julius summoned Gaius. "Take your turma to Eboracum I have a message I need to send by boat. While there find out what you can about Marcus, Livius and the Governor. I am also interested in the whereabouts of the Governor's wife and his nephew. You will also need to inform all the posts about Morwenna. When you have completed that you may return to Morbium. Spend time with your wife I believe the two of you will have some decisions to make."

Gaius looked across at Macro who had barely spoken since his return. "Could I make a request?"

"Of course."

"Let me take Macro with me. I know him better than any now and he may listen to me. He should be part of the conversation with Ailis for it is his son we discuss."

"You are right and I apologise. I should have thought of that."

Giving a wry smile Gaius added, "I think you have enough to think on having put the Legate's nose out of joint. I can see the ala being given all the most dangerous and challenging roles in the spring campaign."

"I thought we always received those anyway."

"True Prefect, true."

The snow had begun to melt as they made their way south. Their road took them on a ridge that was windswept and bleak. Below them, in the valley sides, they could see tendrils of smoke as the settlements went about their daily routine. Gaius wondered if they even thought about the Romans and the security they brought. He remembered twenty years ago when this region suffered raids from Ireland and Caledonia when people lived in constant fear.

The turma had dropped back from the two Decurions allowing them some privacy. Each trooper felt for Macro. They knew that Decius had been very close to both Macro and Gaius. "You are going to have to talk about it sometime."

Macro shot a sharp look at his friend. "I am not ready yet."

"That is fine then. Continue to mope and feel sorry for yourself after all the ala doesn't need a weapons training officer, your turma does not need their leader back and the Prefect doesn't need his charismatic warrior leading his men."

"You don't understand."

"What don't I understand? Listen you arrogant brute, was I not Decius' friend as much as you?" He intended the words to sound harsh and they did.

"Yes, but your wife did not kill him!"

"He is dead, murdered, whoever struck the blow. Is this what this is all about? You blame yourself for his death?"

"Who else can I blame? She was my wife."

"And you, of course, knew that she was Fainch's daughter?"

"Do not be ridiculous; how could I have known?"

"Precisely. And I met her and did not know. Gaelwyn met her and did not know. It seems like the only one who did see the resemblance was Decius and, I suspect, that had he met her then Marcus would have known."

They rode in silence for some time the only sound coming from the horse's hooves on the stone road. "I will have to kill her."

Shaking his head Gaius said, "Did Marcus kill her mother?"

"He ordered her death."

"Yes and that is the difference. If you kill her it will be murder. How would your son view that? When we catch her, and we will, then she will be punished by Rome, not by Macro."

"I will look for her then."

"And she will have won, for if you spend your time looking for her you cannot fight Britannia's enemies. I have no doubt that her aim is the same as her mother's. She wishes us to die and Rome to be gone. Make that your aim. Make Britannia safe for your son, and my children and Ailis who is now your son's mother."

Macro sat upright in his saddle, his shoulders no longer slumped. He had forgotten his son. His son would be Decius, he would shower his boy with all the affection he had given Morwenna. "Thank you Gaius and thank Ailis."

"I have not yet asked my wife to continue to care for your son but I know my wife and I believe that she will give him as much love as her own children." He paused and pondered whether to remind Macro of his rash words in the Prefect's office. "So you have a son now?"

Smiling for the first time since he had heard the terrible news he said quietly, "Yes and thank you Gaius for reminding me that being a father is important."

At that moment Morwenna was less than ten miles from Macro and the turma. The isolated hut where they had spent the night was tucked away in the fellside. The couple who had lived there lay outside, murdered. The four of them had not needed to kill the couple but, as Morwenna had said, they needed to mask their trail and they could not risk the couple reporting their passing to the Romans.

"We need to get home, back to Lulach and give him the news."

"And I need to find shelter for the winter while I plan my next steps."

"Will you not return with us north?"

"Eventually I will but there are things I need to do now. Come with me west and then head north."

"Why?"

"They will look for you north. In the west, it will be easier to pass their patrols."

Aodh had already decided to do as the young witch asked for he was falling under her spell. As with her mother she had a power that commanded loyalty. He determined that he would serve her as long as necessary. "Very well we head west."

Morwenna smiled at Aodh and touched his cheek. "Thank you. I will not forget your loyalty."

Marcus and Livius were just grateful to be on land once more. It was not dry land and, as they trudged through mud, their captors gave them neither sympathy nor shelter from the harsh rains and wind. As far as the guards were concerned they needed little for they were dead men walking. Tethered behind the wagon they could at least talk. "I am sorry to have brought this upon you Marcus."

"You did nothing. I am not even sure that your uncle did anything. The evidence the Legate gave was flimsy, to say the least. Governors have been taking a little for themselves since they first came to Britannia and, even had he wished it, he could not have rebelled against Rome."

"Why not?"

"Because of the very people he thought he could count on. Us. Cominius and Furius would never have rebelled and I know the legions; soldiers like Decius Brutus would have fought against the Governor. Your uncle had about as much chance of rebelling as I have of becoming Emperor."

"Then why are we here and why was my uncle arrested?"

"The Legate was given a job. If he did not find treachery then he had no job. Do you think he will conduct a better campaign than Cominius and Furius?" Livius shook his head. "No. It is politics. The Legate may have been a soldier but he has forgotten the soldier's code. He is now serving himself."

When they arrived at the town they found themselves in a city which was bigger than Eboracum. The only acknowledgement they had of their existence was the guard of the cell block putting his thumb on the wax tablet. The cell they were thrown into had only a tiny aperture to let in light. They were hurled to the straw and faeces covered floor. As Livius tripped over a warm form he heard a moan. As their eyes became accustomed to the light they saw the bloodied figure of Sallustius Lucullus.

"Uncle."

"Is that you Livius?"

As they peered at him in the half-light they could see that his eyes had been removed as well as his fingernails. "It is uncle and Tribune Marcus Maximunius."

"What are you doing here? Wherever here is."

Marcus spoke for Livius was almost in tears at the sight of his uncle. Would he end up looking the same? "We are in Germania Inferior and we are here because we have been accused of joining in your plots against the Emperor."

"What a fool I was! I am sorry. I know that sounds pathetic and weak but there is nothing else I can say." Marcus could not help but agree. "My wife?"

"She has disappeared along with your nephew Decius."

Sallustius laughed sardonically. "The two people who have acted honestly and nobly throughout this are in a prison cell and those who helped betray me are free. The Gods must be laughing at me now."

"What is to happen to you?"

He shrugged, all hope gone. "After they extracted the confession, they left me. I overheard one of the guards tell the other that the Emperor was on his way here. He was returning from the campaign against the Governor of Germania Superior; the man who put me in this position."

"Then we can expect the interrogators soon."

Livius shuddered as he looked at the broken body of his uncle and pictured himself once they had finished with him.

Aula and Decius had managed to get their ill-gotten gains to Calleva Atrebatum. The town had been civilised for thirty years and was as Roman as any city in the province. It was vibrant and thriving. New settlers were arriving daily to take advantage of its market and its new businesses. Aula and Decius did not stand out. Perhaps the age difference might have caused comment but the wagging tongues had Aula down as a rich widow and Decius as the new love of her life. Neither did anything to deny the rumours. They purchased a modest villa on the outskirts of the town. As Aula told Decius, "We keep a low profile. We need to blend into the town. I want us to be anonymous."

They had paid off their guards when they reached the outskirts of Lindum giving them the impression that they were heading for Gaul. The fugitives had done everything in their power to throw any pursuers off the scent. With more money than anyone could imagine they intended to, eventually move to Rome where Aula could finally live the life she felt she deserved.

# Chapter 17

The weather had changed for the better when Macro and Gaius finally rode into the walled enclosure of Gaius' home. Gaelwyn had spotted them and, by the time they arrived, Ailis was waiting in the doorway with their new son in her arms and Decius clinging to her leg. Ailis' forehead creased in a frown when she saw Macro. Gaius leapt off his horse and embraced his whole family. "I have missed you. It was not until I saw you that I knew how much I had missed you."

"And I have missed you husband. Let us not stand here the cold is no good for the child come to the fire."

Macro and Gaelwyn followed the family into the cosy room with the welcoming fire. Ailis pointed to the crib in the corner. "There is your son, Macro. Morwenna did not name him properly but when she comes to join us we can have the naming ceremony." Gaius gave a slight shake of the head.

Macro went over to the sleeping child and laid his huge hand on the baby's head. Gaelwyn looked over at Gaius the question in his eyes almost shouting. Again Gaius shook his head and then said, "Why Decius you have grown and see what we have made for you." He took out a beautifully carved horse. "Sergeant Cato spent many long hours carving that for you, son." The boy's eyes lit up and he gently took it and turned it over in his hands. "You can play with it. It will not break."

Ailis put her baby, now sleeping, in his crib and then tenderly kissed Gaius. "I really have missed you." She then whispered in his ear, "Morwenna?"

"Come outside and I will tell you." Loudly he added. "Gaelwyn and I will see to the horses. Macro you need to be with your son. There will be much you wish to tell him." Macro turned his tear-streaked face towards Gaius and nodded.

While the three of them put the horses in the stable Gaius told them of Decius' murder and Morwenna's betrayal. Ailis buried her face in her husband's chest murmuring, "Poor Decius and poor Macro."

"I thought there was something familiar about her. Now I know I wonder why I didn't see it more clearly."

"I think we all said that. We need to pick the big man up. He has to get over this however there is worse news than that to tell."

Ailis looked up, shocked. "What news can be worse than this?"

"Marcus has been arrested for treason and taken, with Livius, to be questioned by the Emperor."

Gaelwyn snorted, "Marcus a traitor! What fool thought that?"

"The new Legate. The Governor was fermenting rebellion and I think, because Livius is his nephew, they felt he had something to do with it."

"When they question him they will realise the error of their ways will they not?"

Gaelwyn and Gaius exchanged a knowing look. "Sometimes the truth does not matter. Sometimes things are done which are wrong but which encourage everyone to toe the line."

Gaelwyn nodded. "How are the men taking it?"

"Badly. Julius almost came to blows with the Legate and I feel he has made an enemy there."

"Loyalty cannot be bought it has to be earned and Marcus has certainly earned it. I am pleased that the Prefect stood up to the Legate. I think I might have taken more direct action."

Gaius laughed and slapped his old friend on the back. "You are getting too old to be picking fights."

"I do not pick my fights, I choose them."

By the time they went back into the house, Macro had composed himself. "I think I will call the child, Decius."

Ailis nodded, "I think that Morwenna called him that a couple of times but, "she paused not knowing if she should go on. Gaius nodded encouragement, "she was never comfortable with him. Looking back I think that she did something to make the child cry; she must have learned potions and tricks. I think she wanted to be away."

Macro nodded. "I know it is much to ask Ailis and you Gaius, old friend but I cannot look after my son would…"

Ailis' face broke into a smile, "Of course. Your son is a lovely child and he can play with," she looked up at Gaius, "Marcus as they grow to be men together."

Embracing her Gaius said, "You are the wisest and most thoughtful wife a man could have. Now I hope there is food for we are starving. It was a long ride from Eboracum."

Ailis said, "Of course," and scurried out to organise the slaves.

"Eboracum?" questioned the Brigante scout.

"The Prefect wanted us to see what the city was like without a Governor and to deliver some despatches for the Rome packet."

As the Legate and his escort trekked across the uplands of Northern Britannia, they were unaware that they were being stalked by a second warband sent south by Calgathus. Their original role was to have been to join the first warband and raid further south to disrupt the Roman supply lines before the forts could be stocked with winter provisions. Once they realised the futility of that they had joined with the first warbands and were waiting for a supply train. When they saw the column of cavalry they recognised them as the famous Marcus' Horse. The number of Caledonii and Selgovae allies outnumbered the Romans considerably. They had chosen the valley a few miles south of Trimontium as the best place for the ambush. They had chosen it wisely for the steep banks meant that all travellers slowed down and when they rested at the bottom, in the shallow river they would be vulnerable. They had also deduced that, because the fort was so close by, they would relax. So it was that, as Septimus waved the turma forward the Legate called a halt. "It is time for a rest. We will water the horses here for the fort must be close."

Remembering the Prefect's words of warning Septimus said as calmly and reasonably as he could, "With due respect Legate we can rest in the fort. This is not a good place."

"Are you a coward man! We are still in the Roman Empire. The border is many miles hence."

# Roman Retreat

"The border you speak of is a figment of a Roman mapmaker's imagination. When we left Coriosopitum we left the Empire."

Before the Legate could reply there was a whoosh and an arrow embedded itself in one of the Legate's bodyguards. "Shields!" The turma went into the familiar defensive routine each pair protecting each other. The bodyguards had no shields and the ambushers quickly targeted them. They died without drawing their swords. Because the Legate had been moving forward to reprimand the Decurion he avoided an arrow but the banks were suddenly filled with the screaming warband who finally had the turma where they wanted it. "Ride downstream!" Septimus knew that their only chance was to outrun the barbarians and downstream the river became deeper which would enable their horses to swim away from their pursuers.

The Legate had not fought for many years; the last battles he had been involved in had been when he directed the soldiers from the rear. This was the hand to hand fighting which he had not endured since he was a young man. He was now also much older and slower. The Caledonii warrior swung his war axe straight through the Legate's horse's legs and it went down in a screaming flurry of blood. The Legate found himself face down in the water and he would have died there and then were it not for Septimus who wheeled his horse around and thrust his javelin into the barbarian's back. "Get on my horse now Legate!"

As the Legate struggled out of the water and onto the back of Septimus' mount Septimus held off the warriors who surrounded him. Five of the turma saw their Decurion's plight and heroically rode back to help their leader disengage. "Ride. Make it back to the prefect."

The small party found themselves clear and they splashed their way downstream. With screams of rage, they were pursued. The Legate screamed as an arrow plunged into his leg. One of the turma was hurled from his horse by a spear. Two warriors leapt up to pull a second from his horse and then they mercilessly hacked him to pieces. Septimus saw the bend in the river looming large and, for the first time since the ambush began, started to believe he would survive. Fate can be cruel for, as they turned around the bend three warriors jumped from the overhanging branch and brought the Legate and Decurion from their horse. Neither had any chance for the wind was knocked from them and the pursuing barbarians caught them. The remaining auxiliaries could only watch from downstream as the two men were hacked and stabbed to death. Aulus, the chosen man, took charge. "Right lads you heard the Decurion, back to the fort."

The Emperor had had enough of Germania both Inferior and Superior. He longed to be back in Rome. He sat with his clerk reading the various reports from the Empire. "We have some letters from Senators in Rome Caesar."

"I will read those when Julius Verinus has made his report. Where is the man?"

"He has had to travel many miles sir but I believe he has arrived."

"Then why isn't he here?"

"He is probably making himself presentable, Caesar, you know what the roads are like."

Shrugging his agreement he murmured. "Before we built these roads I wonder that they moved at all."

When the Legate did arrive he was clean and presentable. Caesar wasted no time." Well!"

"The rebels are defeated. The ex-governor is dead and my men are mopping up the survivors. "

"Good. Then I can get back to Rome." The clerk gave a little cough. "By the gods, what is it, you annoying little man?"

"There is the problem of Sallustius Lucullus."

"He is not a problem. Have him executed."

"On what charges Caesar?"

"Why treason! Rebellion!"

"The problem there is that they didn't actually rebel and if we say he did then others might get the idea that they ought to rebel. We have had one rebellion, brilliantly put down, I might add, can we not leave it at that?"

"You mean let him live?"

"Oh no Caesar but for another crime."

"What crime?"

"There is the fact that he did name a lance after himself without your permission."

Julius Verinus snorted, "Sounds a bit thin to me."

Domitian said, "Go on explain. I suspect there is some plan behind all this."

"There is Caesar. This tells the world that you make all the decisions, large and small in the Roman Empire. If any citizen whether Governor or soldier wishes to do anything, they should seek your permission."

Even Julius Verinus nodded. "Excellent. Yes, that is my decision. He is to be executed for naming a lance after himself."

Marcus had lost track of the days. From his beard, he felt that they had been down there more than a week but he could not be sure. Sallustius rarely spoke. Livius made sure he ate and drank each day but his uncle was dying little by little. They had become used to the smell of urine and faeces but the lice which infested the straw and their clothes were a constant source of irritation. Even worse were the rats which were bold enough to try to steal the morsels of food which they were allowed."Sir?"

"Yes, Livius although after what we have been through I feel Marcus might be more appropriate."

"I am not sure I can go on much longer."

Even though they were in almost total darkness Marcus felt he could see the abject despair on the boy's face. "Yes, you can Livius because we are still alive and, as long as we are alive, we have hope."

"What hope is there?"

"I don't know but I will keep on hoping. I know it sounds foolish but I have learned that life is too precious to give up. We may well end up being executed but until I see the manner of my death I will believe that I might still live."

There was a silence only disturbed by the erratic breathing of Sallustius and the rats ferreting around in the straw. Suddenly they were blinded when the cell door was thrown open and six legionaries stood with blazing torches. A Centurion stepped forward with a wax tablet. "Sallustius Lucullus, one-time Governor of the Province of Britannia, you have been sentenced by Emperor Domitian to death for the crime of naming a lance after yourself. Take him away."

Before anyone could speak to question the punishment or even say goodbye Livius' uncle was dragged away and the door slammed shut. "Naming a lance?"

"I know Livius it seems so petty somehow but the sentence is still the same. Now we have to await our fate."

Since he had met his son, Macro seemed more at peace with himself. Prefect Demetrius had noticed the change. In the weeks since he had returned he had become the rock, he had always been. He no longer laughed as much as he once had but he went about his job with a fervour which surprised all, even Gaius. The news of the Legate's death had not concerned anyone save Julius, who had to send the report back to Rome and detail the circumstances. What did sadden them all was the death of Septimus who had been one of the most popular Decurions and had been with the ala for a long time. The ala found comfort in the heroic nature of his death. He had died trying to save a comrade and that meant he would now be with the Allfather, Decius and Ulpius sharing tales of brave deeds.

"Any news of the Tribune?"

"No Gaius. A trader who passed through Eboracum said there was a rumour that the Emperor had had him executed after the rebellion in Germania Superior was suppressed."

"I suppose no news is good news."

"I hope so Gaius, I hope so."

Marcus felt his beard. He had never had a beard before and he wondered what he would look like. Perhaps he would resemble a pirate or, more likely, one of the Caledonii he had fought so many times. He had had a good life he knew that. If he had stayed in the Cantabrian village where he had been born he would probably have achieved little and died in some petty war. At least he had achieved things. He had been promoted higher than any other auxiliary. He had married a princess. He had had a son. He had carried the Sword of Cartimandua and he had never lost a battle. Probably more than that however he was proud of the ala, the ala which now bore his name, and he hoped that they were proud of him. What would they say when he died? And he knew he was destined to die in this prison cell despite the lies he told Livius. Would they say he was a good leader? He hoped so. Would they say he was a brave warrior? He prayed so. He would never know for by then he would be dead.

He heard the sound of caligae coming down the passageway. So this was it. His death was imminent. "Livius wake up I think they are coming for us."

"I wasn't asleep sir. I was just wondering about Britannia and the ala."

"Me too. Isn't that strange?"

Their reflections were rudely interrupted as the door was flung open and the room filled with torchlight. "Right you two on your feet we are going to see the Emperor." As they stood two legionaries hurled buckets of ice-cold water over them. The Centurion laughed evilly. "Don't want you stinking up the place do we?"

As they walked down the corridors Marcus kept his head held high. He was going to die and he was going to die an innocent man but he would, at least, die with honour. He just felt such sorrow for Livius who was dying for a corrupt uncle and cousin. The boy deserved to live.

Livius turned to him. "Thank you Tribune for I have seen nobility whilst serving with you."

The Centurion's vine staff crashed against Livius' face. He drew it back for a second blow but Marcus grabbed it. "Praetorian, I know not if you have fought for your comrades in battle but your actions suggest that you have not. This boy does not deserve your cruelty. When we meet in the afterlife look for me for I will show you a warrior."

The Centurion pulled his arm back to strike down the Tribune but something in his eyes stopped him and he pushed them both forward. "Get in there for you are both dead men!"

The Emperor was seated on a raised dais and the Centurion thrust them to the ground so that they looked up at Emperor Domitian from their knees. "When I discovered that two traitors still remained in my dungeons I asked my guards why you were not yet dead. And I was told that there was no evidence presented. You would have died anyway but I received two letters, one from Prefect Julius Demetrius of Marcus' Horse and a second from his father, the renowned Senator Demetrius. Remarkably I find, Tribune," Marcus suddenly brightened when he heard his title, "that you are truly a hero in the old fashioned sense. You have fought for Rome even though your home is in Cantabria. You have fought against great odds and yet never surrendered and the loyalty of your men make me wish to trade my Praetorians for your ala." Marcus noticed with pleasure the Centurion blushing and shifting uncomfortably. "And you, Livius Lucullus. My Legate died but had he lived he would have been before me for he accused you because of your name. Both of you are now free men. Please return to Britannia for you are both men who will make the province not only safe but great."

As the shackles were removed the two men looked at each other in surprise both had expected death. Turning, they left following the clerk. As he passed the Centurion, Marcus paused. "This is not over Centurion. Look over your shoulder for, should our paths ever cross again…you will die." The Centurion paled and for the first time in his life felt true fear.

The Emperor's clerk leaned over. "Excellent Caesar. Senator Demetrius and his supporters will ensure now that no one will question your authority again and you will have their backing for your new wars in Dacia."

# Chapter 18

Aodh had sent his men back to Caledonia. He was completely captivated in every sense of the word by Morwenna. Since the birth of her son, she had blossomed into a young woman who was even more beautiful than when Macro had fallen in love with her. Aodh justified his decision to stay with her by remembering the faith which Lulach and Calgathus had in the young woman. He would, however, happily have deserted his brethren he was so enamoured of Morwenna.

They spent the rest of the winter in the cave which Morwenna had shared with Luigsech. Aodh was an accomplished hunter and they ate well. Morwenna honed her skills as a witch and spent long vigils where she visited higher planes. In the days which followed these vigils, she lay in an exhausted sleep and Aodh watched her motionless body, admiring her beauty all the more. She talked with Aodh of his family. "Are your brothers also warriors?"

"Alas, I am the only boy. My mother had seven daughters."

"Daughters run in your family then?"

"On my mother's side, yes. My father was an only child, his mother died bearing him and he was killed in one of the battles against the horse warriors."

Aodh noticed that following their conversation Morwenna became more affectionate and soon after the moon bleeding she took him to her bed and they made love. For Aodh, it was the most remarkable experience of his life. None of the hags he had experienced came close to the exciting Morwenna. Every night for the rest of the month they made love in the long dark nights. Then one morning Morwenna announced, "Now we will travel south to Mona. It is time I met with my sisters."

Aodh felt confused and he did not know what to do. "Am I to come with you?"

Laughing Morwenna kissed him. "Of course you are for you are to be the father to my daughters. "You have left the

Caledonii and are now a member of my tribe." She looked at him and fixed him with her dancing green eyes. "Or do you wish to return north?"

There was no pause, not even for a heartbeat. He was ensnared. "No my love I will follow you beyond the seas if needs be and I will be a father to our children and I will protect you with my life."

"I know you will." Then she said something which chilled Aodh to his very bones. "But we will have only daughters. Any sons I bear will be left on the hills as a sacrifice to the Mother."

As the first spring flowers struggled through the thawing ground Morwenna headed south for she had waited for a sign from the Mother and as the frail white flowers peered unsteadily at the low sun in the sky she knew it was a whisper from the Earth. She would return to the sacred groves.

Spring brought unwelcome visitors too in the lands to the north of Coriosopitum; it was the warbands of the Caledonii who had roused the tribes after their success in the autumn and winter. Calgathus was seen as a symbol of the rebellion against Roman rule. The tribes from the north flocked to his banners but, more importantly, the Selgovae and Votadini from south of the wall of forts also joined and suddenly the two Tribunes were trapped. In Coriosopitum Prefect Julius had finally replaced all his casualties and his turmae were at full strength. Cassius Crispus, Macro's old chosen man took over the turma who were determined to revenge themselves on those who had killed their Decurion.

Julius called a planning meeting of his officers and sergeants. "We are going to have a harder job this year for we have to keep the supply route to the north open. Our fleet can bring in supplies but the weather can make life far harder for them than for us. We will operate as we did last year. Four turmae will keep the eastern route open. Decurion Princeps Gaius will command those and Decurion Macro the western. The remaining four turmae will be a rapid deployment force ready to go wherever danger threatens. I have secured a cohort of Tungrians who will garrison the fort and patrol the military way south of the forts but make no mistake gentlemen as the only cavalry in this theatre we will not stop. Sergeant Cato, I need you to bring as many horses from the stud at Derventio for last year we took too many casualties amongst our mounts."

Cato nodded, "They are learning sir that a dismounted rider is easier to kill and our horses are unarmoured."

"Any questions?"

The Decurions all looked at each other. Gaius eventually asked the question which was on everyone's minds. "What about Marcus and Livius? Any news?"

"No. We heard that Sallustius Lucullus had been executed but there has been no word of our two friends." Their glum looks let Julius realise that they thought that their friends were indeed, dead. "They may not be dead. I am taking the lack of news as a good thing. Anyway, there is no point brooding about something which is outside our control. I know that the Tribune would not want us to waste time on idle speculation so let us ride."

Gaius looked at the Prefect with newfound respect. He seemed to be able to be calmer and more objective. Gaius knew that he could never have been so sanguine about his oldest friend. As he led his patrol north he knew that his job was more important than it had ever been for if the barbarians went south then his family would be dead for Morbium was the best place to cross the Dunum. He determined that he would do all in his power to protect them.

His chosen man, Servius Maro rode next to him. "How will this patrol work then sir? Up to Trimontium and back?"

"No Servius. Up to Trimontium and spend the night there then up to Veluniate and spend the night there. We will be away for four days and three nights. This way it saves us having to build a fort and, more importantly, we are visible to many more people."

"And I thought we had pacified this area."

Shaking his head Gaius said, "These people are not ready for pacification yet. In the south, the legions only made them Roman when they massacred the Iceni and the tribes who rebelled against them. We have not inflicted a big enough defeat on these barbarians yet and, until we get greater numbers we are unlikely to."

"That is a depressing thought."

"I agree. I had thought that by the time I took my pension this land would be peaceful."

"Your pension sir? That must be years off."

"Not so long now, Servius. In three years I can go and live with my family."

"Three years? As soon as that? Would you not consider signing on again?"

"I might have done but the death of Decius and the way the Tribune was treated mean that as soon as I can I will take my bounty and become a farmer."

"I can't see you as a farmer sir."

"At the moment neither can I but if Gaelwyn can do it then so can I."

When they came to the river where Septimus and the legate had met their demise they scoured the river and banks for any sign of the bodies but there were none. "I expect we will see their killers wearing the Legate's fine armour."

"Yes sir. It will stand out like Decurion Macro on a horse for these barbarians seem to like blue paint for armour."

"They did but I think they are learning."

The patrol met nothing on the road but they sensed they were being watched. The tribes were not as friendly and the Centurion at Trimontium told them one of the lakes they used had had dead animals thrown in to spoil it.

Gaius was relieved to arrive at the solidly built Veluniate and his friend Tribune Sura. "Glad to see you Decurion Princeps."

Gaius saw this Cominius was greyer and had more scars than hitherto. "Bad winter?"

"Bad winter? It is relentless, like the snow. The constant attacks; flames in the night and sentries murdered. It takes its toll. The sentries grow older each day."

"And it will not get any easier now Cominius."

The Tribune smiled. "Thank you for your honesty, Gaius. No, it will not. They will keep attacking. At least we will be able to improve the defences and thank the Allfather that Marcus sent the fleet to support us or we would have perished. And yet they took many casualties. Ships were wrecked on the stormy rocks but we survived. Furius and I thanked the Tribune many times." He looked at Gaius askance, "How is the Tribune?"

"We know not. The Prefect hopes that the truth will emerge and he will be vindicated but the Governor was executed."

"Rome is an ass! It knows nothing but the gossip of incompetent officials and hearsay! Marcus could no more be a traitor than you or I."

"Which is the worrying thing Cominius, for if Marcus could be accused then what of us? I spoke with my men on the way up here. I will take my twenty-five years when it comes and live as Gaelwyn, on the farm."

"When is that?"

"Less than four years old friend."

"I envy you. For me, the auxilia is my life. I will die up here in the badlands where every rock and stone is an enemy and no one is your friend."

The ship bringing him home gave Marcus Aurelius Maximunius a more pleasant journey than the one he had suffered travelling to Germania. It gave him time to reflect on his life for he had come as close to losing his life as in any battle and this time it had been his so-called friends who would have killed him. He glanced at Livius; poor Livius who was nearly killed because of his name. What a tragedy! He swore that he would make it his mission to ensure that Livius was safe and then he would retire. His promise to a dead Governor was no longer valid. It had expired along with the strangled, misguided man. He would devote his life to making Stanwyck and Morbium a safe place for Romans, auxilia and native Britons. The Roman army was an offensive beast, in every sense of the word! Marcus would protect the people he loved. The Brigante he had married into and the retired soldiers he had fought with. Decius would love to be part of it and Decius too had only promised to stay on for a short time. When he landed he would meet with Decius at Coriosopitum and ask him if he too, wanted to retire.

When the Decurions returned from their patrols the Prefect held a celebratory dinner. He wanted the informality of his men having a drink but he wanted the intelligence from their patrols. He had ensured that the food was as they would have wished. A fine doe and magnificent wild boar both hunted within five miles of the fort. He had secured some good Gaulish wine, which he knew his officers preferred and he had sent for some delicacies from Rome which would titillate their taste buds. His father would have done anything for his only surviving son of whom he was immensely proud.

"The west is becoming dangerous Prefect. The tribes there, the Novontae and their allies want to be Roman but the Selgovae, Caledonii and the Irish are raiding all the time. Calgathus makes the chiefs offers which they have so far refused but it will not continue."

"I will ask permission to build up the forts over that side of the coast and, perhaps, ask the Classis Britannica to patrol there."

"If you do that Prefect, then Tribune Sura will find it hard to hold off the assaults of Calgathus. He is sorely pressed."

"I know Gaius."

"And the tribes on the east coast are very belligerent. Our raid last year merely delayed the inevitable. They will rise and they will rise this year."

Sergeant Cato normally kept quiet when the strategy was being discussed but he felt obliged to speak. "It seems to me that Julius Agricola had the right idea."

They all looked at the normally quiet horse master. "Speak on."

"It seems to me, Prefect, that he made sure that the Selgovae, Votadini and the Novontae did not attack us by taking hostages from their families. It is not honourable but it may save lives." There was a silence that echoed around the room. "Just a thought."

# Roman Retreat

"And a very good one Sergeant. In fact quite brilliant. It worked before, it will work again."

Macro coughed and shuffled in his seat. "Yes, but it does not solve the problem. It just makes them hate us even more. Sorry Sergeant." Cato shrugged.

"The longer we can keep the peace the more Roman the tribes will become. I think it is a good idea." The Prefect raised his beaker. "Well done Sergeant Cato."

Quite drunk, after a few hours drinking, the officers all stood, cheering Sergeant Cato's suggestion. Suddenly the door swung open and every man fell silent as Marcus Aurelius Maximunius and Livius Lucullus stood in the doorway.

"Gentlemen. Thank you for your warm welcome."

Macro was the first to react; he had lost his mentor, he had lost his wife and now to have the man he revered the most in the whole Empire returned to him was too much and the huge warrior picked Marcus up bodily and began to cry in uncontrollable sobs and the tears coursed down his cheeks. The other officers followed suit and the two men were greeted as men having been to Hades and back, which of course, they had.

By the time the furore had died down and Marcus and Livius had been given a drink, Macro was in the corner with Gaius comforting him. "There is a tale here Tribune." Prefect Julius understated as ever smiled at his old commander.

"There is. We landed at Veluniate and met with Tribune Sura. He was glad to see us."

The laughter was out of proportion to the comment and reflected the relief all of the officers felt. "I know of Decius' death and." he looked over at Macro, sympathy etched in every line of his face, "of Decurion Macro's betrayal. I feel guiltier than any man here." Everyone bore a shocked look on their face and Macro began to protest. "No Macro, I mean it. Decius saw what no one else had and remember, I had been closer to Fainch than anyone. Do you think that, if I had met her, I would not have recognised her? No, believe me, I feel guilty. I was too busy trying to save Britannia when I should have been trying to save my friends." He looked up at the roof. "Decius old friend, I am sorry."

Each man silently raised their beakers and gave a silent toast to their dead Decurion Princeps. "So Tribune what is your tale? How did you escape?"

Smiling he said, "Prefect, we have three men to thank. Firstly you for your letter and secondly your father for it was his letter to the Emperor which saved the day. "

"And the third?"

"The Emperor himself for he could have had us executed to save face but he did as his father would have done and thought of the soldier."

They all toasted the three men and Gaius looked at Julius with new respect. He had carried the message to Eboracum. Had he known the import of the missive he would have ridden even faster but he was impressed that his quiet Prefect had done so quietly and without fuss.

"And now sir what will you do? Will the Tribune be fighting the tribes again?"

"No Julius. I will be securing Livius a post in an ala." They all grinned for they felt as though he was one of them anyway. "And then I shall retire and this time I will watch over Ailis and Decius, and Marcus and," he looked pointedly at Macro and nodded, "young Decius."

Livius came over to Marcus and embraced him. Macro came over and said simply, "Thank you, sir. I will sleep much easier."

"As I suspect we will be degenerating into a Bacchanalian frenzy ere long, can I say that as of this moment Livius Lucullus is appointed Decurion in Marcus' Horse and Macro is to be promoted, once again, to training officer."

Calgathus had planned his invasion over the long cold winter months. His spies had counted the Roman soldiers and identified the weak spots. He knew that the fleet posed a threat that could not be negated and he aimed his strike at the forts in the middle of the chain. His son, Lulach had told him of the one fort which neither tribune seemed to control and that was the weak spot. His warriors spent the nights before the attack filling the ditch with brush and undergrowth. To the soldiers in the fort there appeared to be no change but the dead and dying material meant that the spikes were covered with a cushion of harmless branches. Calgathus began his attack with a feint at the fort closest to the Clota. Tribune Strabo immediately moved his reserve cohort to the west to counter the thrust. In the east Lulach himself launched an attack against Veluniate. The ships of the Classis Britannica moved in closer and a message was sent to Coriosopitum to bring up the ala of Marcus' Horse to counter the threat.

The forts closest to the incursions transferred their attention to the flanks and the warband in the centre crept closer during the hours of darkness as the auxiliaries in the fort of Inchutil breathed a sigh of relief that their fort was not the focus of attention. As the dawn broke on the late spring morning fifty thousand warriors rose as one and hurled themselves at the walls. The bolt throwers and onagers had no time to fire for the warriors formed pyramids and leapt over the walls, their first targets, and the dreaded artillery. With the artillery negated and the walls breached the cohort manning the fort soon succumbed and died as they fought, to the last man. Deigning to burn the fort the hordes flooded through the breach into the hinterland. Calgathus had a simple aim, to breach not only the first line of forts but the second. The second line of forts was but half finished and would be unprepared for an onslaught. There was nothing between the fifty thousand warriors and the Stane gate forts. The attacks on the extreme ends of the defences ceased and the warriors raced to the breach. The auxiliaries were too busy feeling superior to notice that the undefeated warriors moved towards the centre of their defences. Following the fifty thousand assault troops another twenty thousand barbarians emptied into the lands of the Novontae, Selgovae and Votadini and wavering tribes joined the inevitable attack on Rome.

Prefect Julius and the ala reach Veluniate to find an embarrassed Tribune Sura. "I am sorry Julius the attack seemed so intense that I felt sure this was the spring offensive."

"No matter Tribune better a wasted ride than a breach in the defences. Did you lose many men?"

"No. A handful and from the other forts too."

Just then a bleeding and clearly wounded despatch rider crashed into the gate. Julius and Cominius looked down in alarm. The sentry who came up was ashen. "Sir, the enemy warriors have broken through in huge numbers in the centre. Inchtutil is no more. The enemy warbands have destroyed it. They are heading for the south."

Tribune Sura looked at Julius. "It is up to you friend. We can rebuild Inchtutil and stop them returning but the warband will move too quickly for our infantry. Marcus' Horse must stop them although I know not how." He looked sadly at his friend for he knew the task was almost impossible." The Allfather be with you."

As Julius led his men from the fort he, too, wondered how he would stop this unstoppable wave of barbarians. This was not the time for indecision. "Decurion Cilo, your turma has the best mounts. Ride south and warn the forts between here and Coriosopitum about the invasion. Then head west and warn the Stanegate forts. Send four riders to Morbium and Eboracum."

Gaius looked at his Prefect. "But there is only a cohort at Coriosopitum."

"I know and all we can do is to warn them. Go Decurion! Go!"

Macro glanced at his leader and asked calmly. "And us Prefect, what do we do?"

Taking a deep breath Julius knew that his decision could affect the next thirty years of campaigning in Britannia. "We are on the east side of the high hills. We could waste time trying to fight across the trackless barren lands to the west but we can make quicker time on the road in the east. If we encounter any enemies we will be approaching from their rear. If we find no one before Coriosopitum then we head west and hope that we can meet them on favourable ground."

Gaius looked at Julius. "Sounds risky."

Macro laughed, "Risky? Sounds suicidal. A thousand men against sixty thousand. Nice odds. Let's go Prefect!"

The roar from the ala told Julius that his men were with him and Marcus' Horse would have a glorious end. They might not succeed but people would remember their ride. On a whim Gaius drew out his sword and held it, gleaming in the afternoon spring sunshine. "The Sword of Cartimandua goes to war!" The roar which greeted the gesture was even louder and Julius nodded his approval.

"We ride!"

# Chapter 19

Calgathus was exultant. His plan had worked far better than he had hoped. "Lulach. Take your men to Coriosopitum while I will take mine to the land of the lakes and Luguvalium. Destroy the enemy and take as much plunder as you can. Stop for nothing. Speed is of the essence. We will meet at Morbium when we have destroyed the Romans before us."

"I will my father and my lance will be adorned with so many Roman heads I will need help to lift it."

Lulach and his eager war band hurried down the Roman road south heading for Trimontium. Cilo had made good time and reached the outpost in plenty of time. The Centurion grimly nodded as the Decurion headed south. "Right lads I want a line of brush building fifty paces from the ditch." If any thought to question his orders one look at his face dissuaded them from voicing that thought. "I want the onagers to target the brush line and the bolt throwers to aim between the ditch and the brush line. Second century, take water and pour it into the ditch." His Optio questioned with his eyes. "I want a muddy morass out of which they cannot climb. Cooks! I want the men fed now." The Centurion looked at the sky. Three hours to sunset. The barbarians would be here in less than an hour. It would be tight but if he could delay them then the forces south might be able to muster a defence to defeat them. His fort would be destroyed, along with him and all his men but they would die a glorious death.

In the event they had almost one and a half hours which meant the men were fed, the ditch was muddy and they had had a couple of practice shots to ensure they had the range. The Caledonii and their allies did not expect that their invasion would have been noticed for they had moved quickly. They raced over the brush not noticing that it was unnatural. When the onagers began to hurl their missiles of fire they were taken totally by surprise. When the brush erupted into flame they were engulfed. Lulach urged them on. "It is but one fort and we can take it."

Once his men were in the killing ground the bolt throwers sliced lines through the attackers and Lulach watched with horror as his best men fell. He was even more worried when he saw them entrapped in the muddy morass of the ditches. His father had chosen him for this role because of his quick mind. This was one fort with less than a thousand troops, all infantry. They could not follow him. "Pull back and head south-west"

Even though they were reluctant to retreat from a fight Lulach's charismatic power was such that they all followed him, retreating back through the killing ground and heading down the valley sides away from the bolt throwers and onagers all facing north.

The Centurion in the fort was just happy that he and his men had escaped unscathed but, as the warband headed south, he began to worry about the unsuspecting forts to the south. "First Cohort. Clear the lines and dispose of the bodies."

The prefect reached Trimontium just as the defenders had cleared the bodies from the ditch. "Well done Centurion. Which way?"

"It is thanks to your warning sir. They headed south west about two hours ago."

"Macro and Livius take your turma and find them. Watch them and we will follow." Macro and Livius headed southwest following the clear trail left by the huge warband. "Ala! Rest your horses and eat. We have an hour."

Livius was exhilarated to be riding with his turma. He felt no resentment that Julius had sent Macro with him. Although the turma had accepted him he was under no illusions. Macro was still their leader whether Livius gave the orders or not. Macro had incredible balance and Livius was certain that the huge man would fall off his horse as he leaned over his horse's neck to look for signs of the warband. "Slow up lads. They are not far off. "A hundred paces later Macro held up his hand and they halted. At first, it appeared to be silent but then Livius heard the unmistakable noise of human activity. They had found the warband. "Servius ride back to the prefect and tell them we have found them. Right lads dismount. We move quietly until we can see them and then wait. Have your javelins ready in case they spot us." The big man's confidence and enthusiasm were infectious and Livius felt himself growing in confidence. Macro leaned over to Livius and whispered, "That's the secret. Make them believe you know what you are doing even though you are shitting yourself." He gave Livius a huge wink and a grin.

Livius met the Prefect and halted the ala. "The warband is halted in a dell a mile away. Mac... the Decurion asked me to halt you here."

"Well done. Gaius, come with me. The rest of you feed and rest your horses."

Livius led them off the road and they found the two troopers guarding the horses. Leaving their own mounts there they began to make their way through the undergrowth. The warband obviously hadn't come down the slope for the brush was thick and tangled, ripping at cloaks and unprotected limbs. Macro appeared like a wraith from nowhere and Gaius was reminded of Gaelwyn the Brigante scout. Livius noted that the well-trained turma was also well hidden and he knew the enormity of the role he had taken on. How would he take on Macro's mantle?

Macro squatted and they copied him. Whispering he said, "They are down there about five hundred paces. Most of them are sleeping but they have got guards out all around and an ambush laid up the back trail. With this undergrowth, there is no way to surprise them and our mounts would not cope with this terrain."

The Prefect popped his head up and looked around. "You are right. The good news is they are not going anywhere at the moment and our horses need the rest. Let us go back to our horses where we can talk."

Livius' mind was working overtime as they slipped through the tangle. He was desperate to impress these hardened warriors. "How about an ambush of our own?"

Julius looked with interest at Livius. "How would we work that?"

"I don't know the terrain down here but we know where they are heading, don't we? Morbium. Is there somewhere that we could ambush them with Macro's archers while the rest of the ala attacks the rear?"

Gaius looked at Macro. "Remember the place where Drusus died near the river? Well just down from there the valley narrows quite a lot and it is steep ground. Fifty archers could cause problems."

"That's right and the land this side is quite wide and will allow us to manoeuvre. "

"Right. Macro leave two of your men to trail the barbarians when they leave. You and Livius take Gratius' turma; they are competent archers and lay your ambush." As Macro eagerly sprang on to his horse's back the Prefect gripped the reins. "And Macro you are not Horatius on the bridge. You are an ambush. Kill as many as you can but when they work out how to outflank you then flee. Release your arrows as you do so but do not get caught. We haven't got enough men to be able to throw away two turmae." Macro nodded sulkily. "Retreat to Morbium. They could use the extra men and we will continue our pursuit."

Gaius and Julius were glad for the rest, Gaius even more than the Prefect. He felt his age these days and the back of his horse did not seem as easy and comfortable as it once had. When he did retire he would save his horse riding for special occasions.

"Will the plan work Gaius?"

Gaius looked over in surprise. The Prefect was having doubts. "It doesn't matter, either way, sir. It is the only plan we have. We slowed them up at Trimontium. If we can slow them up at Morbium then they may not get south of the Dunum and that is all we can hope."

"There will be another warband, Gaius, in the west and there will be no one to stop that one."

"Remember the land of the lakes Julius? That is a hard country. There is a large garrison at Luguvalium which may slow them down and a small garrison at Glanibanta. Those and the terrain may well make it harder for Calgathus' men."

## Roman Retreat

"But Gaius there is no one coming to aid us. Once they brush aside those two forts then they are into Britannia, Brigante country."

"This isn't like you, Julius. Don't look too far ahead. Let us deal with this warband first and then we will look at the next problem."

"You are right. One warband at a time."

The problem the ala had the next day was staying out of sight of the warband. The Roman road ran along a ridge and any troops would be clearly seen. The warband stayed in the valleys moving swiftly along the lush new growth. Eventually, Julius decided to move the ala east and ride parallel to the road relying on Macro's scouts for warnings of any deviation from the route they had predicted.

"The funnel is about two miles away sir."

"Right Gaius." Raising his arm the Prefect led them down the slope along to the valley bottom. At first, it was hard going until they came to the area trampled by thirty thousand warriors. The two scouts found them.

"Still heading south sir but they keep leaving forty or fifty warriors along the trail to ambush any pursuers. They nearly caught us until we worked out what they were doing."

"Decurions Valerius and Galeo. Go with these men and eliminate the ambush. The rest of you, unsling your shields we are going to battle."

The land fell away before them but they could see, about a mile away, the wooded copse in which the ambush was being set. The ala halted in two lines and waited. The two Decurions had split their forces and Julius could see the horses tethered on the outside of the woods. The troopers slipped in and after what seemed like an age but was probably a few minutes he saw a trooper emerge and wave his javelin. The ambush had been cleared.

The two wings of the ala swept around the outside of the copse and reformed on the other side. The turmae of Cilo and Galeo formed up behind them. Julius led the ala slowly towards the funnel and the trap. He needed Macro to ensure that the barbarians were pressing forward before he attacked.

## Roman Retreat

As they came over the rise they could see the horde pushing forward. In the distance, the Prefect could see arrows, few in number plunging into the warband. Drawing his sword Julius ordered the charge. Gaius drew the Sword of Cartimandua and, as he felt his turma start to edge forward, he smiled at their enthusiasm. Marcus had always said the sword was worth another turma in battle and he was right.

The barbarians were too eager to get at the men who had halted them and did not see or hear the horses thundering at their backs. The first javelins were hurled at thirty paces distance and the second twenty. Even as the last javelins flew they drew their spathas and, as their mounts trampled the dead and dying they stabbed and thrust into unarmoured and unprotected backs. Their blades slipped easily down the sides of their horse's heads killing all before them. They were a killing machine four hundred paces wide. The second line threw their javelins ahead to create an enormous killing ground. As Julius found a gap before him he looked over the barbarians and saw Macro's men retreating, firing arrows as they went. The charge of the rest of the ala had slowed down and the barbarians were now turning to fight their tormentors. "Fall back!"

The order was repeated and the ala withdrew up the slope out of arrow range. The Caledonii waved their fists and weapons at the Romans but they were in no position to attack. Julius watched as a group of chiefs and leaders met behind the barbarian's lines. "Looks like we have given them a problem Prefect."

"Aye. They can't move forward with us here and they can't attack us because we can evade them."

"They will probably try to outflank us."

"No, that would take too much time."

Lulach's solution was simple, he kept moving through the funnel but the men at the rear were spearmen who planted their long shafts of ash into the ground whenever the ala approached making a hedgehog of spear points. Although this stopped the ala from attacking it meant that the warband was moving incredibly slowly. Macro had chosen to disobey his orders and was harrying those at the front and peppering them with arrows. Unfortunately for Macro the funnelling effect did not last long and the warband began to spread out; the turmae were in danger of being enveloped and, holding his bow above his head as a signal Macro led his men south to the safety of Morbium's walls.

"Well we slowed them for a while but they can move on to the river now."

"But much more slowly Gaius. By the time they arrive, it will be dark and they will have been warned by Macro. Look at the field. They have left almost an ala of their own men dead. The problem is they now know we are pursuing and we will have to watch for ambushes. Take your turma as scouts, we will follow."

Calgathus was having less success than his son. The legionaries and auxiliaries at Luguvalium had inflicted many casualties on his warband and, like Lulach at Trimontium, he had been forced to leave the siege and continue south to raid. Already herds of cattle and other animals were being driven north to the lands of the Selgovae and Votadini. Calgathus might not have caused a major military problem but, economically, he had hurt northern Britannia.

Decius Brutus arrived at Eboracum with the cohort from the Ninth. "Who is in charge here?" He looked around and could only see Centurions. "Who is senior then?"

"Me, First Spear, Centurion Annius Servilius."

"Where is the Prefect?"

"He was taken ill last week. He died last night."

Groaning Decius looked around the walls. "Who do you have here then?"

"Two cohorts of Tungrians."

"That it?"

"There is a camp outside with the four Cohortes Equitatae waiting for orders. They have been trained but no prefects!"

"Why haven't they moved north then?"

Before the man could answer there was a shout from the gates. "Riders approaching. Stand to."

Decius heard the challenge and the response. As soon as he heard, "Marcus' Horse." He shouted, "Open the gate and let them in."

The two troopers were exhausted. One of them Julius Calpius recognised Decius. "Am I glad to see you, sir? We are from Decurion Cilo's turma. The Caledonii have broken out and two warbands are heading south. The prefect was trying to slow them down. One of them was heading for Morbium."

"Well done son. Get these men some food and water. Centurion, I want one of your cohorts ready to move at dawn. Take me to these four cohorts. They are going into action tomorrow. We will march on Morbium."

"But sir it is sixty miles."

"Then we will double time. If we don't stop them there soon they will be able to destroy Eboracum in a heartbeat. Send messengers to Lindum and Deva. They need warning too."

Prefect Demetrius was proved correct. Lulach's warband arrived at Morbium after dark and they made their camp in the Roman style with a ditch and stakes. "They are learning Gaius."

"Yes, I had hoped they would just collapse and then we could have attacked them while they slept."

"I want us up that ridge. The last thing I want is for a sneak attack at night and undo all the good work the lads have done. Set the sentries and make sure everyone is rested."

"At least Macro will have a comfortable night."

"I think he would rather be here with us."

Decurion Macro was, indeed longing to be outside the walls. "I tell you Livius I am never happy inside walls. I feel trapped."

Decurion Cilo laughed. "Well if you will go outside then Livius and I will have four times the room to sleep."

"No, I will put up with the discomfort."

The Camp Prefect now had almost three full turmae in the fort. While this made it crowded he had a much better chance of defending against the warband which seemed to fill the horizon and their many fires dancing closer to the fort than they would have liked made the night seem like day. He hoped that the two troopers sent south had reached Eboracum but more than that, he hoped there was even now, a legion marching from the south. The giant Decurion, Macro had stressed to the Centurions and the Camp Prefect that they needed to ensure that the bolt throwers were well supplied, well manned and well-aimed. "They could be the difference between winning and getting our arses kicked. Make sure the men have the ranges for the onagers and get plenty of water from the river otherwise we will burn. "

Decurion Cilo and Livius just smiled at the befuddled expressions on the Prefect and Centurion's faces. Macro looked so big and muscular that everyone assumed he had no brain. As Decurion Cilo said to Livius, "He might not be sharp about some things but he is a military marvel right down to his toes."

Lulach was in a foul mood. He knew that the Roman cavalry was just watching him and waiting for him to attack. His plan to sneak up on them as they slept had failed when they moved out of sight and his scouts had been found butchered. The fort still stood there and he knew that his father would have expected him to have passed it already and be heading for Eboracum. He looked towards the road where his tired men were planting sharpened stakes. If he couldn't eliminate the cavalry he could at least neutralize it. When he attacked the fort he would not have to worry about cavalry causing him problems.

Julius was up well before dawn. Gaius had told him of the traps laid by the Caledonii. "That gives us a problem then doesn't it?"

"We could go upstream and cross the river at the ford it is only twenty miles upstream."

"All that does Gaius is to get us across the river. No, we need to cause the Caledonii problems here. It seems that we shall have to fight on foot." Gaius looked quizzically at the prefect. They had done it before but the men were not happy about it. "We shall do as we did in the north. Half the men mounted and half on foot. The mounted use javelins and the foot use bows. If, sorry I meant, when the Caledonii attack, the mounted men race in with spare horses and take our men out."

"We won't be able to destroy large numbers."

"No, but we will wear them down and stop them bringing their full force against Morbium. It is no Alavna or Coriosopitum. Unless Eboracum can send reinforcements it won't last a day. I just hope Macro and Cilo can do something about the bridge. If they can get men across there then the south is open to them."

Gaius looked south as though he could see the miles to Stanwyck. "Where my family and Tribune Marcus wait."

Lulach had learned from his wars against Rome. His men had constructed huge shields made of logs. In the night they had moved forward and placed them within arrow range of the fort. The men who had waited there had had a long cold night but were rewarded in the morning by not having to face the gauntlet of enemy fire. Lulach stood out of range of the Romans and signalled the assault. The first warriors popped their heads over the log shields and fired their arrows. There was no reply and they looked back at their leader who urged them on. Soon the archers were firing constantly until their arrows were exhausted.

Inside the fort, the Camp Prefect was looking at Macro and Cilo. "When do we loose arrows back?"

"Have you taken any casualties?"

"No."

"Then why waste missiles? Their arrows are wasted. Save our arrows and bolts for targets too big to miss."

Lulach had been prepared for his first attack to fail although he had not expected it to fail because the enemy did not fire back. The wagon had been filled with straw and pitch. The front had had the shafts removed and replaced by ten long spears. He nodded and the forty chosen men began to push it down the slope. It began slowly at first but soon its momentum and the warriors pushing it caused it to move quite rapidly. Suddenly the fort's archers began to release wave upon wave of arrows and soon the forty men had been whittled down to a handful but the damage had been done and the wagon was on its way. Archers stepped from the woods and launched fire arrows at the out of control vehicle lurching down the paved road. Some arrows missed but enough struck and soon the wagon was an inferno. Despite the Roman's attempts to stop it, they failed and it crashed into the gate the wood and dried kindling bursting into flame.

As soon as it hit, a number of things happened: Lulach launched his attack, the Camp Prefect ordered the buckets of water standing by to be poured onto the conflagration and Gaius began to attack the Caledonii lines. The barbarians were so intent upon the gates that they failed to notice the men at the rear dying. The ala archers caused many casualties but the Romans were not having it their own way and the Caledonii archers now had targets. The auxiliaries with the buckets began to take casualties. Macro was busy both killing the archers and shouting orders. "Keep the buckets coming! You men in the fort, throw as much water as you can. Piss on it if you need to!"

The tide began to turn when the mass of men passed into the killing ground where the bolts and artillery sliced through whole files of men. Brave as they were it was hard to keep going. "Get to the walls. They cannot send arrows and stones at you there!" Lulach's powerful voice echoed across the noisy, screaming battlefield. Enough men made it to the walls so that they started to climb and engage the auxiliaries in hand to hand.

A small group of a hundred or so warriors evaded all the missiles and the defenders and raced to the bridge. Their leader raised his staff, the signal that Lulach had been waiting for. They had secured the bridge. Lulach called his men back to avoid further casualties. He could now cross the Dunum at his leisure. He would send over ten thousand of his best warriors in the hours of darkness and they would lay waste to the surrounding land. It would then be a matter of time before their flimsy fort fell.

As night drew in each leader reviewed the day, Julius was disappointed that they had not killed more men. The camp Prefect and Macro were pleased that their walls had not been breached but were disturbed by the men on the bridge and the still glowing Porta Praetorium which had held, but only just. Only Lulach was truly content. The morrow would see victory and his warband would flood into the gentle vales and rich lands that surrounded Eboracum.

# Chapter 20

Decius Brutus was angry and frustrated. His legionary cohort could have made the fort in one day but the lack of leadership and training of the new cohorts appalled him. Sallustius Lucullus had kept them idle for too long and they had barely managed forty miles. Those forty miles were hard-earned with more moans and complaints than Decius had ever experienced. His vine staff had been in constant use. Rather than risk them making a mockery of building a camp he had headed for Cataractonium swearing, as he lambasted them, that they would be up before dawn and make the last twenty miles by mid-morning.

"What is on your mind Macro?"

"What?"

"I have known you long enough, known you since you trained me at Derventio all those years ago, to know that you are plotting and planning."

"And I have not known you long Decurion but I too know that your mind is working."

Grinning Macro nodded. "It is the bridge. They can move over their whole army and we can do little to stop it. I have but one son who lies less than ten miles from here. I do not want him or Ailis and Gaius' children, to die."

"What can we do? The best men in here are the ninety men we brought and there are hundreds out there."

"I know and I do not intend to waste men's lives. I intend to steal an idea from the Caledonii."

"How?"

"Simple Livius. We will fill the four wagons which we have here in the fort with our own flammable material. Open the Porta Decumana and send them flaming towards the bridge. They may kill men but, more importantly, the heat will crack the concrete of the blocks and weaken the whole structure."

"But if the bridge falls then we will be stranded."

## Roman Retreat

"Any Roman soldier can build a bridge but these screaming half-dressed cockerels cannot. At the very least we will kill many of their warriors and, if we reduce the odds we may yet be able to evict them."

Despite being dubious about the whole concept the Camp Prefect could not come up with a powerful enough argument against it. They spent half the night building the bridge destroyers and it was just before dawn when they were ready. Unbeknown to Macro and the defenders, Lulach had been busy sending warriors across the bridge, slithering on their bellies like snakes to avoid being seen by the sentries. Over three thousand had made it by the time the gates opened and, like a scene from Hades, the four flame-filled wagons lurched, spat, crackled and rumbled down to the bridge. The night was like day and the other barbarians attempting to cross the bridge were spotted. Macro quickly raised the alarm and bolts, arrows, javelins and slingshots pummelled the shocked warriors. Those on the bridge died in a screaming inferno of burning pitch and oil. Men, who were able, threw themselves into the river and continued to burn as their dying, blackened bodies were carried downstream.

As the survivors gathered on the far bank Lulach decided to launch his attack. There was little point in waiting. There would be no surprise but this time he would fight until the walls were taken, knowing that the force he had ferried across the river would cause huge damage. He could only hope his father had been as successful. "Brothers today we will attack and win. Yesterday we tested them and found that they are weak. Why I alone could knock down their damaged gate. With you, besides me, we could knock down their very walls. Are you with me?"

With a roar, his men raised their arms and rushed down the slope. Their speed was such that the auxiliaries were slow to react and Macro had to scream at them. "Release, you dozy bastards! They will be on us."

The men began to release javelins and arrows and inflict heavy casualties but the Caledonii closed with the walls and leapt on each other's shoulders to reach the ramparts. As soon as they were close then the power of the artillery was nullified. A party led by Lulach paused to pick up a log shield and, using it as a ram, smashed it into the door. The fire had cracked the wood and it began to crumble. Encouraged by the brittle, blackened nature of the barrier they hurled the logs again and suddenly the gate was breached and it first cracked then crashed open, the warriors flooding in like water unleashed from a dam.

Julius had nearly been caught off guard but one of the alert sentries had spotted the wagons and awoken the Prefect. "Gaius, get the men mounted."

"But Julius, the stakes!"

"It doesn't matter they aren't guarding them. We walk through and then charge. You take turmae one, two, three and four and chase down those on the bridge. I'll take the rest to the fort."

"Sir!" Gaius nodded his thanks for he would be able to get to his villa and save Ailis!

Macro had the men from the ala ready with arrows and javelins. They stood in front of the Praetorium in three ranks. The rear ranks launched arrows as soon as the door fell and many warriors fell but still they came on. Livius was in the front rank with the javelin men and he cursed his lack of skill with a bow. Waiting until the warriors were but twenty paces away he yelled, "Loose!" and thirty javelins found their marks. They had no time for another volley for the enemy were upon them and Livius found himself facing a huge red-bearded, blue-painted warrior wearing a nose ring. In his hands, he held a fearsome-looking axe and a small sax. He felt like running and he almost panicked until out of the corner of his eye he saw Macro fighting two warriors with a smile on his face. He remembered when Marcus had asked Macro to test him and he suddenly became confident. This was no Macro. This was a barbarian with no more idea of fighting a soldier than he had of reading Homer. Livius waited until the warrior committed himself with a vicious swinging blow from his axe and he deflected it with his shield to slice harmlessly into the soil. At the same time, he blocked the sax with his sword and then head-butted the bare face of his opponent with his helmet. He heard the nose break and felt the blood gush but he had no time for self-congratulation; his enemy would soon regain his sight. Bringing his sword up he drove it through the man's throat and into his brain. He twisted his blade to free it and moved on to the next warrior.

The ala was not having it all its own way and neither were the defenders on the walls. They soon found themselves attacked from in front and behind. Livius noted that the men on either side of him were dead but he remembered his lessons and fought each man as he came at him. The three lines were shrinking until Macro ordered the rear rank to join the others. As soon as he had fellow troopers on either side Livius noticed that it became much easier.

Lulach left the fort and slipped, almost unnoticed out of the Porta Decumana. With six of his oath brethren, he hacked his way towards the bridge where the inferno had finally died down to little pockets of fire and burning bodies. In the distance, he could see his warband marching down Dere Street. His lieutenants could continue the fight at the fort; Lulach wanted the glory of Eboracum.

Gaius and his turmae struggled to pass the stakes and the detritus of the barbarian camp. Loath to lose a mount to a broken leg the Decurion Princeps took it steadily. Their problems really started when they found themselves in the killing ground in front of the fort. The warriors were twenty deep and trying to get at the walls. When they heard the horses behind them they vented their spleen on those foes. "Wedge!" Using himself as the spear point Gaius hacked his way through the seething maelstrom of men. The horses themselves became a weapon as they trampled and kicked all before them in their terrified attempt to escape the blades and barbs which cut and sliced them. Gaius also had the advantage that he was not heading for the fort but the bridge and its sickening smell of human roast.

The horses were afraid at the bridge because of the smell and the smoke. When Gaius looked at the bridge he could see the cracks starting to appear. Macro's conflagration would mean weeks of work to repair it. Gaius leaned forward and spoke gently to his mount which made its way gingerly across the bridge. Once he had made the journey, the rest of the turmae followed.

As the turmae came over Gaius saw the empty saddles and empty spaces. He had less than eighty men left. "Form up. Column of twos but be prepared to get into line when we catch up with them."

Lulach's long legs and his fitness soon enabled him to catch up with the warband. "Rest for a few minutes and then we run down this road the Romans have so thoughtfully built for us." He glanced back at the fort as his men laughed. There would be no pursuit; the burning bridge would ensure that. The Romans had unwittingly helped him achieve his ends. Cataractonium would be the next settlement that would be put to the sword.

Decius Brutus grinned as the new cohorts struggled along the road. The legionary cohort was finding it an easy stroll but, having been marching for four hours the unfit auxiliaries were ready to vomit. Suddenly he stopped and ordered the column to halt as his scouts came racing down the road. "A warband sir and Morbium is aflame."

So he was too late to save the fort but he would destroy the warband. "How many?"

The man shrugged, warbands were notoriously hard to count. "Half a legion?"

"Ninth we will take the centre, three lines!" He pointed to the left and right and the Centurions of the auxiliaries led their men to their prearranged positions. The auxiliaries were just glad to be halted.

Decius glanced along the line. Whilst he was not confident about the auxiliaries, no one would get past his cohort and, holding the middle of the line, that meant the warband would be halted.

Lulach and his band came over the brow of the hill and looked with dismay at the forces before them. "Legionaries!" This would not be an easy fight. The only advantage he had was the slope, gentle though it was, which would give his men impetus. He could see that the legionaries were in the

# Roman Retreat

centre which meant the weaker auxiliaries were on the flanks. "Boar's snout!" The men quickly formed up with more men on the two flanks and the best warriors in the middle. "Once we are through this pitiful force we will have a free run to Eboracum. Charge!"

Decius was not concerned with the men of the Ninth for they would withstand the onslaught easily but the untried cohorts on his flanks were a different matter. He had only had a couple of days to give the Centurions advice on fighting the fearsome barbarians. He hoped they would heed his words which came from over twenty years fighting in the province. He was gratified to see them watching for his signal. He had impressed upon them the effect of a volley of javelins. He raised his arm and every soldier in the five cohorts raised his javelin. Decius had to time the volley just right for he had a majority of inexperienced men. Waiting until the first ranks were forty paces away he yelled, "Loose!" His legionaries had their second javelins in their hands almost instantly and Decius yelled, "Loose!" again. The volley was more ragged this time because the auxiliaries had not been as quick as the well trained Ninth. "Lock shields!" The command was probably unnecessary but Decius wanted the Centurions on his flanks to do the same.

The volleys had been devastating but there were still many in the warband. They hurled themselves at the Roman line; some of the warriors jumping high in the air to strike down on the soldiers before them. The second and third lines of the legionaries braced their shields against the backs of the men in front and the barbarians, who hit that part of the line, fell back, many of them unconscious with the force of their strike. As soon as they were stationary the legionaries went to work with their gladii. They were ruthlessly efficient. The unarmoured Caledonii could find no target for their blows which bounced ineffectually off armour or shield while the razor-sharp gladii slid between locked shields to find the vulnerable parts of the enemy's bodies. Soon the middle part of the Roman line moved inexorably forward.

Unfortunately, the flanks were not secure and the extra warriors of the boar's snout were pushing back the looser line of the auxiliaries. The Centurions screamed their orders and the cohorts fought bravely but as quickly as the legionaries moved forwards so the flanks were pushed back. Soon the Ninth would be outflanked by the whole warband. To their credit, the auxiliaries did not run but they were losing the battle.

Lulach could sense the battle swinging his way and he shouted at his lieutenants to finish off the flanks. He just hoped that his men assaulting the fort were doing as well. The battle at the fort was on a knife-edge. Julius and the ala were using their missiles to thin out the barbarians but the bolt throwers and onagers could no longer fire as the Caledonii were on the towers and walkways. Macro and his archers had run out of arrows and it was a slogging match with warriors fighting soldiers in a deadly fight to the death. Livius wondered if he would have the strength to lift his sword again but as he felt his comrades around him find reserves from somewhere so too did he.

Gaius halted his remaining men at the top of the slope. "One line." Looking down he could see that the flanks were about to give. He could also see that the warband in front of the legionaries was thin and if they could manage to avoid being flanked they could fight the foes on their flanks. The land to his right was rocky and steep, leading up to a heavily wooded area and would afford no advantage to his men. "We will attack their left flank. We have to relieve the pressure on those auxiliaries." He hoped that by attacking one flank he would give the legionaries the chance to sweep around to the other flank.

The horses were fresh and the ground open; soon the thundering of the hooves could be heard by warriors and Romans alike. It gave the Romans heart but the barbarians began to look around nervously, not knowing from which direction the danger was coming. The cavalry only had swords but the spatha had a good long reach and the slicing scything blades found easy targets. Their horses crashed and crushed their victims and the beleaguered auxiliaries suddenly found new heart and began to push hard against a foe that was visibly weakening. Like a weakened dam wall,

## Roman Retreat

the Caledonii left flank and centre collapsed in an instant and the Caledonii right flank, amongst the rocks and brush, was isolated.

Lulach was a pragmatist. He had lost this battle but he would not waste his life. The rocky bank behind him led to a thick stand of trees and pursuit would be difficult. He would live to fight another day. "Caledonii follow me!" Suddenly disengaging they ran up the rocky bank, scampering like mountain goats. The auxiliaries were too tired and shocked to do anything other than watch. The remaining warriors were soon slaughtered and Gaius and Decius greeted each other like the long lost friends they were. "As soon as I heard horses I knew we were safe."

"And when I saw the standard of the Ninth I hoped it was you."

Decius looked up the road and the smoke spiralling in the distance. "Aye Decius it is not yet finished. We will have to leave those in the woods for it is still not decided at the fort. They are within the walls."

"Ninth form up. Auxiliaries take position behind us. You," Decius grinned at Gaius, "can choose your own place."

"We will take the left flank just in case the remnants of our skirmish decide to join their comrades in the fort."

"Sir, the horses are exhausted."

Julius looked at Sergeant Cato. "I know."

"Sir!" there was pleading in the man's eyes and Julius knew that the horses were now more of a hindrance.

"Withdraw." The turmae withdrew reluctantly, the Caledonii cheering, thinking that they had defeated them. Inside the fort, the defender's spirits slumped as they heard the cheer for they knew it spelt the end for them.

"Dismount we fight on foot. These barbarians think they have won. Let us show them that Marcus' Horse can fight as well on foot as a horse."

With a roar they hurled themselves at the shocked warriors who moments ago thought they had finally won, finally defeated the vaunted ala after so many attempts. At the same time, Decius and his legionaries marched across the rocky and smoking bridge. Inside Morbium Macro heard Decius' stentorian tones ring out. "Forward."

"Right lads we have reinforcements let's get these bastards out of the fort!!"

Attacked on three sides by three forces the warband, still more numerous than the defenders in number, crumbled. Panicking many threw themselves in the river whilst others raced north towards the woods, desperate to evade the disciplined force which was inexorably ending the life of the warband. The survivors were slaughtered until the only ones still living in Morbium were the Romans. They had won. Weeks later those who eked out a living at the mouth of the Dunum saw the decaying and battered bodies of the Caledonii washing out to sea.

Macro, Livius and the other members of the ala looked around at the death and destruction in the fort. There were dead bodies lying five and six deep. None of the survivors had emerged unwounded. Even the mighty Macro was bleeding heavily from a head wound and a slash on the arm. Decurion Cilo had lost three fingers on his left hand and the remains of the shield showed the force of the blow.

Decius Brutus was the freshest of the senior officers who remained and he took charge. "Right Centurion I know your lads did alright, eventually but now they can do a little bit more work. Take all these barbarian bodies outside and make a pile. We will burn them later." He glanced over at the other Centurions from the Ninth. "Make sure there are no survivors." The officers from the Ninth drew their pugeos and sent those almost at death's door or feigning death to the great hereafter.

Julius and the rest of the ala dragged their weary bodies towards the river. Gaius was already drinking upstream from where the bodies lay and the rest of the ala joined him and his turmae. "That was closer than I like Gaius."

"They nearly had us. If they had concentrated on the fort they would have taken it."

"They were too keen to get into the Southlands."

Gaius pointed at the wooded ridge. "A lot of them escaped up there and I think their leader was with them."

"We'll get after them in the morning."

Gaius shook his head as Macro and Livius walked up to them. "No. I'll take those who are fit tonight." Macro looked curiously at Gaius for he seemed determined and he rarely argued with the prefect. "Because if they head west they will come to Stanwyck!"

Macro understood and leapt to his feet. "Come with me, Gaius. Our horses have been resting." Ignoring the Prefect he shouted. "Volunteers to ride with the Decurion Princeps and me."

If Julius had wanted a measure of the loyalty of the men and the popularity of Gaius and Macro he had it when, almost to a man, all those at the river rose and followed the two decurions to the mounts. Livius looked at the prefect. "Did they just disobey an order?"

"No Livius I didn't give an order they just wrote their own, but in truth they are right and I should have thought of it first but I am so very tired." Julius slumped to the ground and Livius ran over to him. He could see no wound but as he lifted the helmet from his head he saw a long savage wound running across his forehead oozing blood.

"Pontius! Get the surgeon."

Gaius led the way. "They were heading west so if we swing southwest and use Dere Street we can be at Stanwyck before them."

Macro urged his horse on. "If anything were to happen to Decius…"

"Gaelwyn and Marcus are there and we have armed men guarding the walls."

"How many?"

"Ten but they are good men."

"Ten? Against these Caledonii butchers? We had better hurry."

The road made the short miles fly and, as they neared Stanwyck they looked for signs of war; there were none. Gaelwyn and his men were on the walls with torches as

Gaius rode up. Marcus emerged from the hut his sword in his hand. "We thought it was the barbarians. I am glad it is you." He looked at the smoke rising in the north. "Have they succeeded? Are you the survivors?" He opened the gate and the fifty troopers rode into the walled enclosure.

"No we won, but only just. There is a chief with the remnants of a warband. Almost a thousand of them and they are loose somewhere around here."

Ailis ran out and threw her arms around Gaius. "You are safe." They embraced and kissed as Macro and Gaelwyn smiled at each other.

"Macro, what do we do? Stay here and hope that they don't come or head for Morbium and hope they don't catch us."

"I think we stay."

Marcus nodded, "It is the wisest course. Here we have sound walls and ditches. They have fought one battle they will not want another."

Gaius turned, holding his wife in the crook of his arm. "I agree. They took a beating today and they have been fighting since before dawn. Even if they do come here, I think we will discourage them easily enough."

"But we need food and rest Gaelwyn. We have fought all day as well."

Gaelwyn looked at the exhausted ala and opened his arms. "We will stand guard and we will get you food. But worry not. I can smell the Caledonii."

Macro grinned at his friend, "Is that why you and your guards came out tooled up for war as we arrived?"

Sniffing Gaelwyn said, "No but you do smell like a barbarian."

When they were indoors Marcus turned to Gaelwyn. "It never ends, does it? I thought that when I finished with the ala I would have a peaceful life but it is not meant to be."

"Peace is different things to different men. To me, it is not having to fight and survive each day but knowing that some days I may have to fight."

"So it makes most of your days peaceful."

"Yes and, with Ailis and the bairns, rewarding. It will come to you Tribune. It just takes time."

"I can see that and you are more content."

Nodding Gaelwyn added, "And these raids, they will lessen. They will tire of being beaten by the Romans."

Lulach and his men were still hiding in the woods. They had watched the cavalry riding south and suspected a trap. "They mean to send out others west and the two forces will converge on us."

"Perhaps your father will arrive," one of his men said hopefully.

"I think not. Our plan was for us to go down two roads and divide their forces but if we can head south and west we might find him in the land of the lakes. Find food and water. We need rest. When it is dark we will travel."

Macro and Gaius did not realise how tired they were until they had eaten and were sat with their babies on their laps. All four fell asleep together, much to Gaelwyn's amusement. "Look at them, four babies together!"

"Leave them be uncle. I am just glad that they are still whole."

Gaelwyn cast his eye over their wounds. "Yes but only just. Well, I had better check my guards."

Gaelwyn was taking no chances and not only did he have his guards out but he had dogs in the outer ditch. If any strangers came they would let him know and loudly. The night was dark and moonless; the barbarians had the advantage. "Do not look to the light; it will spoil your night vision." The men smiled. They knew that Gaelwyn was worried when he stated the obvious. Suddenly one of the dogs started to bark. "Here they come. Watch for them and I will get the Romans." He slipped into the hut and woke Gaius and Macro. Already their men were rousing, having heard the barking.

"Grab your weapons and spread yourselves out around the wall."

The Caledonii who had awoken the dogs had been sent by Lulach to find food. The woods had been barren and without anything which might sustain a hungry and thirsty warband. He knew that his men need sustenance if they were to trek across the spine of Britannia. The first warriors he sent were attacked by the dogs and the yelping told Gaelwyn that they had been killed. His guards were armed with bows and as soon as they saw lightness in the dark their arrows flew straight and true. The first five scouts died silently but, as more warriors crossed the ditch they saw the arrows and their comrades die. With a roar, they raced at the walls. They expected a farmer and his slaves. There was a sudden shock as they realised they had awoken a hornet's nest and it was a party of Roman soldiers. After a short and intense skirmish, the survivors raced off.

"So we will not eat tonight."

"Let us return with the warband and finish off these soldiers. There cannot be many. Let us kill them."

Lulach shook his head. "We have lost too many warriors already. A full belly is not worth another dead warrior. Now that we know there are Romans here we will move west. There will be easier pickings there for there are fewer Romans..."

# Epilogue

Mona was as she had dreamed it and as Luigsech had described it. The majestic mountain of Wyddfa, so sacred and powerful, a symbol of the power of the Mother, seemed to stand guard over the verdant little island. So detailed had the description been and the paths that she must take that she easily found the sacred groves on the holiest of isles lying just off the main one. Nervously they crept towards the sacred grove. Aodh had no idea what to expect but Morwenna had been feeling its power as they had made their way across Mona, heaving with spring life. Her heart fell when she saw the whitened bones lying like sand on a beach. These were all that remained of her mother's sisters and the Druids who worshipped there. As she reverently gathered their remains Aodh could only stand mesmerised by her devotion. When he attempted to help she waved him off. "Your hands are those of a warrior. This needs the hands of a priestess. Go and make us a shelter. You should find a cave just around the headland."

Aodh knew that Morwenna had never been to Mona and yet the cave was exactly where she said it would be. The entrance was cunningly hidden but once inside there was clear evidence of human habitation. The fresh breeze going towards the sea told Aodh that there was another entrance on the land side. He quickly moved the debris from the floor and placed their few belongings on the rock shelves in the side. By the time he emerged there was no sign of the bones. He was going to ask where they were but one look at her face told him that would not be greeted well.

"You will need to forage for food and find out, without giving our presence away, where the women are who live on the island. I will speak with my sisters for the child kicking deep within me tells me that the Mother wants me to begin my work."

Aodh began his appointed task and, leaving Morwenna to go into her dream world, he headed north to spy out the rest of the mysterious land of Mona.

Calgathus and his warband had fared better than Lulach and he had more of his band intact. They met in the long valley close to the barren mountain. Calgathus and his son embraced. "I see you did not do as well in the east as he had hoped." There was no censure in his voice for he knew his son to be a cautious warrior who would not waste men's lives. His dead brother Ninian had been another thing altogether.

"No father. Their cavalry pursued us and some legionaries came from the south to attack us from two sides. We could not defeat their forts. They are stronger here in the south; they have used more stone."

"You are right son. I fear that this strategy may not be the right one. Let us take the positives from this campaign, which is just the beginning. We have taken much plunder and given it to our allies to make their support stronger. We will raid this region and take this plunder back for us. When we are back in our lands we will continue to attack their forts. Our success in breaking through has given me heart. With our Selgovae and Votadini brothers, we can make the Romans regret coming so far north. This is not the end. We have only just begun to fight."

Calleva Atrebatum was a bustling and thriving town. Aula and Decius had been there long enough not to attract attention as newcomers. Aula had changed her looks and hair colour so that not even her now dead husband would have recognised her. The greedy, grasping pair had not retired from the business of money-making. Decius still knew where there were rich pickings to be had. "We are not going to live here in this poor land as rich citizens Decius. I want to return to Rome and be rich in a rich land."

Decius set about recruiting the disenchanted and disenfranchised; those who had lost money and position and were eager to regain it. Decius promised them much and in the late spring he took his little caravan to the area around Wyddfa and the gold his engineers had found there; the engineers whose bodies now littered the lakes and high streams of the mountains. Decius was the only one who knew where to find the gold. All he needed were the people to mine it for him. His mercenaries would ensure the cooperation of anyone he found who could mine for him.

While Decius Brutus helped to organise the repairs to the fort and the bridge, Prefect Julius Demetrius took the ala on long patrols to ensure that their enemies were indeed gone. The east was indeed devoid of any sign they had been there. One evening when he and Gaius were talking at the fort Marcus arrived. "You saw nothing to show where they had been or where they were going?"

"It is as though they vanished into the air like spirits."

"But we know, do we not Julius that the Caledonii do not disappear? They are a plague like the locusts which devour the crops in Egypt."

Julius smiled. His old leader could never stop being a leader. He was still doing what he used to all those years ago when he tried to get Gaius or himself to reach the same conclusion as him. "I do wish Marcus Aurelius Maximunius that you would just tell me what you are thinking. We have been comrades too long for this, as Decius might have said, 'dicking' around."

"He would you know Marcus." Gaius smiled in memory of his dead friend.

Smiling at himself and remembering fondly the friend who had died whilst he had languished in a prison cell, he continued." West. That's where they would have gone. It has far fewer forts and soldiers and yet it is rich. Remember when we came up the west side with Agricola? There was nothing between Deva and what is now the fort of Luguvalium. "

"And Julius it is more pleasant travelling that way now than in winter."

"You are right. Gaius, you keep four turmae here and I will take the rest on an extended patrol."

As soon as they dropped down the other side, past Brocauum they could see the devastation wrought by the barbarians. They passed barely a living creature all the way north to Luguvalium. When they reached that northern outpost the camp Prefect, who looked like an empty shell, told them of the siege which had kept them trapped in their walls for the past three weeks. "We saw the warband and their plunder head north but we could do nothing to stop them and then the siege was lifted. They took cattle, sheep and slaves." Apologetically he repeated, "We could do nothing. It would have taken a legion to defeat them."

"I know we had a similar story in the east."

When Julius finally returned to Morbium he told a sad tale of Carvetii and Brigante families dragged away into slavery and whole populations wiped out. "When I reached Strabo's forts we could see the effect of the invasion. There were three forts badly damaged. They will not see another winter."

Marcus sighed. "That fool Sallustius played politics. Had those four cohorts been committed to the north this might never have happened. I think Julius you ought to write a report for the new governor, whoever he is. We need a line of defences from Coriosopitum west for mark my words Tribunes Strabo and Sura will either have to seek sanctuary in the south or they will die with all their men."

"You are right Marcus. I thought that we could hold them north of Veluniate but I was wrong. We will take no more land. Rome has started its long retreat."

The End

# Maps

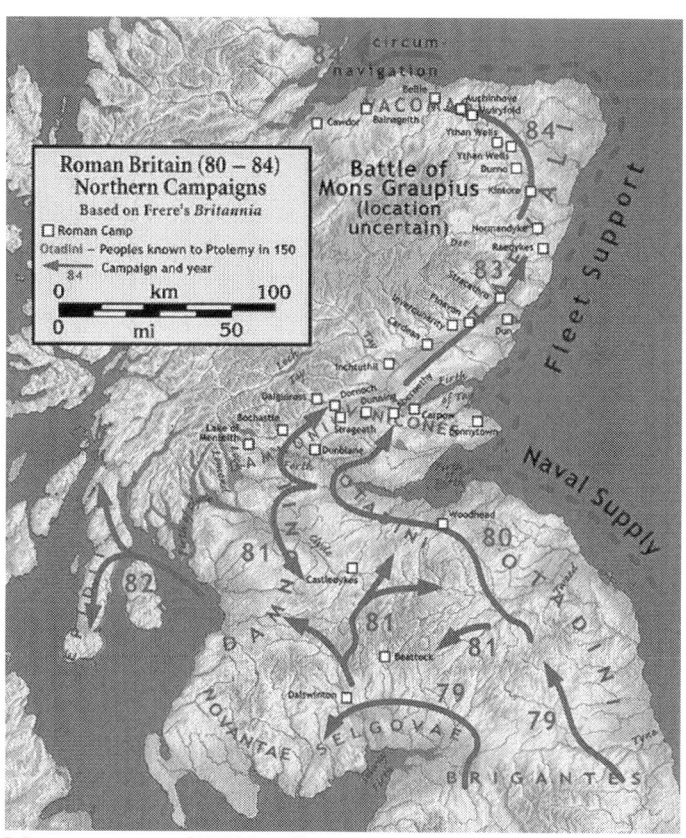

Map courtesy of Wikipedia
This file is licensed under the Creative Commons Attribution-Share Alike 3.0 Unported license.

Roman Retreat

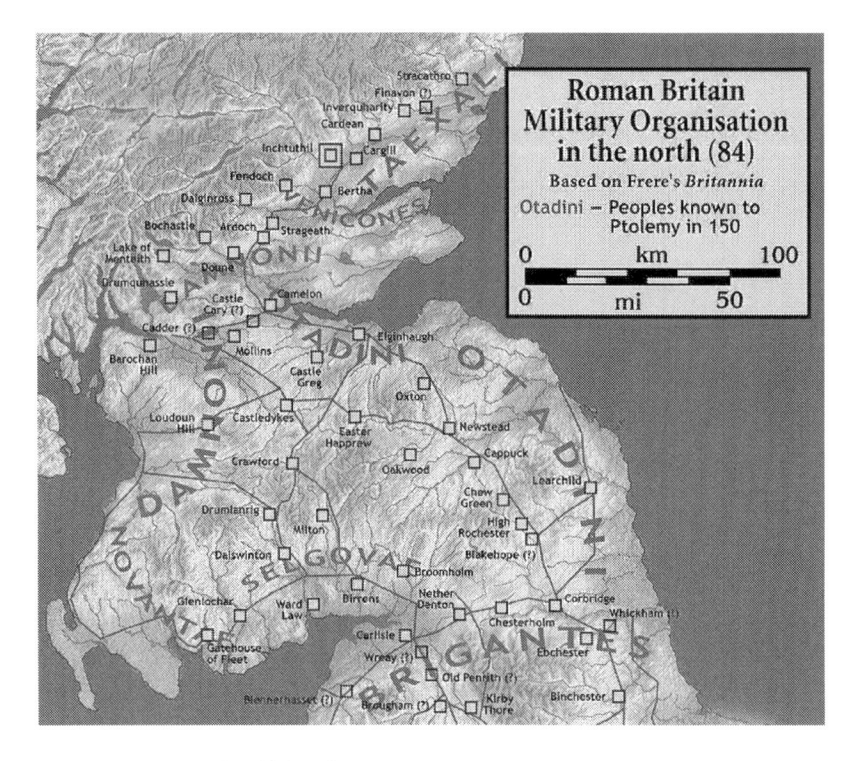

Map courtesy of Wikipedia
This file is licensed under the Creative Commons Attribution-Share Alike 3.0 Unported license.

If you have enjoyed this book and wish to know what happens next then read the opening chapter of the next book: Revolt of the Red Witch.

# Revolt of the Red Witch

Book 5 in the Sword of Cartimandua series

By

Griff Hosker

# Chapter 1

Lulach looked at the Roman fort of Coriosopitum. It was over five years since he had failed to capture and destroy this symbol of Roman power in the north of Britannia. It still rankled with him that he and his warband had been defeated south of Morbium and that defeat had begun at Coriosopitum where the garrison foiled his attempts to take and destroy it. In the past five years he, and his father King Calgathus, had built up his armies to their former strength attacking and harrying the Romans wherever possible. Lulach had urged his father to allow him to redeem himself for his former failure and rid the north of the blight that was Coriosopitum.

His men were hidden in the many wooded areas around the fort and the settlement of Corio. They had spent the night moving secretly into position. He would not assault the fort as he had attempted previously; he had a more cunning plan. He and his elite force were hidden in the settlement of Corio. During the night they had silently entered the houses and huts and murdered all the inhabitants. A gory and grisly task, especially when it came to killing children but he had reminded those few of his men who had qualms about such action that these people were Roman lovers and, as such, deserved the same treatment as Romans. The sentries on the walls had detected and heard nothing of the slaughter in the civilian settlement.

As dawn approached the raiders could hear the sounds of the fort coming to life: the guards were changing and the garrison preparing for another day on the frontier. Having watched for days they knew the familiar and well-practised routine. Once the guards were changed the Porta Decumana would be opened and sentries stationed outside the walls to inspect the visitors who wished to enter or pass through the fort. Lulach had identified several regular visitors taking food and other goods to clients in the fort. Once the Porta Decumana had been secured the Porta Praetorium would be opened and a larger number of sentries would march to their sentry points.

The gates nearest the settlement swung slowly and ponderously open, Lulach and five of his men wandered haphazardly towards the gate; their hoods and cowls protecting their identity and disguising their short saxes. The sentries had become complacent for most of them were a new auxiliary cohort brought from the south. They saw what they wanted to see; the same villagers with the same goods for they saw the northern tribes as being identical, they were all barbarians. Lulach and his men held their goods in front of them and, when the sentries inspected them, they were stabbed quickly and died without a sound. Time was of the essence and the six warriors raced for the open gate. Behind them, the horde emerged from the settlement and raced along the road. The guards on the tower shouted the alarm when they saw the mass of men descending upon the gate but before they could be closed the luckless sentries were savagely and ruthlessly slaughtered. The warband raced through the gates and the auxiliaries, just awakening to a new day, barely had time to register that there was an attack.

Lulach and his men did not pause in their stride as they raced towards the Porta Praetorium. Barely dressed and half asleep auxiliaries tried to stop the horde of ferocious warriors but the speed of the assault took them by surprise. Outside the unopened main gate, the rest of the warband shot the sentries from the towers and by the time the gates had been opened the battle was already decided. In the open the cohort might have fought off a warband; on the walls of the fort, using their artillery they might have withstood the onslaught but fighting in tiny groups they were overwhelmed and slaughtered. The First Spear and his century held out the longest, fighting shield to shield around the Praetorium but Lulach remembered the devastation by the bolt throwers and the Romans suffered the final irony of being destroyed by their own weapons as the Caledonii climbed the towers and turned the hated ballistae on to the last stand of the auxiliaries.

"Strip the bodies of all that we can use and then burn this fort!"

Warriors eagerly seized the swords and javelins. Others stripped the bodies of the leather armour and daggers. Some took the shields but most left them where they were. Within the hour the fort was a burning pyre. The wooden fort on the eastern end of the Roman defences was no more and the only bulwark against the barbarian invasion was Luguvalium on the west coast.

"Now brothers, we will not make the same mistakes. When we last came here we left a trail of brave warriors in our wake. This time I want to leave Roman bones to rot. Go with your chiefs, they know where they are to raid. We return with slaves and plunder. Kill every Roman and burn every building."

The cheer from his warriors was an affirmation of the popularity of his actions. He and his father had spent long months in the winter deciding upon this strategy. If they made the mistake of one warband then the Governor would send out forces from Eboracum and they knew that they could not defeat the Roman behemoth in open battle. By using smaller bands they could still defeat the patrols they met and flee before being caught. Their only fear was the cavalry, Marcus' Horse and Lulach knew that it was the weak part of the strategy. They had yet to defeat these thousand horsemen who could move swiftly and bring deadly retribution on raiders. He just hoped that they would not run into them.

Five years had passed since the most northerly fortress in the Roman Empire, Inchtuthil, had been abandoned and since that time northern Britannia had seen a series of reverses and misfortunes. The line of forts between Luguvalium and Coriosopitum now represented the uneasy northern frontier of the Roman world. Five years in which the relentless Caledonii had ravaged and destroyed the Roman presence north of the Tinea. Many forts and their garrisons had been destroyed whilst others had been withdrawn further south where rebellion was fermenting.

Prefect Julius Demetrius now showed the signs of his time in Britannia and, as he looked northwards, he couldn't help but think of what they had held and what they had lost. The charred line of forts was just a reminder that the frontier had receded. A little like his own receding hairline which made him look much older than his thirty-eight years and appeared to be receding at the same rate as the frontier. He had lost many friends, family and brother officers since he had first joined Marcus' Horse almost twenty years previously. As he removed his helmet to let the cooler air refresh him, he peered along the bleak moorland rising away to the west. He had crossed this land many times; he had fought and bled in this land many times but he had always thought that one day it would be safe. It would be a place where the people who farmed the savage uplands would be able to do so without worrying about enemies coming on slave raids. The land was more dangerous now than at any time since the Brigante revolt of twenty-five years ago. He had not even been in Britannia then but Gaius, the old Decurion Princeps, had told him of those dangerous times when the only law was the cavalry of the Pannonian Ala.

"Sir?" He turned to see the new Decurion Lentius Gaius Servius. He was one of the many new, unfamiliar faces who had replaced some of the older officers who had served with him for so many years. He found it hard not to call him Gaius, for he commanded Gaius' old Second Turma.

"Yes, Decurion? What is it?"

The Decurion had come from one of the southern tribes and he had only known Roman rule and Roman peace. In the sixth months, he had been in the north he had found it hard to adjust to the frontier way of life. "Why doesn't the Governor or the Legate just bring the legions up from the south and stop these raids once and for all? We aren't doing much good are we sir? We are like the man trying to plug leaks in an old barrel, as soon as one is plugged another erupts."

Julius remembered when he had first arrived and been full of aggression. "The Legions are guarding those parts of the land which we have conquered, ensuring that the Roman businesses in that part of Britannia prosper. Here we have yet to conquer and believe me, Lentius, if we were not here then the Caledonii would raid all the way to Deva and Eboracum and the barrel would not just have leaks, it would burst."

"Sorry, sir. I didn't mean any offence."

"None taken. I, too, long for the day when we march north with legions and auxiliaries side by side and retake the land we once won with so much blood but that may not be for some time."

"Is that why we are split into three groups and patrol so far apart?"

"Yes, Decurion it makes the most of what we have got. Decurion Princeps Cilo patrols the south and west whilst Decurion Lucullus covers the east and the north. Four turmae can cover more ground than the whole ala. It keeps our presence over a wider area of this vast and empty land." He glanced around to make sure that the turmae, men and horses, were rested and then signalled for them to follow. "Keep a keen eye out for those raiders. I know they may have returned north but something tells me they are still close by and watch out for ambushes; we have to travel close to the trees and they have learned that horses do not cope with the narrow trails in these dense woods."

They dropped down from the windswept ridge top and followed a small trail through the pine trees. Someone had cut some down at some point and in places they almost found space to breathe. This was where Julius missed Gaelwyn, for the Brigante scout would have been able to smell the Caledonii. Julius and his men would have to make do with their eyes and their mounts that would whinny if they were afraid of something or smelled something alien.

Down in the valley, the raiders watched the horsemen disappear into the forest. Their leader, a huge grey-haired giant called Modius, had once been a member of the ala until he had deserted. His knowledge of the ala and the way they operated had saved his little band of robbers and brigands on more than one occasion. They had slipped over from the west a month earlier and had spent their time quite profitably robbing caravans of merchants moving small, but valuable cargoes like jet and copper. Some had even had gold taken, ironically, from the rivers close to Modius' camp and following Modius' route to Eboracum. He was a cunning leader and he knew when he ought to cut his losses. Since the ala had sent their patrols out for him he had found the pickings harder to come by. Turmae escorted the larger caravans and kept the main routes open. Modius knew the Prefect; he had served with his brother and, later, been one of the warband which killed him. As much as he would have like to do the same to his little brother he could not take on two turmae with the bandits he controlled. Now he was an independent as he styled himself, a robber baron who answered to no one but took advantage of the unrest and the raids from the warlike tribes further north.

"Right. They are out of sight. Single file back along this track. I want no noise and I want the last man to clear the trail. Now let's move."

There was no loyalty amongst the band but Modius was an effective leader. As long as he brought them success and cowed them with his strength of arms, they would follow him. They were not warriors as Modius had once led, but they served his purpose. When they were sure that they had lost the patrol Modius headed them up the rocky gully which would eventually take them to the high waterfall. The route was hard for his men but he knew that they would fare much better than the horses of the ala.

## Roman Retreat

Seonag was the wise woman of the village. Nestled in a little dell close to the sea moors the prosperous little village made a good living mining the much sought after jet. Prized by both royalty and mystics its value exceeded that of gold. In the last three years they had sold much to traders from the area around the holy mountain of Wyddfa. Seonag had her own theory about this but she kept her counsel for she was the last of the priestesses in this part of the world. In her heart, she knew her sisters were once again rising to take back the power they had once possessed. Despite being a widow, her husband having died young in Venutius' first rising, she was not poor for her medicines and wise words were much sought after by the people of the village and nearby valleys.

Despite her age, she was the one who sensed when the band of Caledonii raiders was close by. She was afraid neither of them nor of death. She had outlived all those with whom she grew up and she knew she still had power over men. She went to her secret place and took out her magic amulet made of intricately carved pieces of jet skilfully shaped into ravens and crows. She walked out into the daylight prepared to meet whoever came.

Manus, as his name suggested, was a big warrior; he was one of the biggest warriors in Caledonia. At his birth, his prodigious size had given him his name as soon as he emerged screaming into the world. He had loyally served Lulach for many years as a bodyguard and had earned the right to choose his own warband. Once they had crossed the Dunum he had made straight for this village despite its proximity to Cataractonium. He was gambling that the dreaded ala would be elsewhere but he had visited the place to buy jet many years earlier and he knew of high and steep paths which would enable him to escape pursuit should they stumble upon him.

He and his men rose like wraiths from the tree line. The village was totally surrounded and the fifteen or so men unarmed. They were slaughtered where they stood. "Round up the women and the children kill the old. You eight go and gather the jet it will be in that hut over there then burn the houses and huts."

Just then he noticed Seonag who just stood like a rock, her old piercing eyes taking in the murder and mayhem around her. One of his men was walking up to her, his sax already ready drawn. "Hold!"

"But you said to kill the old and this one is older than the rocks and as ugly."

Manus backhanded the shocked warrior to the ground. "You are a fool, Lugh! Do you not see she is a holy woman! Would you bring the curse of the Mother on to us? I am sorry mother we mean you no harm."

"I know. Do not take all of the jet for the sisters will need some."

Nodding he shouted to his men. "Bring the jet to me."

When the slaves were tethered and the jet packed onto the two small horses used in the village Manus handed over a large quantity of jet. "Thank you. The Mother will watch over you."

The warband headed north at a steady lope heading for the river crossing. Manus was already thinking about the three villages he had skirted whilst heading south. He had lost no men so far and he could gather more plunder there.

Decurion Livius Lucullus had grown up since he had languished in a cell awaiting the whim of an Emperor. Having faced death at close hand he was a far more mature leader than his age would suggest. He had spent much time with Tribune Marcus Aurelius Maximunius and picked up not only wisdom but intimate knowledge of how the ala could and should be used in Britannia. As a native of the island and a relative of the last king, Cunobelinus, he was passionate about protecting its people. His turmae trusted his judgement implicitly. His scout had reported the smoke as they were descending from the eastern moors heading back to Cataractonium. He sensed that his men were ready to return to barracks and a little comfort after a week in the saddle but he knew that it was his duty to find out what had caused the pall of black smoke on the horizon. He wondered if the Prefect and the Decurion Princeps felt the same. He also knew he would have to investigate.

They rode warily into the still burning village. They saw some bodies near the road and an old woman laying others into a hole in the ground. "Let us help you mother."

"Thank you. I am too old for this."

"When did they leave?"

"They came just after dawn and they did not stay long. We were a small village and it did not take them long."

"Caledonii?" She nodded, there was little point denying it although she did not want to help the Romans if she could avoid it. "Which way did they go?" She waved a hand in the vague direction of north. "Thank you. Would you like my men to escort you to the fort?"

"Thank you for your offer but I have a journey to make and it will be my last." The young Decurion thought that this was a journey to die and he nodded sadly but Seonag had no intention of relinquishing her hold on life until she had delivered her precious cargo to the sisters who had re-invested Mona. Her journey was not one of death but of rebirth. She would rejoin the community on Mona. Her life was far from over.

"May the gods watch over you."

"She will."

His men had finished burying the bodies and they awaited his orders. Decurion Cassius chewed idly on a liquorice root he had taken from his bag. "Will they head for Morbium do you think?"

"Possibly but there is a garrison there."

"There was a garrison there."

"True but I think we will follow their trail for a while. If Morbium is their destination then the Prefect will intercept them, for that is his patrol area no we will follow them for I feel they will head for the Dunum and the narrow place."

"The water there can be deep."

"I know but in high summer it is often low, especially at low tide and there are bluffs on the other side to afford protection. It is but two extra days in the saddle. I think it is worth it."

Cassius sniffed. "Just means the turmae of the Decurion Princeps will have the first choice of food and we will be left with scraps. They will get back to the fort before we do."

Livius laughed. "Always thinking of your stomach."

"If I don't then who will?"

As the troopers rode away the old woman waited in the village. When she saw that they were out of sight she gathered her possessions together. She was leaving the settlement and leaving forever. Before she left she needed to make sure she had enough money to support her on her journey west. She went to the headman's hut and moved away the dead ashes from the fire; taking a mattock she scraped away until she struck wood. The villager's money and valuables had been hidden there in case of such a raid. She felt neither guilt nor remorse in taking the wealth of the village for the inhabitants were either dead or enslaved and the money would do them no good. She would be able to pay for herself to be transported on a merchant's wagon leaving Eboracum for Deva and once there it was but a short journey to Mona and her sisters.

Decurion Princeps Cilo was a very contented leader. As a trooper he had incurred the wrath of a martinet Decurion and almost been dismissed from the ala. If it were not for the weapon's trainer, Decurion Macro, then he would have had to do something else other than this job that he loved. He, like the whole ala, loved Decurion Macro for both his skill as a warrior and his genial good humour; he was great fun to be around. Decurion Macro did not resent the fact that one of his protégés had been promoted he preferred to be a weapons trainer and to be given all the dangerous jobs. His turma were all as madcap as he was and were both feared and respected by the rest of the ala. Macro also had a son to think about and that was more than enough responsibility for him.

The Decurion Princeps had brought his quartet of turmae further north than he would normally because he had heard of bandits and raiders operating west of Cataractonium. The burnt-out villages and dead Brigante were a clear trail to follow. Decurion Macro had been more than happy to take his turma north-west to find the trail and might also bring him along the line of the Prefect's patrol. The only nagging doubt in his mind was that two-thirds of the ala were being dragged north-west leaving only Livius and his four turmae to protect the rest. Cilo reminded himself that Livius was well over to the east. The central vale was devoid of cavalry. He shook his head, angry with the Imperial penny pinchers who begrudged paying for more troops for Britannia. Perhaps the new Emperor, Nerva, might be different but the Decurion Princeps had heard that the new Emperor was having difficulties in Rome so it was likely they would have to make do with what they had.

The trooper from Macro's turma came galloping up. "Decurion's compliments sir and we have found the trail of the bandits. They are about five miles across the moors."

"Right column of twos." Perhaps their luck was about to change and they were actually going to catch these elusive bandits. But at the back of Cilo's mind was the thought that they may be a Caledonii warband trying to draw the ala away.

"Modius!" Without bothering to speak the giant glared around. "Roman cavalry, to the south."

"Did they see you?" The downward glance told the leader all he needed to know. "Shit!" He had one patrol to the east and now there was another one to the south. "How far away?"

"Three or four miles."

"Damn!" That meant they could be with him in less than thirty minutes. "Ditch everything that is too heavy and double time. We have cavalry after us. If we can make the waterfall we stand a chance. If not then we die. Anyone left behind…." The unspoken reality was that they would die.

There was no loyalty in this band. For a big man who was ageing, Modius could move swiftly. He had no need to discard anything as the only plunder he carried was the gold he had taken. The ten men who formed his bodyguard had also done the same. Soon the eleven men were pulling away from their weaker comrades. As the path began to climb towards the falls the gap became even greater. Halfway up Modius paused behind a straggly thin elder to survey the horizon. He could see the cavalry now; it was a turma and even from that distance he recognised the enormous figure of Decurion Macro. He remembered him from his days in the ala. He was surprised that the big man was still alive; he had always been volunteering and Modius had convinced himself that he would be dead by now. The turma was within four hundred paces of the rearmost men and, further away Modius could see the rest of the ala. Perhaps the tail-enders would hold up the pursuit but he determined to make the most of the gap. "Run you whoresons! Run!"

Decurion Princeps Cilo could just see figures climbing the precipitous path adjoining the waterfall. If they managed to cross it then they would gain a lead. "Trooper. Ride northeast. Find the Prefect tell him we think we are on the trail of bandits. He will know what to do." As the trooper galloped off Cilo felt confident that they could catch and destroy most of the raiders but it irked him that some might get away.

A small party of the bandits had decided that they were too exhausted to climb the steep rocky path, in addition to which these fifty had been loath to leave their hard-earned loot behind. The large lump of a warrior who fancied himself leader should anything happen to Modius took charge of the rabble who remained. "There's only twenty or so we can have these." They turned and faced the approaching cavalry with weapons at the ready. They had an eclectic mixture of weapons from spears and axes to swords and bows.

Macro had already ascertained what they were going to do; it is what he would have done. He would have to dismount at the bottom of the falls and pursue on foot. He glanced over his shoulder and, in the distance; he could see the red plumes of his comrades. That decided him he would destroy these and then pursue the rest up the path. "Thin them out with arrows but be quick we want to catch the others."

His men grinned; this was why they loved their leader, it was either death or glory with Macro, there was no halfway. Their arrows did indeed thin them out and when they hit them with their horses and swords the survivors threw their weapons away and prostrated themselves on the ground. "You four guard them until the Decurion Princeps arrives. The rest of you follow me on foot. When the others have taken over the guarding of the prisoners you four take the horses around the bluff and meet us at the top of the waterfall."

The shell shocked survivors huddled in the midst of their slaughtered comrades. Any thought of escape had ended with the first flurry of arrows. Macro glanced up. The bandits were spread out in a long line negotiating the treacherous and slippery path which wound up the steep sides. The pursuers had barely gone twenty paces when they saw how treacherous it was as a bandit fell screaming to a bone-crushing death amongst the rocks at the bottom of the falls which waited like some huge predator with its sharp and jagged teeth bared.

Modius had reached the top of the falls. One of his men started to cross. "No, not here they will find our trail too easily. It will take them some time to get to us. We go upstream and then cross."

The first few bandits encountered by Macro proved to be no problem. They did not know he was behind and he was able to cut them down as they struggled to escape. The screams of the dying rose above the stormy thunder of the falls and three of them turned to face the foe who stalked them up this rocky ladder of death. They had spears and the advantage of height. With any other turma it might have gone ill for the leader but Macro's men raced to fight, perilously close to the edge of the falls, to give support to their enigmatic Decurion. Climbing the falls with three men together slowed up their pursuit but ensured that all that they caught died.

The situation was clear to the highly experienced Decurion Princeps Cilo as he rode up to the bundle of bandits sitting miserably at the foot of the falls. Macro's chosen man told him what Macro had asked. "Good plan." He turned to his own chosen man. "We will join Decurion Macro on the other side. You escort these vermin back to Cataractonium." He dismounted and walked up to the sullen-looking prisoners. "Where are you from?" There was a silence more from bravado than any conviction that they would not tell. None of them wanted to be the first to betray their comrades. Nodding Cilo pointed to the large ugly warrior, the erstwhile leader, who looked more sullen than the rest. "You where are you from and who is your leader? Are you Caledonii? Is your leader Lulach?" The man shrugged and gave a half-grin to his comrades. "That is your choice, is it? Silence?" The man, still grinning, nodded. With almost no effort Cilo sliced his spatha backhand and removed the man's head, still grinning. After a few moments, the body crashed to the ground and rolled into the river whilst the unseeing eyes stared at the clouds.

Cilo said to two of his men. "Pick him up." They both grabbed the nearest man whose eyes rolled pleading into his head.

"No please, please!" He screamed.

"Same questions; where are you from, and who is your leader?"

The terrified man looked at his comrades, all of whom looked at the ground. "We came from the west, the land of the lakes and our leader is Modius."

Suddenly Decurion Princeps Cilo stopped and stared as did the older members of the turmae. "This Modius. Did he fight with the Romans?" Having given some information the man found it easy to give more and he nodded, pleased to be alive still. "Well, the Prefect will be interested. Rest your horses and then escort these back."

The last thirty warriors had no energy left when they reached the top of the falls and they could see no sign of their leader who appeared to have been swallowed up by the river. Below them, they could see the fifteen troopers struggling up the side and a few of them decided to brave the stones which made a crude if dangerous path across the shallow bed of the falls. The rest decided to see if they could despatch the fifteen and then continue more safely. It was an uneven contest. The bandits had only fought farmers and merchants; they were facing the hardened elite troopers of Marcus' Horse.

Macro, although out of breath was keen to follow the ones who had half waded, half run across the river. The small rearguard died to a man. Before he pursued the rest Macro glanced down the path and saw Cilo leading the rest of the turmae around the bluff. As he had expected, Macro would be leading the pursuit with his fourteen troopers. "Well lads, until they bring our horses up we are going to have to run. Rip up some of the bandits' clothes and we will leave a trail for them to follow." Already the ones across the river were making good their flight and opening up a lead. Unencumbered as they were by arms and armour they thought to make good their escape.

Further up the river Modius watched as the auxiliaries crossed the river in pursuit of the last of his men. "Looks like we made a good decision. We'll stay this side of the river a bit longer and then head south towards Brocauum. Another few days and we'll be home and safe.

The end of the foot race was inevitable; Macro and his troopers were far fitter than the bandits they were chasing. Inexorably they caught them up one by one and they were despatched one by one. Macro could afford no mercy for he only had fourteen men. Once he could see there were only four remaining he shouted over his shoulder, "We take these prisoners. Find out where they are from and who their leader is."

The last four accepted the inevitable when they heard the shout to stop. At first, they had thought they would escape but as they had heard their fellows being killed they knew it was only a matter of time. As they squatted on the ground trying to catch their breath all of them wondered what had happened to their leader.

"Good run lads. If you had been auxiliaries you might have outrun us. Now I'll give you a while to get your breath but then I want two questions answering. Which of you is the leader and where is your home?"

The looks on their faces and the blank looks they gave each other told Macro that none of these was the leader. Resentful of the fact that they had been abandoned to slow down the pursuit, they all happily volunteered the information requested. "We come from the land of the lakes and none of us is the leader, he is Modius who fought with the horse warriors."

"So the treacherous bastard is still alive. Right if you can talk you can walk. Let's get back to our horses."

Decurion Princeps Cilo was waiting with their mounts when they arrived back at the falls. They were both pleased that their information matched but both surprised at the leader. "Last I knew he was still with Aed."

"Aye, and I thought he died in that last battle."

# Author's note

The battle of Mons Graupius was the high-water mark in the Roman occupation of Britain. Julius Agricola was summoned back to Rome. Although some authors argue that Agricola did not do as much as his son in law Tacitus claimed, the fact remains that he was the successful general who fought all the way from Wales to Scotland and, following his removal, Rome had to retreat. The fort at Inchtuthil was abandoned before it was finished and pots of nails were found buried to prevent them from falling into barbarian hands. The Glen forts, as they were called, had been there for a few years but the date of their abandonment is open to conjecture.

Emperor Domitian did indeed withdraw legions from not only Britain but other parts of the Empire to help him fight in Dacia. These wars were not successful and it was not until Trajan that the Empire began to recover some of the lost territory. With the legions gone it was left to the auxiliaries to defend the island. Agricola held these soldiers in great esteem and felt he could conquer the whole of Britannia with such men. They had the same officer structure as the legions but fought in smaller units, the cohort.

The Governor of Germania Superior did rebel against Emperor Domitian in the late eighties. When the rebellion was put down he was executed. Sallustius Lucullus was the grandson of Cunobelinus. Bizarrely he was actually executed for naming a lance after himself. I found this hard to believe for an Emperor who, until the last years of his reign, was quite a reasonable Emperor. There is no evidence that he attempted to rebel against the Emperor but, as the grandson of a king of Britain and as another Governor did so at the same time I thought it was a legitimate storyline.

As with all my books, I use many facts and real events but essentially, they are stories. Stories which I hope you enjoy. I will continue to write about the ala, the witch, Morwenna and the wars the Romans fought in the north of Britain.

*Griff Hosker February 2014*

# Glossary

### Characters and places mentioned in the novel

Decius Flavius — Decurion Marcus' Horse
Julius Demetrius — Decurion Marcus' Horse
Gaius Metellus Aurelius — Decurion Marcus' Horse
Macro — Decurion Marcus' Horse
Domitian — Emperor of Rome
Rufius Agrippa — Envoy for Lucius Saturninus
Morwenna — Fainch's daughter
Lucius Antoninus Saturninus — Governor- Germania Superior
Sallustius Lucullus — Governor of Britannia
Calgathus — King of the Caledonii
Luigsech — Morwenna's nurse
Cominius Sura — Prefect Batavian auxiliary
Furius Strabo — Prefect Batavian Auxiliary
Marcus Aurelius Maximunius — Prefect Marcus' Horse
Luentinum — Pumsaint gold mine in west Wales
Livius Lucullus — Sallustius' nephew
Decius Lucullus — Sallustius' nephew
Parcae — The Roman fates
Aula Luculla — Wife of the governor
Alavna — Ardoch in Perthshire
Bodotria — River Firth
Clota — River Clyde
Coriosopitum — Corbridge
Corio — Corbridge-civilian settlement
Danum — Doncaster
Derventio — Malton
Deva — Chester
Dunum Fluvius — River Tees
Eboracum — York
Glanibanta — Ambleside
Hen Waliau — Caernarfon
Luguvalium — Carlisle
Mamucium — Manchester
Mona — Holyhead
Morbium — Piercebridge
Taus — River Solway
Tava — River Tay
uncia — Roman inch

# Other books by Griff Hosker

If you enjoyed reading this book, then why not read another one by the author?

## Ancient History

### The Sword of Cartimandua Series
(Germania and Britannia 50 A.D. – 128 A.D.)
Ulpius Felix- Roman Warrior (prequel)
The Sword of Cartimandua
The Horse Warriors
Invasion Caledonia
Roman Retreat
Revolt of the Red Witch
Druid's Gold
Trajan's Hunters
The Last Frontier
Hero of Rome
Roman Hawk
Roman Treachery
Roman Wall
Roman Courage

### The Wolf Warrior series
(Britain in the late 6th Century)
Saxon Dawn
Saxon Revenge
Saxon England
Saxon Blood
Saxon Slayer
Saxon Slaughter
Saxon Bane
Saxon Fall: Rise of the Warlord
Saxon Throne
Saxon Sword

Roman Retreat

# Medieval History

**The Dragon Heart Series**
Viking Slave
Viking Warrior
Viking Jarl
Viking Kingdom
Viking Wolf
Viking War
Viking Sword
Viking Wrath
Viking Raid
Viking Legend
Viking Vengeance
Viking Dragon
Viking Treasure
Viking Enemy
Viking Witch
Viking Blood
Viking Weregeld
Viking Storm
Viking Warband
Viking Shadow
Viking Legacy
Viking Clan
Viking Bravery

**The Norman Genesis Series**
Hrolf the Viking
Horseman
The Battle for a Home
Revenge of the Franks
The Land of the Northmen
Ragnvald Hrolfsson
Brothers in Blood
Lord of Rouen
Drekar in the Seine
Duke of Normandy
The Duke and the King

Roman Retreat

**New World Series**
Blood on the Blade
Across the Seas
The Savage Wilderness
The Bear and the Wolf
Erik the Navigator

The Vengeance Trail

**The Danelaw Saga**
The Dragon Sword

**The Reconquista Chronicles**
Castilian Knight
El Campeador
The Lord of Valencia

**The Aelfraed Series**
(Britain and Byzantium 1050 A.D. - 1085 A.D.)
Housecarl
Outlaw
Varangian

**The Anarchy Series England 1120-1180**
English Knight
Knight of the Empress
Northern Knight
Baron of the North
Earl
King Henry's Champion
The King is Dead
Warlord of the North
Enemy at the Gate
The Fallen Crown
Warlord's War
Kingmaker
Henry II

Crusader
The Welsh Marches
Irish War
Poisonous Plots
The Princes' Revolt
Earl Marshal

**Border Knight**
**1182-1300**
Sword for Hire
Return of the Knight
Baron's War
Magna Carta
Welsh Wars
Henry III
The Bloody Border
Baron's Crusade
Sentinel of the North
War in the West
Debt of Honour (May 2021)

**Sir John Hawkwood Series**
**France and Italy 1339- 1387**
Crécy: The Age of the Archer
Man at Arms
The White Company (July 2021)

**Lord Edward's Archer**
Lord Edward's Archer
King in Waiting
An Archer's Crusade
Targets of Treachery (Due out August 2021)

**Struggle for a Crown**
**1360- 1485**
Blood on the Crown
To Murder A King
The Throne
King Henry IV

Roman Retreat

The Road to Agincourt
St Crispin's Day
The Battle for France

Tales from the Sword I

**Conquistador**
**England and America in the 16th Century**
Conquistador (Coming in 2021)

# Modern History

**The Napoleonic Horseman Series**
Chasseur à Cheval
Napoleon's Guard
British Light Dragoon
Soldier Spy
1808: The Road to Coruña
Talavera
The Lines of Torres Vedras
Bloody Badajoz
The Road to France
Waterloo (June 2021)

**The Lucky Jack American Civil War series**
Rebel Raiders
Confederate Rangers
The Road to Gettysburg

**The British Ace Series**
1914
1915 Fokker Scourge
1916 Angels over the Somme
1917 Eagles Fall
1918 We will remember them
From Arctic Snow to Desert Sand
Wings over Persia

Roman Retreat

**Combined Operations series
1940-1945**
Commando
Raider
Behind Enemy Lines
Dieppe
Toehold in Europe
Sword Beach
Breakout
The Battle for Antwerp
King Tiger
Beyond the Rhine
Korea
Korean Winter

Tales from the Sword Book 2

**Other Books**
Great Granny's Ghost (Aimed at 9-14-year-old young people)

For more information on all of the books then please visit the author's website at www.griffhosker.com where there is a link to contact him or visit his Facebook page: GriffHosker at Sword Books

Printed in Great Britain
by Amazon